Advance Praise for *Dragons Suck*

"In Benjamin Gamble, readers may have found the next Terry Pratchett. The self-aware humor and deconstructed fantasy of *Dragons Suck* show flashes of true depth and an epic heart."

—D.J. Butler, author of *Witchy Eye*

DRAGONS SUCK

BENJAMIN GAMBLE

PERMUTED
PRESS

A PERMUTED PRESS BOOK

ISBN: 978-1-68261-857-8
ISBN (eBook): 978-1-68261-858-5

Cover art by Cody Corcoran

PERMUTED
PRESS

Permuted Press, LLC
New York • Nashville
permutedpress.com

Published in the United States of America

ook, I'm gonna sound twelve different kinds of screwed up for saying this, but standing in the charred, smoking remains of my village, I wasn't upset. I wasn't even furious.

Mostly, I just felt kinda hungry.

I mean, yeah, I get that those were burnt *people* I was smelling, but it really did remind me how long it had been since I actually had cooked meat.

Nobody else seemed to be taking it as optimistically (or maybe opportunistically) as I was. There were a bunch of women screaming and wailing, some guys desperately trying to clear the blackened ruins of their homes or whatever. Honestly, I wasn't that torn up, as you may have ascertained. There wasn't much of value in our lame-ass village. Somebody probably lost their grandfather's trusty war sword, or a ceremonial urn that had been passed down for sixty generations—

Okay, that made me laugh. Losing an urn in a fire? I just love irony sometimes.

Somebody bumped into me and I almost got pissed—I don't care if there was a crisis going on, a man's got to draw the line somewhere—until I saw who it was. Elaine was shuffling through the ash, and even though I only turned around in time to see the back of her head, I knew what her face looked like.

You know how sometimes, you get sad—to the point where you can't even cry? You just feel...numb? That's where she was. Numbness.

I'll admit it was a sad sight, and I felt my first twinge of pity about this whole catastrophe. Poor girl was heartbroken. Her tunic was absolutely filthy, her red hair a ragged mess—and normally, she tried so hard to look all prim and proper. Looking nice was pretty hard, considering 1) bathing's like a biannual thing, and that's, like, the every two years kind, by the way, and 2) she was the daughter of a sheep farmer, and sheep farmers are not renowned for their cleanliness. I had another rare moment of empathy—her dad tended the sheep and she and her mom made the wool into mittens or something. Must've really sucked, making all those nice clothes for people and still having the worst wardrobe in town. The only piece of somewhat nice clothing she had on was a little scarf, pink and meticulously cared for. Come to think of it, I think it had been her betrothed—I dunno his name—that gave it to her. He must've worked his ass off for it, and bought the scarf from some other village.

...and then he had to go and get abducted.

Eh. Life sucks, and then you die. It's pretty much the status quo here.

Well, everybody's wardrobe was the same now—whatever they had on their backs, all stylishly refurbished with ash and soot. The Reckoning had come once again, and the whole town was acting like it was the end of the world. I alone seemed to have a clear head.

I felt a hand clasp my shoulder—the sort of grip that conveys how strong the person is while being gentle and reassuring. Not a rude, Let-me-dislocate-your-shoulder-lesser-male grip, more like a Heya-pal-how's-it-going? grip. I mean, both were equally annoying, just in different ways.

I turned and saw Aldric, one of my...friends? I don't know if friend is the right term. Aldric and I hung out sometimes, we did whatever together. I wasn't too keen on emotional attachments, so seeing Aldric had survived the Reckoning was kind of like seeing a friend show up to a party after they had said they couldn't make it. It was cool, but...you were still planning on having the party without them, ya know?

Don't give me that look. When your life expectancy is maybe forty years if you're lucky, and the leading causes of death are unknown diseases we can't cure; ravaged by wild animals in his own home; and now, roasted like a goose by a dragon, it's pretty tough to get emotionally rattled by someone dying. *Oh, so and so died? Huh. Lasted longer than I expected.*

Coincidentally, the bar in town was full pretty much every night. Good thing nobody had invented AA yet.

"I'm so sorry, Harkness," Aldric croaked, gripping me in a tight embrace. I awkwardly returned the hug, clapping him on the back. "There was nothing you could've done."

Aldric had his moments of being a pretty chill guy. Mostly, I hung with him because he didn't ramble on about dumb stuff like the majority of people here (you can only deal with so many "Aye, gonna be a rough winter this year" or "Did you hear that Abraham's sow died?"). He was also not blessed with good looks, so having him as a wingman was helpful. Between the nose that was more crooked than a lightning bolt with scoliosis, the oversized hands, and the slightly uneven blue eyes (he got those from his mother, though—and she was dead, so I didn't give him any crap about that) he wasn't making any of the village girls swoon when he stumbled on by.

It took me a moment to figure out what he was talking about. I couldn't have done anything about…Oh! *Oh, shit.* My girlfriend, Marisa! Well, fiancée, technically. Yeah, she was kinda abducted by the dragon, too, along with Elaine's husband-to-be. That one had totally slipped my mind. I managed to cover my awkward silence by looking mournful.

"Thanks, Aldric. It, uh, it means a lot."

He gave me a half-hearted, I'm-torn-up-inside-but-I'm-trying-to-make-you-feel-better grin and another quick squeeze. "What friends are for, mate. Look, you want to go after that monster, I'll be right there beside you."

Oh…did people expect me to do that? To actually go after a freaking dragon to save my girlfriend (and I guess while I was there, I could save Elaine's boyfriend. I mean, might as well)? Sure, I was all for trying to do the right thing when it's convenient, but c'mon now. First off, it was me. I got in a fight *once* before, and that was because I was legitimately just really bored and wanted to see what would happen. Second, even if I was some mighty warrior, that dragon had just handed our entire town its own ass. How was I supposed to stop that thing? Not to mention I had stuff to do. I mean, I wasn't sure if my parents had survived the attack, so maybe I was actually off the hook in terms of work, but still. I guessed I'd be spending the next few weeks clearing away what used to be our house/tannery. Tannery? Is that the right word? The place where they tan stuff, make fluffy animals into boots and saddles? I probably should know the right word, being the tanner's son, but I don't really have the best attention to detail.

"...Yeah. Uh, nobody I'd rather have along for the journey than you."

Aldric clapped me on the shoulder again—oh, and by the way, that's the primary way of expressing affection here. It really gets old after a while (unlike most of the people who live here).

Aldric went off on his way, conveying size and strength with his thundering footsteps and conveying being a Goody Two-shoes with how he stopped to help people move debris. I didn't bother asking where he was going or what he was doing, because even before our village got turned into a tinderbox, there weren't that many recreational options available. You could drink yourself into a stupor, knock someone up, or sleep. Or, if you were one of the three literate people in our town, I guess you could read. Or maybe even write! The possibilities for a lower-class Plagiaran peasant were truly limitless.

I massaged my temples, trying to guesstimate how much time was left before I was going to sleep. I wasn't a fortune-teller, but something told me none of our straw mattresses had survived the dragon's attack. It was gonna be a long night.

No, wait. There was probably going to be a vigil or something with the whole village, for us to remember the terrible events that had happened early this morning. Just in case someone had, you know, forgotten already. If any mead had survived, people would probably get blackout drunk, which wasn't much different from what people normally did.

We may not have electricity, but we have a few things figured out.

After that, I just wandered around for a while. Now that I knew what people were talking about when they said "Oh, I'm so sorry for your loss," or "It's a real tragedy what happened, son," I could respond more accurately. *Yeah, Marisa's dragon chow. I'm losing sleep over it. 'Tis a shame.* Also, I found my parents—they were busy burying one of our horses, who'd died in the convection oven that our barn was turned into. I was pissed—mostly because, hey, I was still *really* hungry.

Also, I thought it was a little unfair that he died from the fire but wasn't cremated by it. Burn a man's horse to death, but leave enough for him to have to bury? Dick move, dragon, dick move.

Lots of people were just standing around, staring at the wreckage. Lots of crying and hugging, lots of attempts to make people feel better. I guess the people here were decent, even if it was the most boring place in Plagiar. Well, normally the most boring place. If a dragon wipes out everything you've ever known, you can't really call it "boring" anymore. *Optimism, people. It's all about optimism.*

I passed Aldric a couple more times—the big blond oaf was going around, checking in and trying to see who was left alive. It was a bit of a waste, because the dragon normally didn't kill that many people during the Reckoning—or so I was told. I'd been a little kid when the last one occurred. Widespread killing? That's not the flying lizard's MO. Same thing with human hunters. They don't go in and kill every single deer in the woods. They pick off one or two at a time, give them a chance to screw and make more baby deer, then they go pick off those guys. The circle of life is beautiful like that.

The dragon, however, was a little more sadistic about it. He'd burn down all the buildings, generally make a mess of things, but he'd leave most of them alive. Normally, if you pissed him off—shooting arrows at him or whatever—he'd kill you for being insolent, but not much else would happen. Then, to put the salt in the proverbial wound, he'd scamper off with one guy and one girl, each of marrying age. This had a couple of different effects. For starters, our village's matchmaker had really shitty job security. Also, it generally dampened the mood for a while, because people can handle adults being killed way better than kids for some reason. I don't really get why. Adults can sometimes do useful stuff, like make mead or cook food. Kids just talk and ask questions and eat all the time. I say this as a proud adolescent/societal dead weight myself.

Eventually, my feet, filthy and ash-coated, carried me to the house of another of my tagalongs, Karla. She wasn't much of a looker, but she did live fairly close to me, and our parents would hang out sometimes, which meant we hung out sometimes. She didn't talk too much, and aspired to be a troubadour. I guess those were her defining traits or whatever. Her being a troubadour was never going to happen (Quick—name a world-renowned celebrity from our lovely hometown of Sorro. Nope? Nobody? See, that's why she's going nowhere.), but whenever somebody's practicing singing and dancing, they can't make small talk, so she was all right in my book. *Go chase those dreams, Karla.*

Her house had fared better than most—there was still a vague "shell" of a home left, whereas most of the other buildings had been completely obliterated. She was sifting through the wreckage, maybe hoping for a piece of jewelry (correction: *the* piece of jewelry) that survived, or a childhood relic. She saw me walk up and flashed me a smile, wiping some of the sweat/liquid ash off her face and coming over. I gave her a hug, noting that her hair still somehow smelled nice.

How do chicks manage to do that? Everything else smelled like mourning and broken childhoods.

She pulled away, grimy and ragged. Her red hair was bound back in a ponytail, she was sorta slumped over—most people in the village had been up all night after the dragon attack. Well, the attack was early morning. So up all morning? Look, our timelines are a little fuzzy without watches—and we were nearing the late afternoon. Her brown eyes were bloodshot and drooping. The scrawny girl looked like she might fall over from exhaustion. She paused for a second, her beak-like nose twitching as she felt a sneeze coming on. Had I any food—*gods, I was still so hungry!*—I might've given her some, which is the sort of thing I don't do that often. I mean, c'mon, a dragon just curbstomped my known world. I don't have time to give handouts to people. I had my own problems to handle. Where was I going to sleep tonight? Did I need to go talk to Marisa's parents, clear the air, discuss who keeps the dowry now? Lots of stuff.

"You hanging in there?" Karla asked, holding my hand. It was a total friend thing, no romantic weight to it. This was fine by me. There was enough drama going on with holocaust-by-dragon without throwing a romantic triangle into things. Her fingers were warm, either from hours of work or from handling the smoldering leftovers of her house.

"Yeah, I'm all right. You?"

Karla nodded, blinking a couple of times. "Yeah. It's just…well…I lost my lyre…." She reached up and brushed some hair out of the way, glancing up at the smoky skies.

I tried to figure out why that was so import—oh, shoot, the whole minstrel-lady dream. "Uh, well, I don't think you need one to win over a crowd."

Karla beamed, hugging me again. Crisis averted. "Thanks, Harkness. I appreciate it."

I did that hug-with-a-pat-on-the-back thing, which seemed to be the ace-in-the-hole for awkward emotional encounters. "Anytime, Karla. You need anything?"

"No, I guess not." She turned away for a second, appearing to check out the well-done remains of her old life. "Well, actually, what time is it?"

I glanced up to the sky. All grey and black, like carcinogenic curtains pulled over the sun. "Hell if I know."

"Ah. Well, I heard the village's gathering around the town center. They're gonna have a vigil, ya know." *Called it.* "Old Man Granger's gonna speak."

Now that would be actually interesting. Even moreso than Aldric and Karla, Old Man Granger was one of the few people in the village I actually enjoyed being around. He was also the only person I really had respect for, because he was old, and you don't get to be old in Plagiar by being a pushover. I'd never seen him fight or anything, but I bet he could've taken anybody else in our town, even with a ten- to twenty-year handicap slowing him down. Everybody was more or less amazed by him because he was black. I don't wanna make this a race thing—socially, I don't think we have that construct yet—but we got new travelers into town maybe once or twice a month, and normally they were hopelessly lost on the way to somewhere else. Everybody here was also whiter than albino snow (I mean, count it, we've got two redheads so far), so that means that Old Man Granger came here from a long, long ways away, and had also stayed here for a long, long time. Both of which were things that I couldn't really fathom. Looking around at people, busy trying to fix the scorch mark of a hometown we had—who would leave some faraway land for here? Who would stay here once they got here?

No sane human would, that's for damn sure. He was the town's resident wise old man and also our kickass story-teller—normally, at festivals (or, apparently, vigils for dragon attacks) he would regale everybody with some cool story of one of his travels. Nobody was ever sure how true any of them were. But hey, he was fun to listen to, and people were generally too leery of being smacked with his cane to question the accuracy of what he said.

"Well, let's get to it, then." Karla and I walked along the streets, and—this is me being a glass-half-full kinda guy here—I have to say the ton of ash that fell onto our village actually *improved* the quality of the roads. I mean, before they were just dirt, but maybe all this ash would help make them a little more manageable in the rain and such. It'd be easier for the horses to carry stuff now.

Well, not our horse.

Optimism, people, it's all about optimism.

We didn't talk about much that was interesting, mostly just discussing how other people had fared in the attack. Which really got boring fast, because it was repetitive. The answers were either A) They got roasted or B) they lived, but lost everything they owned. And then Karla kept repeat-edly and not-so-subtly trying to see if I was taking Marisa's absence okay. *Yes, if I was upset, I would have told you back when we'd passed by the tavern, and then you could've bought me beer.*

Oh, yeah, that was the one miraculous thing about the dragon attack—somehow, and I honestly have no idea how—the one building full of alcohol was unscathed. The entire village was pumped about it. The bartender was being uncharacteristically nice and giving out drinks for free, probably because no one had any money left to pay him with. It's easy to be compassionate when you've got no other options. The village center was already pretty full when we got there, and people were making the best of things. A couple of barrels of mead had been rolled out and mugs passed around. They were heartily drained by people sitting on top of charred logs or charred stones or charred anything else they could find. Most people were resting on the dirt, which was a relief after all those hours of standing on your feet and digging through ashes. Karla and I found Aldric, who was doing some annoyingly helpful thing like letting a kid sit on his shoulders so they could have a better view. We sat next to him and scanned the crowd, seeing the same story repeated on all sides—there were beaten faces, worn and weary, people falling asleep on each other or casually sipping at their mugs, but overall, people had made it. A few old people took their usual perches on rocking chairs, which, also surprisingly, had survived. The chairs, I mean, not the old people. Well, the old people too, I guess. There were laughs and smiles, even if they were somewhat subdued, and there was a general sense of "Hey, we might bounce back from this."

…all things considered, it was probably the booze.

The only exception to this was Elaine, who was standing against what was left of the fletcher's shop, staring at her feet. Nobody went over and comforted her. What could you even say?

As I glanced around, I saw people eyeing me the same way I was eyeing her. Elaine and I—we were in the same boat, although it seemed her end of the boat was filling up with water a lot more than mine was.

After a little while people quieted down and our village's leader—well, he wasn't really the official leader, he was just the guy that people went to with their problems, and he was an okay public speaker, so I guess he was the leader—got up and started speaking. "Everyone, please, settle down. I know this is a time of great tragedy for us all…"

On either side of me I could feel Aldric and Karla listening in to every word—the kid on Aldric's shoulders had dozed off, and he gently laid the brat down next to him. Karla sniffed a couple of times and Aldric glanced at her to make sure she was okay. *Oh, those two.* I zoned out, mostly because they say the same sorta stuff after every tragedy, and if you pay attention the first time, you can coast through the rest. It's not like any of this stuff really applied to me personally, anyways.

Well, aside from Marisa.

I only started to tune back in when there was a bunch of clapping and enthusiastic cheers (similar to the slapping/pounding on the back, our society was fond of yelling like drunken banshees to express any given emotion) after our village leader guy stepped down, and Old Man Granger hobbled his way up on the platform.

His dark, weathered features were outlined with a silvery beard and bushy white eyebrows, his usual half-smile on his face. He was in on a joke, and the rest of us were just waiting for the punchline. There was more raucous screaming and whatnot until he smacked his cane against his perch and cut through the noise. His wrinkly face scrunched up as he surveyed the whole village—a few hundred people, as everyone and their brother had come as a result of the attack. Old Man Granger didn't have the best vision anymore, so maybe to him it only looked like a couple people showed up. He ran a hand through the beard that engulfed the bottom half of his face and covered most of his torso, and spoke in a low rumble.

"Don't know to quiet down for your elders, eh?"

That shut more people up than the cane-smacking had. There was a reason I liked Granger. He continued, and, when he spoke—I can't really describe it. But have you ever heard somebody talk, and their voice just has a flow to it? Most pretty girls sound that way, coincidentally enough, but Old Man Granger's voice just seemed to slide on into your mind and paint the clearest picture of whatever he was saying. He was deep and loud and easily heard, even on the far side of the plaza—but that was mostly because everyone was in total silence when he got to telling his stories. The best understanding we had of acoustical science was "talk louder."

"There was a time, back before my grandfather, and before his grandfather. In those days the world was different. The gods walked alongside men, instead of hiding away in the heavens like they do now, only interfering at the rarest and direst of times. No, then, you were likely to see a god in a tavern, drinking alongside his loyal followers—or see a goddess blessing a young bride."

I glanced over at Elaine and saw a hollow look on her face. Her face was supposed to be round and warm and gentle. It was skeletal. Even in the warm summer air she shivered and curled up on herself, arms clutching at each other across her chest. I looked away and stared at my feet for a while.

"But there was also terrible evil in the world. Great beasts, more monstrous and cruel than any grizzly bear, any pack of wolves. So the gods, they decided to help the mortals. They bestowed upon them weapons, tools, armor—everything they would need to fight back the darkness. And for a time, it worked. For a while, there were the great heroes we know, strong of heart and body, and they kept us safe. But eventually the gods came to understand they had given man too much power. There were swords whose wielders could never be slain. There was armor so awful any man who laid his eyes upon it would run for his very life. There was power that men were simply not meant to have. Not for very long."

There was an uneasy silence over the crowd—everyone was transfixed by Granger's slow, steady retelling, but there was also a sense of apprehension. *Uh, isn't there supposed to be a feel-good message at the end of this?* The faces of the crowd, their already shoddy clothes frayed and burnt and filthy, faces sunken…well, they needed this. I was counting on the old man to deliver, but I don't know if everyone else was. If only for Elaine, he needed to. The rest of the town could keep on trucking—I wasn't so sure she could.

"So, the gods and goddesses, they came together. Assembled in the heavens, and discussed what had to be done. For you see, their gifts had worked too well. No longer was there any great evil, no longer was there a reason for mortals to band together. *We* had become the great evil… once the darkness in the world had been wiped out, people just started going to war over the light. The gods, seeking to bring balance to mankind, created a beast, one single being that the mortals could never destroy. It was a creature that would bring death and destruction wherever it went—and in its wake, the mortals would have no choice but to join together to survive. They came together, each divine bringing a different part of the beast into creation. Karvos, the god of war and strength—he gave the beast its bones and muscles, so that it might be stronger than any man on earth. Daome, the god of wisdom, of strategy—he gave the beast its scales, thicker and tougher than any steel that could be forged."

There was a collective side glance at the town's blacksmith, who rolled his eyes.

"Gaerde, the Lady of Secrets, she gave the beast its eyes, so that it might see through any hiding places the men had, see into any schemes or plans the mortals whipped up. Remos, Lord of the Seasons, gave the beast its voice, one with more force than any winter storm, any summer heat. Aurea, the Goddess of Prophecy and Fate, gave the beast its ears, so that it would hear when the time had come for it to once again return to the mortal realm. Catalya, the Lady of Change, whispered her blessing upon its right side, that it may always cause catastrophe wherever it went. Gaius, the Father of all Life, whispered his blessing upon its left side, that it may have authority over any living thing. And finally, Skavor, the dark lady of Death and That Which Lies Beyond.... She gave the beast its teeth, sharper than any man's sword, and capable of breathing a flame that would bring death to all it touched."

The crowd had grown quiet once more, everyone somber, everyone soaking in the pain of what had happened the night before, the cold truth tearing past what little hope they'd pieced back together. There was a gust of air, making the fragile houses creak and sway in the grey twilight.

"They decided this beast would be called a dragon. And they decided that once every ten years, the beast would visit our world, and that it would utterly wipe out one village. It would be a reckoning, a reminder that one atoned for hubris with blood. And when it came, it would take one boy and one girl back to whatever darkness it came from. Word would spread of what had happened, of what had occurred. The other towns and cities, they would know and fear the beast. And they would be reminded of those dark days, when all the monsters had been wiped out, and the humans had stepped up to fill their place."

There was a tense quiet as everyone waited for the happy ending. Old Man Granger, however, seemed to have no intention of continuing. He did that thing old people do sometimes, when you can't tell if they're done talking or not. We teenagers do not have that same problem.

"Wait," somebody asked, a lone voice in the crowd. "What about Layana! You forgot to say what Layana did!"

Old Man Granger beamed, showing off a few missing teeth and a smile that made him look fifty years younger. *Sly old bastard.* He'd planned that. "Oh? I did forget, didn't I. Well, you see, Layana didn't quite agree with all the others. The Goddess of Love thought the whole plan was a bunch of hogwash. She refused to help make the dragon…which is why the beast has no heart. It cannot bleed, or feel…" Granger placed one hand over his chest, almost absentmindedly. There was a strange quality to his face, and his half-blind eyes stared everywhere and nowhere at once. His head tilted just so slightly, and if I hadn't known better, I thought I might've heard a touch of pity in his voice. "It can only wonder what it is that makes the mortals weep, what drives them to come hunting for it. Mortal souls, life, happiness, love…they're beyond its ken. But more importantly, Layana refused to take back her gift from the mortals. She wanted them to have a fighting chance against the dragon, an opportunity to stop the Reckoning, so she changed her gift, kept its newfound powers secret from the other gods and goddesses. Layana had given the humans a sword—a blade sharper than any other. You see, no matter how badly war might wound you, or how terribly winter might gnaw at your fingers and toes…" Granger held up his right hand, which was missing the last part of his pinky and ring fingers. I told you the old man had seen some shit. "…there is no pain worse than heartache. Losing the ones you love."

If I hadn't seen her moving, I would've thought Elaine a corpse. She was clinging to her precious pink scarf with one hand and shakily trying to clear her eyes with the other.

"But by the same token, there was no army or magic in this world more powerful than love." There were a few snickers, mostly from the young boys, and Granger glared them down. He went from grandfatherly storyteller to decades-old-survivor in a heartbeat. "Don't you laugh at me, boy. Number of years I've been alive is higher than your fool ass can count to. Interrupt me again and I'll give your mother heartache, understand me?" He paused for a second, brow furrowed. "Where was I? Oh, yes." He immediately resumed his previous, melodic tone. "You can have all the money in the world, all the beer and mead…."

There was a collective side glance at the bartender, who rolled his eyes.

"…but there's a hole inside that you can't fill with anything but love. Layana knew it. That's the dragon's weakness, you see. It can't understand human emotions, can't understand the way we think….it never got a heart. And so the goddess put a spell upon the Blade, one that made it more powerful and more binding than any of the other old gifts. You see, whoever holds Layana's Blade would have strength enough to defeat the dragon, strength that the dragon could never understand and never overcome. But they could only ever wield it as long as they did so for true love. Nothing else in the world would let somebody take up that Blade and carry it into battle. But once it got picked up? There was nothing that was putting it back in its sheath. And so the gods wouldn't know of what she did, she hid it away, waiting for the right mortal to find it…and put an end to the Reckoning."

I started to glance around again and felt my face begin to burn—literally everyone was looking at me. Elaine had her blurry, puffy eyes staring right through me, like she wanted more than anything else to believe that the stupid old myth was real, that the corpses and scorched earth around us were lies and the old man's fairy tale was true. Aldric and Karla were watching with a tentative apprehension, waiting to really react until they saw how I reacted, and everybody was sizing me up, playing out a fight between me and the dragon in their heads, trying to see if I could come out on top.

What the hell, people? I'm not dragonkiller material. No. No way. That Blade probably doesn't even exist. I…I stayed quiet, watching everyone around me, feeling the weight of a couple hundred people's expectations pressing against me, and thought it through.

I could see it then, in their eyes. Old Man Granger had really sold them on that stupid story. Before, people had always regarded it as a…a myth. I mean, you heard about the Reckoning happening somewhere halfway across Plagiar and you didn't really care, but…

I mean, c'mon, I was breathing in more smoke than air. There were fires still burning. Everyone wanted something to believe in, *somebody* to believe in. They didn't want to think about the fact that ten years from now, this could all happen again…more mothers lose their kids, more husbands lose their wives.

But I wasn't that somebody. That wasn't me. I hadn't even been here when the dragon attacked, I'd just wandered back home after the fact. It was possible I was moderately ine-briated. And everyone wanted me to go rescue Marisa and Elaine's betrothed and that just wasn't me, I wasn't a fighter or an adventurer...

I didn't even think I'd known true love. Which, appar-ently, is the only requirement you need for kicking a drag-on's ass.

But they weren't relenting.

I guess...I guess I could set off on my journey and just go somewhere. Never again would everybody be willing to pitch in with what little they had left and send me on my way. The warm air broke around me and a deep cold starting tiptoeing down my spine. I stared at the old storyteller and saw myself in him—a few years out from the grave and staying in the middle of a godsforsaken town, rambling lies about true love and the end of the world.

If you don't go now, the cold whispered, *you never will.*

I could see some of the world, maybe pick up a few cool stories like Old Man Granger. And when I came back, I guess people would be disappointed, but the town would be rebuilt. Everybody would've moved on. I could find another girl, marry her, and live out the rest of my life.

The silence was hard to break—it was tough to push the words out of my throat. "So..." I said, my voice getting louder and steadier with each word. "When do I head out?"

There was a second of hesitation and then another round of unbelievably boisterous screaming. Aldric was slapping me on the back (*damnit, enough with that already*) and Karla was threatening to snap my spine with a hug. They didn't say anything, but I'd known them for long enough that I knew what they meant without saying a word: *We're coming with you.*

That, uh…that threw a wrench in my plans.

They were like accountability partners, which is a really fancy term for "killjoys." I grinned at my newfound admirers (half these people didn't even know my name, or if they did, it was "Oh, the girl that was taken? I hear she was supposed to get married to that Harkness boy, bless his heart.") and hoped their contributions to my little odyssey would live up to their half-drunken cheers.

The rest of the night was something of a blur. This was probably because a lot of different people wanted to give me drinks, which would've meant a lot more had the bartender not been passing them out for free.

The barkeep, by the way, glared at me a little harder with each barrel of mead he emptied out into someone's mug. Glares are less intimidating when it comes from a pudgy guy with a unibrow. *Glare on, you pugfaced prick.*

A bunch of people were coming up to the three of us—either by association or by the crowd spreading the word, it had gotten around that Aldric and Karla were tagging along with me. Everybody wanted to come up to us and wish us luck, and generally asked the same sorts of questions.

"Are you scared?" *Of what? Oh, the dragon! The beast that destroyed the world as we know it in the course of about two hours? The one that like twelve different gods engineered to murder people? Nah, not at all.*

"You think you've got enough for the trip?" *Yeah, I kept a bag ready for adventure in my hou—oh…wait…*

"If you need anything, just let us know. Gods bless you, son." Yeah, nothing smartassy you can say to people actually trying to help. Underneath my snarky outer shell is a less snarky interior.

Then there were a bunch of people trying to live out the glory days through us *("Ah, if I was just a few years younger, I'd be right there beside ya!")* and a bunch of kids with eyes twice as wide as normal *("Can I come on your adventure with you?")* and, off in the distance, I could always seem to feel the eyes of Old Man Granger on us, curious and apprehensive. A few times I saw him try and make his way through the crowd to us, but he never seemed able to. Their total reverence for the man (if Granger even was a man—like I said, the dude's *old*, like, *suspiciously* old) tended to fade a bit when they got hammered.

I don't know exactly what time it was that I staggered back home. Past midnight, before dawn? That was specific enough for me. Our house had been mostly annihilated by the dragon attack, but a small shed we had out back (separate from the barn that had charbroiled our late equestrian friend) had survived. The animals were all sleeping outside, so I figured that's where we were crashing for the night. I stumbled inside and was immediately engulfed in the second bone-splitting hug of the night by my mother. A small candle in the room flickered, being tended to by my dad. Whoa, a candle. They must've been taking this pretty seriously. Those were hard to come by.

"What are you thinking? Harkness you can't go out and—"

"Leave it, Beth." My father sighed. He looked sorta like me, I guess—which made sense, you know. His hair was cut pretty short, streaks of silver fading up through the brown. His face was wrinkled and tan from years and years of work, and he had pretty big muscles, which I guess were what made Mom swoon. Certainly wasn't all that money he didn't have. *Wish I'd gotten Dad's muscles and height instead of Mom's.* I was mirrored in Dad's forever messy hair and sharp jawline,

Mom's round nose and brown eyes. "Boy's got to protect Marisa, simple as that."

Mom didn't let go, her bony little arms wrapped tight around my neck. I was starting to get sorta dizzy, although that may have more to do with the alcohol than the hugs. "I know. I know. I just…promise you'll come back home safe, okay?"

"I mean…yeah, sure, I promise. I'll be back home safe and sound before you know it."

Normally my lies roll off the tongue. I can even trick myself with them. That one, half-hammered and sleep-deprived as I was, still felt hollow.

Mom pulled away, looking much older in the candlelight. "Okay." Dad didn't say much, but rather watched quietly and gave me the wordless nod of his head that conveyed about all it needed to. *I'm proud of you. Don't die.* Something shook in his features. Or maybe it was the blurry vision.

I returned it, my message silent but understood. *Thanks. I'll try not to.*

"Boy's got a big day tomorrow. Let him sleep."

And, for the second time since the Reckoning, I felt genuinely upset—I fell asleep listening to quiet, muffled sobs, ones that continued long after Mom had lain down to sleep.

II

Morning always comes too quickly when you're hungover. It comes even quicker whenever you've been peer-pressured into going on a suicidal journey. Also, it doesn't help if you were curled up on a couple bales of hay instead of a bed.

Which is interesting, because our beds were made of straw. There should've been no difference...

Anywho, I was double-checking my various provisions for the trip. This was a much quicker process than you would expect. We had some food, which was mostly whatever the villagers had leftover and were willing to spare—so some jerky (which was almost like real, cooked meat. Almost), a half loaf of bread, and whatever fruits and vegetables could be spared. There was a wineskin full of water—which, at the first opportunity, would be made full of wine. I had two blankets—one, presumably, was to throw over the oh-so-comfortable rocks and dirt, and the other to cover myself up with. I figured if I tied both of them into a noose and choked myself, I might actually be able to fall asleep with them. A little kit of flint and steel for starting fires, and that was it.

Given recent events, I wasn't really surprised people were giving their firestarters away.

Other than that, there wasn't a whole lot. Shame that the horse died. I'd be hoofing it the whole way. Of course, I didn't really know what "the whole way" entailed—millennia-old legends aren't crystal clear on *where* the great evil dragon would be, so we were going to be winging this one. I hefted my satchel over my shoulders and situated the strap across my chest, momentarily happy to be a tanner's kid. I mean, sure, I eternally reeked of oil and had the traumatizing chore of flaying bunny rabbits as a small child, but I always had plenty of satchels and boots.

Now, where are my sidekicks? I was standing out in front of my house, wondering if they were coming to me, or if I was going to them. I didn't want us to pass each other—then we'd spend half the day trying to figure out what was going on. That'd be awkward. Not a proper way to start questing, not at all.

"Son, hold up."

I turned and saw my dad walk out, holding a bundle in his hand. It was fairly long and, ah, a lesser mind might've commented as to its phallic shape, shall we say. Dad walked slow, wincing a bit as he stepped out of the shed. I hadn't noticed it in the candlelight, but there were some burn marks on his forearms, a few singed spots on his head. His eyebrows weren't all there, either.

I'd only been burned once before, playing near the fire as a kid. I...I was glad I hadn't been here when the dragon attacked. I was becoming increasingly happier I hadn't been in town when the Reckoning happened. It was a little different when it was nameless people it happened to. I wondered how Dad had gotten burned. Running back in to try and save the horse, or maybe looking for me, or who knows what.

"Yeah, what is it?"

He extended the cloth roll to me and I grabbed it, nearly dropping it. Heavier than I expected. I unwrapped it and saw—

...*oh.*

Hell yeah.

A sword! I dropped the blanket around it and tested it out, swinging it tentatively a time or two. "Dad...since when have you had this?"

He shrugged, a rebellious youth coming out behind the aching features. "Eh, I've had it tucked away. Didn't want to tell you about it."

"Why not?" I slashed at an imaginary attacker. Look, all I'm saying, fellas, if you're having any insecurity, go get yourself a sword. You will feel like more of a man in seconds.

He gave me an irritated look, half-eyebrows furrowing.

Okay, yeah, I probably didn't need a sword, all things considered. I went to sheathe it and...

"Uh...don't suppose you could loan me a sheath?"

"Blacksmith's keeping a few that I gave him. Tell him you need it. He should hand it over."

"And if not?"

"What do you think the sword's for?" He grinned and clapped me on the shoulder—(grimacing as a result, but he tried to hide it). "Be careful, son. Dragon's nothing to play around with."

I nodded. "Don't worry." "I'm worried for the dragon. Now go. You're burning daylight." And, with that, he turned and walked back into the shed, perhaps fearing what would happen if we spent too much more time exchanging good-byes. I wasn't going to dwell on that.

Regardless, *I had a sword. Hell yes!* I began walking toward the blacksmith's place, eyeing my newfound toy. It was maybe threeish, three and a half feet long—I've never been good at measurements; they aren't exactly standardized in Plagiar anyways. I'd never held one before so the weight felt kinda weird and wobbly in my hands. We would be relying heavily on the element of surprise to make up for my total lack of skill. Razor sharp, which was good, because I had no clue how you sharpened a sword. I'd seen guys rubbing rocks on theirs, but I didn't know what else was involved in that process. It was edged on both sides, and even though my fencing experience was limited to stabbing Aldric with sticks as a child, it couldn't be that hard to ruin someone's day with it. And if I accidentally hacked off one of my appendages, I was just that much closer to being Old Man Granger.

I whistled to myself, walking back through town. Most people weren't awake (most of them had been drinking even more heavily than I had—and, c'mon, what were they waking up to at this point? If the apocalypse came, would you still set your alarm clock?), so I didn't get too much in the way of fanfare on my way out. A few people smiled and waved, or said vaguely encouraging things, but beyond that, the village was quiet. The day was already beginning to heat up a bit, and I could feel sweat start soaking through where the satchel rested against my back. Lovely. Figures it'd be too much for the gods to throw me some decent weather while I was busy doing their dirty work.

Our village was small enough to move from one side to the other pretty easily, but there was crap all over the place thanks to the dragon. Not like literal dragon crap. I mean broken buildings and stuff. *Oh, man, but that would've been really nasty. And really petty.*

I was taking my time to see if I ran into Aldric and Karla. I began to ruminate on the deeper things in life: the way I was leaving footprints in the ash, only for them to be erased by the breeze. The way I was leaving everything I'd ever known for the outside world, and I'd never get this opportunity again. The unhealthy confidence boost having a sword in my hand gave me. *You guys better hope dragon's not an acquired taste, 'cause I'm bringing back steaks.*

Tripping over what was once the cornerstone of some-body's house made me break out of my reverie and I scanned the town around me. There was a strange sense of familiar-ity as I recognized where I was. Blacksmith's was a little fur-ther, but not far up the road. I saw Karla walking around and caught her eye—she came jogging over to me, stepping around mounds of still-smoking wreckage. She was still wear-ing the same clothes as yesterday, and seemed to be packing pretty light. *Must not have found much in the ruins.*

"Sure you wanna do this?" I asked, hoping she'd say no. Granted, if I had to haul ass for a thousand miles, on foot, with only stale food to eat, it'd at least be all right to have a girl along for the ride. But at the same time, Aldric and Karla were more focused on the whole heroism thing than I was. Not my speed.

"You kidding? You actually pull this off and I'll have stuff to sing about for *years*." She did a double-take. "Whoa, nice sword!"

"I know, right?" I held it up for her to admire, which sounds really messed-up out of context. She ran her finger down it and drew blood, yelping and pulling it back. Huh, that sounds even more messed-up out of context. "Heh, Karla, how many troubadours does it take to change out a chandelier?"

"Oh, shut it." Karla sucked on the finger which was probably unsanitary but was not unpleasant to watch. Platonic friendships have their limits, you know. "Where we headed?"

"Blacksmith's. I have to get a sheath before we head off. Also, we gotta find Aldric at some point. Don't know where the buffoon wandered off to."

"Oh, lay off. He's not a buffoon."

"He's *our* buffoon. We're allowed to call him that."

Karla sighed,but she also didn't contest it. Eh, I gave Aldric too much flak. He was a good guy. And being a good guy just seemed to come naturally to him. I...couldn't really get that.

I couldn't see the blacksmith's shop—we were about to turn the corner when Karla grabbed my wrist and yanked me back (which, by the way, is a really unwise thing to do when somebody has a sword in their hand), making me pause for a second. She pressed up against the corner, fingers digging into my wrist.

"No. *No.* You lying son of a bitch! You said you'd have it for me!" It was a girl speaking—her voice rough and hoarse.

There was the deep laughter of the blacksmith. "You thought I'd have a sword you asked for last night ready *today?*"

"You said you would!"

"To calm you down. Now get lost."

"No. Not until you give me a sword."

"I make it a personal policy not to give weapons to angry women." The blacksmith's voice was overwhelmingly smug, the sort where you can tell somebody's *enjoying* rubbing salt in the wound.

Now I'll be the first to tell you I'm not really a shining paragon of gender equality in Plagiar. Mostly because trying to improve other people's lives would require me to first care about people's lives, and secondly, I would have to put in a *lot* of hard work. Neither of those are really what I'm about.

But even I wanted to call this guy a dick.

There was a moment of no one saying anything—and I could practically *hear* the intensity of those two glaring at each other. "Fine," the girl hissed.

Elaine came storming out around the corner, her face burning hotter than the blacksmith's furnace. It, slightly comically, made her hair match her face, but in a moment of self-discipline I decided not to comment on this fact. Her bruised hands were curled up into fists, her breaths coming heavy and fast. You know how, when people get really pissed, their throat, like, sucks in, but their jaw gets all clenched? She was a couple steps past that, so her whole body was tense and her head looked like it was about to pop off her neck. Elaine stopped dead when she saw us—and the sword in my hands. Her bloodshot green eyes flickered from the sword to me, running the numbers in her head. I tightened my grip on it.

Hey, not saying the blacksmith was an ideal role model, but I barely even trusted *myself* with the sword. *Deep breaths, sweetheart, deep breaths.*

"Sorry you had to hear that," she muttered. It was possibly the most insincere apology of all time. I had given enough of them to know for certain. "Are you going to talk with that pig?"

"Indeed we are. I don't think I have the money to buy you a sword, though."

A smile tugged at Elaine's lips—the sort of smile you might get when you hear your ex got a new haircut that makes them look really, really bad. She cocked her head to the side and her smile widened. *Ooh, Miss Elaine is planning something devilish, isn't she?* Shame I couldn't stick around to be a part of it. "Oh, okay. That's quite all right. Good luck on your journey, Harkness." She nodded her head at Karla and slipped on by us.

I felt bad for her, but Elaine could be kinda weird some-times. Headstrong. She did impulsive stuff a lot. I watched her walk away, just to make sure she wasn't trying anything on us—people in mourning do crazy stuff sometimes—before we sidled on up to the blacksmith. He was standing at the counter of his store, which was broken in half and mildly charred. It would seem a few of his items had survived—probably by virtue of being made of metal, and the black-smith had his place on the outskirts of town. Made sense that nobody would want all that smoke filling up the center of town.

Oh, man. *More* irony. At this point I kinda just wanted to buy that dragon a drink.

"Howdy," I said, an actual genuine smile on my face. Things were going well so far. *Good vibes. Optimism. After this whole mess is over, I've got a career set for myself as a life coach.* "My dad said you could spare a sheath for me?"

The blacksmith eyed me for a minute, scratching his bald head. It was already slick with sweat. "Your father going to pay me?"

"Well, he said he gave them to you. Honestly, I'm not super clear on the details. But, I am in need of something to keep this very fine sword of mine in."

I figured that a little flattery on his craftsmanship would go a long way. *Ah, Harkness, you silver-tongued bastard, you.* The smith stared at the sword, confusion twisting up his lit-tle gorilla face. "Not my sword," he muttered.

"Yeah, it's my sword."

"No, you cretin." *Somebody must have woken up on the polite side of the bed.* "I didn't make that sword. It's not *mine.* And it doesn't look old enough to be something your father got from his father. Which means"—Big Ugly snarled, as he leaned forward on the counter (which somehow didn't burst into a million pieces)—"He bought that sword from another town. I don't take too kindly to that."

Would you take kindly to my sword cleaning out the inside of your ass?

I didn't say that. See, I have self-restraint.

Unfortunately, we were still in one of those "sins of the father" phases of societal development, which meant this particular jerk wasn't about to start judging me on the merits of my own character. *Actually, if he does that, it'll probably be worse for me.*

"Look, we can pay you."

"Well, to make up the loss from that sword, I'm thinking I'll need about twice as much. Given that it would take *your father* a few days to get a sheath made, what with everything he owns being burnt to the ground, I think you'll find my price reasonable."

Karla started to say something to him, perhaps sensing that the blacksmith was a touch grumpy, but there was a loud noise from the back of the forge, like somebody banging a rock against a piece of metal. I had a sneaking suspicion that it was somebody banging a rock against a piece of metal. The quick, trying-to-be-silent-but-failing sound of footsteps scampering off followed. Big Ugly whipped around, faster than I would've thought capable. *I mean, with a forehead that big, there has to be a bunch of wind resistance.* He picked up a hammer off the anvil next to him, rolling it over in his scarred hands. He probably could've fit his hand over my entire face, and it looked like he hadn't been skipping nightly pushups. I wasn't sure if I felt worse for whoever caused the noise, or for the hammer.

He moved slowly to the back of his area, eyes scanning his shop. Problem was, he had his "store" up front and the "smith" towards the back, and the whole thing was more or less open—no walls or anything. I don't know if that was bad or good in terms of *feng shui*, but it was definitely not helpful in terms of preventing burglaries. Racks of swords and armor, some of which were knocked over, some of which were scorched to oblivion, made it even harder to see. Karla and I exchanged a glance, trying to ascertain if this was just everyday life for the blacksmith or if there was actually something going on.

All the while, I noticed a small flicker of movement around the side of the "building," and Elaine ducked in front of us, pressed a finger to her lips, and jumped over the counter. She tiptoed over toward the swords, picking one of the smaller ones and lifting it up very slowly, very quietly. "*Something devilish.*" *Called it.*

"You two see anything?" Big Ugly snarled, raising his hammer in preparation for a strike. "Didn't think it would be this long before godsdamned looters tried to take what was rightfully!" He roared the last word, evidently hoping to startle the aforementioned looters, but there was no one behind the shelf where he kept blacksmith stuff. He moved behind it and Elaine was in the clear, creeping back over to us. I caught her attention and pointed my head at the sheathes—she nodded and moved over, grabbing two.

"Gah. Must've been my imagination."

"No, uh, I definitely heard something," Karla spoke up—a little too quickly, a little too high-pitched.

The blacksmith turned back to us, suspicion somehow expressed through his raised unibrow (maybe he and the bartender were brothers or something—or maybe there was just a very limited gene pool in our village), and saw Elaine stepping over the counter, a few hundred coins' worth of soon-to-be-stolen goods in her hands. There was a moment of silence before Elaine took her free hand and raised one particular finger to Big Ugly. He screamed and threw the hammer at her—which seemed a little harsh. I mean, we didn't have laws regarding beating the crap out of children, but still.

Elaine was too quick—the minute his arm reared back, she'd rolled over the counter and the hammer sailed over her head by a good foot and a half. Where'd she get reflexes like that? No way it was from herding sheep and knitting socks. She scrambled up in a heartbeat, threw one of the sheaths to me—which, you know, was slightly incriminating—and took off, leaping over part of a collapsed building to get cover from Hideous McThrowsHammers, Resident Blacksmith of Sorro.

That, of course, made him turn his attention to us—he reached for a mace—spiked, heavy, and just a touch intimidating. There was no doubt that he knew how to use it. *Hey there, friend.* "You're going to put that sheath down, or I'm going to make things a lot easier for that dragon."

"Hey guys! What's got Elaine in such a hurry?"

Aldric bounded up, doing that thing where you run up and half-jump against two people, resting your arms on their shoulders to stop yourself. She (well, cards on the table, it was both of us, but this looks better for me if I say it was just her) nearly pissed herself. I grunted but managed to take his weight; Karla started to crumple and Aldric staggered forward, still beaming constantly. The blacksmith was now attempting to decide which one of us to smash first. Given that this was a complex thought with lots of possibilities, his face was all scrunched up, the mental exertion contorting his features. Aldric seemed blissfully unaware of our dilemma. "Took forever to find you guys, I—hey, Mr. Darnoth, what's got you upset?"

There was a moment of stunned silence and then Big Ugly—apparently named Darnoth—came at us, lumbering faster than a human should be able to lumber. *When did everyone in this town get so fast?*

Aldric yanked both of us back and we tripped, stumbling our way into a sprint. Big Ugly tried to follow us but he was both carrying a heavy mace and we had a thirty-year head start on him in the fitness department, so outrunning him wasn't too terribly difficult. We stopped at the edge of town, breathing hard and glancing back over our shoulders frequently.

"You," I huffed, "have either really good or really bad timing, Aldric."

Aldric ran a hand over his face, his blond stubble hard to make out against his skin. "Nah. I was watching you guys from a little ways. Second Elaine jumped the counter I started to come on over."

Huh. He was smarter than I gave him credit for. Granted, that statement applies to most people I know. *Expect the worst, hope for the best.*

"Well," Karla said, "I think maybe we should get a little further before we start congratulating ourselves. But hey, if we can outsmart Darnoth, how bad can that dragon be?"

"Fair enough!" Aldric does this thing when he talks where he's just always enthusiastic and it was already pissing me off.

And he just sorta saved my life, so I couldn't say anything about it. Blegh. This was going to be a long trip.

We set off walking, Aldric and Karla throwing the occasional glance back at our hometown. I didn't bother—I'd done plenty of jaunts to the neighboring town of Hammerk, although most of those were in the dead of night, so this was admittedly new. Watching the sun rise up over the blackened, splintery remains of your childhood? Truly breathtaking. We didn't talk much for a while, mostly because being chased out of town by an asshole with a hammer kinda kills the conversational vibe. Karla would occasionally hum a song under her breath, Aldric would attempt to match her and fail horribly, and I would laugh, which made them both quiet down.

This cycle repeated itself every few minutes.

The dirt road was familiar to me but alien to my tagalongs, who were tripping and stumbling a lot more than I was. Ah. I did notice that my boots had survived the dragon attack whereas theirs had not.

"How much further? Is Hammerk an all-day march, or…?" Karla asked.

"It's not far. You can make it to Hammerk and back in an hour or so on foot."

"Didn't realize we were travelling with a walking map." Karla glanced down at her feet—I caught Aldric doing the same. The path was mostly smooth, but twigs and pebbles were doing their best to slow my compatriots down. Not me. I had shoes.

I mean, don't get me wrong, I felt bad about it, but it wasn't like I could carry them both, and giving them my shoes wouldn't really solve the problem. Plus, as the designated dragon-slayer, I probably needed them the most. I figured we'd find a cobbler in Hammerk, get Aldric and Karla fixed up, and then head out on our merry way to…wherever the dragon was. No, wait, the Blade. We had to find the Blade, first. Then the dragon. Heavens forbid the gods make something too straightforward.

"Sometimes my brilliance amazes even me, Karla. Should be just over that hill."

In case your village is on a plateau or something, hills are a sort of rounded landmass that protrude up above the area around it. The important thing about hills is that they are a bitch to climb. I, however, had experience climbing this particular hill, and I must say, I left my companions wheezing for air as I clambered on up to the top. Well, Karla moreso than Aldric. Aldric was the sort who could throw around bags of flour or chop wood all day and not really get worn out, but when it came to running and climbing he didn't do so hot. Karla, on the other hand—well, Kara wasn't really adventurer material at all. I mean she was here, she was trying, I had to give her credit, but she wasn't cut out for this sort of stuff. To be fair, I couldn't tell you which end of a lyre was up, and Aldric's singing was thought by some to be an omen of the End Times, so Karla definitely had us beat in some categories.

Still, her face was scrunched up into a reddened, sweaty sort of defiance, so good on her. I'm sure her "most team spirit" award at the end of this journey was really going to strike fear in the heart of the dragon.

I clambered on top of a smooth, mossy old boulder that must've been around before Old Man Granger could walk. I thrust my hands up in the air, bowed my head, and assumed my victory pose. "I'm king of the rock!" Aldric playfully shoved me aside, taking my spot on the boulder at the top of the hill. The skies above were blue, free of clouds, partially free of smoke—which was good. I did not want to be hiking in the rain. Also, clear skies meant no dragons overhead. The monster was supposed to stay put for the next ten years, but it just seemed wise not to, you know, expect a *monster* to stick to a schedule.

Karla rolled her eyes, continuing to walk along the bumpy, treacherous road. "Boys," she sighed.

"You don't care because you're queen of the rock by default," I said.

"Hey, he makes a good point, doesn't he?" Aldric said. He stopped to glance up at the skies like I had, and I seized this opportunity to knock him back off and permanently seal my authority as king of the hill before we continued on down (which, for those of you still unclear on the hill concept, is less of a bitch than going up the hill). Karla went in front and I let Aldric cut ahead of me.

We, of course, had gotten all of fifteen feet before Aldric had to stop and smell the roses. Being literal here. He knelt down (which put him barely beneath Karla's height) and picked up a few of the flowers.

"Hey, man, tick tock, tick tock."

He glanced up at me, a look of confusion on his face. "What?"

"You know…clock's ticking."

He and Karla exchanged a glance. *Oh, shit, this one is going over their heads. Clocks aren't a thing yet.* "Look, you don't want any of those plants anyway."

"They're everwinters." Aldric had plucked one of the flowers, a rose as white and soft as snow. He went to inhale it and I smacked it away from him. "Aren't they pretty?"

"No they're not, you oaf. They're wise man's willows."

Karla knelt down and picked up one of the flowers as well. "Pretty sure willows are trees, Hark. Like the big one by Old Man Granger's hut?"

I wondered if botanical disputes played a big role in everyone's adventures, or if it was just me. "Yeah, that's the point. Some alchemist's idea of a sick joke. They're not willows, and they're definitely not going to make you a wise man. Don't breathe them in."

I could see Aldric's willpower slipping.

"No, like seriously don't. My dad—who is colorblind as all hell—thought he would be nice one day and pick some everwinters for my mother when she was pregnant with me. Lo and behold, he got wise man's willows and not everwinters. Anyway, Mom had some major cravings. I guess plants look tasty when you're knocked up, and the next thing you know, she's tripping for a straight week. I come out the womb rattling off—"

"Colorblind?" Karla asked. She frowned. "What does rattling off mean?"

"What are you talking about? Why did the plants make your mother trip and fall over?" Aldric asked.

"No, no, like…." I counted to ten. Deep breaths. Lots more adventuring was still before us. "Okay, you know how Old Man Granger goes on vision quests?"

"Yeah," Karla said.

"His eyesight's bad?" Aldric asked out of genuine confusion. He was still rolling the acid-trip dandelions around in his hands exactly how I told him not to.

I ignored Aldric, as I normally did when I needed to get something done in a timely manner. "So basically, he could get around having to starve himself in the woods for a week if he huffed on a few of these for a while. Too many and your brain melts. Just a few and you'll hallucinate for a while. See other worlds, broaden your perspectives, learn weird stuff. And, apparently, if you pop some when you're pregnant, your kid comes out an asshole and a touch socially progressive."

Karla's face scrunched up as she rolled one of the flowers over in her hand. "Good for inspiration, then? I mean, you're always creative."

"Yeah," Aldric said. "I don't even get half the stuff you say, honestly."

"Good gods, how am I the responsible one when it comes to substance abuse? Can we keep it moving?" I made sure Aldric dropped all of the drug-trip-dandelions before we kept pushing onward.

Before us, maybe a third of a mile away, was the town of Hammerk. In terms of easily overlooked villages, it's neck and neck with our hometown. Hammerk, however, has one key advantage over Sorro—while we're closer to the woods, which has let us develop such lovely industries as foresting and lumberjacking and such, they were closer to the main road, which let them develop brothels and bars for travelers. Hammerk was the sort of place that was way more fun to be in after dark.

The village altogether was pretty small: there was one main street, maybe fifty yards long, that had a couple of small shops in it. They had a bar or two, a quaint little whorehouse, a bakery, along with everything a small community needs. Then, there were a bunch of shanty houses kinda haphazardly thrown around the outside, shacks built of piecemeal logs and mud. Hammerk's economy was not exactly booming. The main buildings at least appeared to have some competency behind their architecture, but the rest of Hammerk's residents probably figured a ceiling collapsing on them in their sleep was an okay way to go. Grasses and weeds surrounded the edge of the town, and there were a couple of fences up where people were keeping their cows and sheep and whatnot. One goat gave us a rather irritated look as we passed by, and resumed browsing. I didn't know how much of the farming was for profit and how much was for eating. If I had to guess, I'd say the latter. Neither of our towns were especially well-off, but we at least didn't have a place to easily burn through money aside from our tavern. I feel like a lot of the money in Hammerk got sucked away down that road they clung to—travelers came in and wound up leaving with more than they left behind. Out here, you couldn't tell so much, in the hills and farms.

But inside you got the sense that nobody ever really left.

The adventure was starting to seem like a really good idea. Plus, Aldric and Karla had made it like fifteen minutes before the no shoes thing wore them down. I was in the clear.

In the mid-morning (the sun was an okay distance over the horizon, now), it was a mess of hungover johns and wayward women. *I have found my people.* We walked right on down the main street, eyeing some of the horses that were tied up in front of the bars—even savoring the smell of bread wafting over from the nearby bakery. Part of me considered stealing one of the horses, but I decided against it. Not for any ethical reasons or anything, just because I figured I wouldn't want to piss somebody off at the *start* of my journey. I'd steal the horse on the way back.

The horses were too tired to pull against their ropes, and the people were too tired to take the ropes for themselves. *Welcome to Hammerk.*

"First order of business," Karla said. "I think we should get some shoes. I don't want to complain, but uh, I don't know much further bare feet are going to take us. Especially since I've got a feeling dragon-hunting might take us off the beaten path."

"True," Aldric said, glancing at Karla's feet, black and filthy as they were. He chewed on his lip for a minute. "Hark, do we have enough money for both of us to get shoes?"

I pulled out our coin purse. The town had chipped in to help supply us with what they could, but we weren't exactly loaded. Enough to get two pairs of shoes? Yeah, we could swing that, but it was gonna put a major dent in our budget. Still, shoes were shoes. They needed them, so there wasn't much choice. *This was supposed to be a solo venture.* "Yeah, man." I tossed it to him, seeing the relief on Aldric's face. What, had he planned on going without or something?

Karla snatched the bag out of the air before Aldric could grab it, grinning fiercely at him. "Yeah, who's queen of the rock now? Let's go, Aldric."

Aldric paused, glancing at the purse. It was a small purse. Aldric had big feet. "Shouldn't we check and see how much money we've got?"

A few passersby gave Aldric very curious looks as he said this. Said passersby were dressed about as well as we were—our excuse was the dragon attacking, theirs was mere hard living. I felt the weight of a few sets of eyes on the sword at my belt, and at the size of my tagalong, Aldric. Mercifully, Karla was a little more street smart than he was, and she quickly shut him up with an elbow to the ribs. "Voice down, Aldric. This isn't home." He nodded, muttered a quick apology. Man, we were never going to live it down if we got mugged before we even made it to the dragon.

"Hand me a few coins—I'll try and get us some more food for the journey. What we have isn't going to last too terribly long, especially if Aldric wants to eat."

Aldric opened his mouth to say something, then paused. Kid's like six inches taller and sixty pounds heavier than everyone else in our town. "Yeah, okay," he admitted.

"Good idea," Karla said, handing me a few coins. The little bronze pieces were rusty, some king's face on them. Honestly, didn't really know who. We were a few hundred miles out from anything resembling well-patrolled territory and pretty much governed ourselves. King wasn't making money off backwater towns like this; king didn't care about backwater towns like this. *With that kind of attitude, maybe I'm royalty.*

They disappeared around a corner, leaving me flying solo for a while. I entered the bakery which I guess was nice by Hammerk's standards. Actually, nice by most standards. The building was low—one story—and I imagine the owner lived out the back. It was pretty well-maintained. No spiderwebs clinging to the roof's overhang. The delicious smell of cooking bread wafted out the window, and I had to wonder if he'd baked so much that it just sunk into the heavy logs of the store itself, so that the place just always smelled like fresh bread.

Even with the scent of heavenly warm bread trying its hardest to empty my wallet, blowing all our money here didn't seem economical to me. We had the food the town had scrounged up for us, but it wasn't enough to last me more than a day if I ate until I was full, let alone all three of us. Maybe I could milk the "we're poor survivors of the dragon attack" thing. There was no way they didn't see the smoke from here, and while our villages weren't really that close (emotionally, I mean. We're pretty cozy geographically), there was a kind of camaraderie. If we didn't help each other, nobody would, especially in times of crisis like these. In fact, part of me wondered if anyone else from our hometown had been here so far. We could've claimed we were the only survivors, gotten some food and drinks out of it, and double-timed it down the road before somebody else came along and ruined our little scam.

Hey—we had to eat, all right? And we were saving the world and whatnot, so that allowed for a little moral ambiguity.

I entered the baker's place and smiled at him, which I've found either throws people off or warms them up to you. He grinned back before his face went sober, looking at the soot-soaked, worse-for-the-wear patron he'd just acquired. *So...the latter.* We couldn't have been more opposite—I was lanky and thin, but years of baker's dozens showed on his gut and wide frame. He was fair, blond and watery blue eyes to contrast my dark features. His face was round, jawlines lost somewhere in pudgy flesh. Still, friendly looking guy. Just gave off that vibe, like he wasn't totally annoying. I'd found relatively few people gave me that impression, and I usually rolled with it when I saw it. "You..." the words got lost somewhere in his throat, and he just nodded his head toward what was once a town, a few miles from where we'd come.

"Yes, sir," I replied. "True tragedy. The horror, the horror."

He nodded, turning and pulling a loaf of bread out of the oven, setting it on the counter. He must've noticed my staring at it the same way sailors stare at the shore, and he let out a short little guffaw. "Go on, help yourself."

"I have a few friends coming over in a minute, do you mind if I get some for them too?"

"Take the whole thing. Think you need it more than I need a few coins."

Woohoo! I love the altruistic types. "I can pay you some…"

"No, son, it's fine." My suspicions were right. He sat down on a stool (it creaked slightly under his weight) and looked around the otherwise empty bakery, perhaps running through bags of flour and supplies. The burlap sacks were stacked pretty high in the corner, and I noticed an unapologetically fat cat dozing next to it. Probably kept the rats away in exchange for food. *Now here's a morbid thought—the dragon isn't much different.*

"Any of your people survive?" he asked, a quiet but almost familiar tone to his voice. For all the crap I give people in these parts, they're generally all right. Sure you get some thugs—like the ones eyeing us back on the street—but that's to be expected in a cesspit like Hammerk. Most people are just trying to make it by, and I think life in Plagiar's too brutal for most to bother with malice. *Optimism, people.*

I nodded my head, tearing off a chunk of bread and chewing a mouthful of divine blessing. All hot and chewy and…*damn.* I shifted around the "attractions of Hammerk" in my mental travel guidebook. The bread just jumped up ahead of the beer and the whores—I can see how this guy and his kitty had gotten so heavy. "A few. My folks did, but it…" I paused, remembering I needed to be way more upset about this than I really was. "Took my girl. Another guy out of my town, too. A few people…you know."

The baker's face darkened and he shook his head, wiping his flour-coated hands off with a rag. "That's terrible. You…"

Aldric and Karla chose that moment to enter the bakery, clad in what looked like cheap but functional leather boots. If my father had more time, he probably could've made them a replacement pair, but I'm actually glad he didn't. Dad's a pretty considerate guy, underneath the gruff exterior. He would've woven bells or something into Little Miss Troubadour's shoes and I would've had to hear those stupid things jingle for the next thousand miles. Or…leagues? What were adventures measured in?

The baker glanced up at them, quickly pieced together that they were with me (*we all look like death's bastard children and reek of smoke—guess who's from out of town*) and gave them a reassuring smile. "C'mon in, have some. You three look like you've been through hell."

"Plan on marching right through it!" Aldric said, flashing the guy a smile and ripping off a hunk for Karla before he gnawed on a piece. She smiled quietly, and under the dirt smears on her cheeks and the sleep-deprivation bags under her eyes, there was a sort of…glow. She ate quietly, watching the cat snore almost jealously.

"The name's Aldric, sir." He offered a hand to shake— oops, I probably should've done that. I hadn't even introduced myself. One dragon attack and my manners go right out the window. "Thanks for the bread."

"Dirk," he replied. "No problem. I've got some grain to move in—"

"Need any help?" Aldric offered.

"No, son, I'm good." Dirk grinned—I'd never noticed it before, but Aldric had a way with people. Something about his happy-go-lucky, gentle giant getup just set people at ease. Of course, it got annoying at times, but he was charismatic in his own, weird way.

I heard laughing. Girls laughing. The door to the bakery was propped open, letting the heat of the ovens get sucked out by the breeze. Not good. I zoned out of the conversation entirely, accidentally biting into my fingers along with the handful of bread. *No, no, no, no.* There was another bout of giggling, and it sounded closer. *Shit. Shit. Shit!* Footsteps hammered against the path outside and I realized how close they were. *Please don't let them come in for bread. Please don't let them come in for bread.*

I ducked my head down, which made Karla glance up at me curiously. I frantically wiped bread crumbs off my shirt to make it appear natural. She studied me for a minute—I think she caught on that something was up—but said nothing, returning to watching the cat after a second or two. Aldric and the baker carried on as normal, laughing about something Aldric had said.

An eternity passed and the women moved past the front of the store, the laughter fading as they walked further away. *Oh thank the gods. That was...that was close.*

My voice came out a little fast and a little squeaky. "We appreciate the help, sir, but, uh, I think we've got to get going soon."

"Where to?"

"Going after her. My girl, that is."

Dirk's jolly grin and soft features darkened for a moment, his eyes growing wide with...disappointment. It was a lot easier for people to rally behind you when they had nothing else left—it was easy to buy into Old Man Granger's tale, that there was actually hope to get out of this, when you'd been through the worst. But this guy?

I mean, aside from the morning breeze smelling like bar-becued peasant, the dragon attack hadn't affected him at all. If I'd seen three homeless-looking kids, hell-bent on saving a girl that was in all likelihood dead, I'd have given them the same look. "Wish you luck," he said quietly. "You can, uh, take some more bread, if you like. I've got plenty." He gave us a little nod and we muttered our thanks, the warmth of the bakery all gone. The faint smell of smoke reached us—I saw Karla flinch and Aldric whip around to the front of the store, eyes frantically checking the street outside.

It was the oven—our conversation made Dirk miss pulling something out of the oven. He hurriedly grabbed it before it was charred to a crisp, cursing his stupidity as he set it on the counter to cool.

"It's okay," Karla said softly, standing up and moving over to Aldric. Aldric nodded and took a few deep breaths.

"I'm gonna, uh, step outside," Aldric said, his skin a few shades paler than normal. "Fresh air. Thanks, Mr. Dirk." He hurried outside, breathing deep once he got out of the smoky bakery.

I sat in silence for a minute, feeling the sword's weight tug at my hip, and wondered what, exactly, had pushed them to come on this quest. Even with more food than I could eat in a year lying around us, I didn't feel hungry. Not anymore.

Dirk muttered something I didn't quite hear and he stepped into the back room, helping to end the awkward little incident.

"Seemed to have a lot of faith in us," Karla said quietly enough to not be heard by the baker. She took our waterskins and refilled them with a pitcher the baker had. She looked rattled by the smoke, but it seemed…put to the side for now. Consequential. Karla may have been all shaken up, but she was still carrying on. It'd catch up to her at some point, I figured. When she lay down to sleep or when she ran out of songs to keep her mind off it.

And it's going to catch up to you too, Harkness. Can't run forever.

I heard the faint echo of a woman's laugh and it broke me out of my stupor. "Yeah, well, don't mind him. Let's just get out of here." Karla nodded and I grabbed the wineskins from her, slinging them over my shoulder. "Thank you once again!" I shouted to Dirk. The cat opened one eye, clearly irritated, as we hurried out.

III

By the time we'd gone back out onto the street, the sun was up and stirring, drenching us in the lovely heat and humidity that this section of Plagiar has to offer. On the positive side, Aldric was looking better, and had given his last bit of bread to a few hungry (ravenous, if you will) crows on the street. They pecked at it furiously, ignoring their benefactor. Aldric didn't seem to mind. I checked both sides of the street, making sure the laughing girls were gone. *Good. Good, good, good.*

I felt Karla watching me again, and spoke to Aldric before she could ask me anything. "So, you good?"

"I'm not good. I'm Aldric!"

There's nothing more annoying than glaring at someone and just having them smile back.

After a long sigh, I continued. "Well, as riveting as Hammerk is, we should probably get going. We're bound to catch syphilis just by breathing."

Aldric blinked. I could practically feel the wise man willow flowing through the umbilical cord and right out my mouth. "Syphilis is, like, a disease you get from whores," I explained.

"Ah," Aldric said. "Well, we won't get that. That'd be a lame ending for Karla's song. Or who knows, maybe my song. I might just take up troubadouring after all this."

We started walking along the main road, although I managed to divert us onto a side road that would hopefully keep us from crossing paths with any of Hammerk's more giggly residents. Karla kept looking around, eyeing me and eyeing the streets. She knew something was up. *Damnit.*

"Oh really?" Karla asked, playful skepticism in her voice.

"Worried I'll be better than you?" Aldric stepped out of the way of a man pulling a donkey loaded with bags of some sort. Even by donkey standards, the donkey looked like he did not want to be there. "I can storytell in my sleep."

"By all means, indulge us!" Karla said, her challenge good-natured. I let them bicker, trying to watch for any pickpockets or the sort. Pretty much all of Hammerk was "the bad side of town" and we couldn't really afford to get burgled. Or robbed? I forget the difference.

"Fine." Aldric cleared his throat melodramatically, and began speaking his best impression of Old Man Granger's low, rough growl. "Once upon a time there was, uh, the selflessly brave hero, Harkness."

My laughter drew the attention of everyone in the alley.

"…the impossibly beautiful Karla…."

"Oh yeah, I'm really turning heads looking like this," Karla muttered.

"…and, of course, the dashing warrior, Aldric."

"You're a warrior now?"

"Hush, I'm telling the story." Aldric realized he'd broken character and hurriedly picked the voice back up. "Uh, they traveled through the dangerous land of Hammerk, aided only by the supreme baker, Dirk…"

You know, I wonder how many people just helped out heroes in the stories for the publicity. Karla nimbly hopped over a sleeping dog who was "keeping watch" over somebody's house. Hey, if I was protecting that little, I probably wouldn't take my job seriously either. Gentrification was happening to this town wherever we and our meager gold purse happened to be walking through.

Aldric paused for a minute, pondering the end of our journey. "…and after emerging from the village without even a trace of syphilis…"

"Speak for yourself," I muttered.

"The heroes succeeded in killing the dragon and saving the day. The end."

Karla brushed some of her hair out of her face, rubbing at her eyes. "Look at you go, Al. You'll be putting me out of business in no time."

Aldric shrugged. "Eh, I'm sure if you had your lyre you could keep up."

Karla winced.

Noticing her discomfort, Aldric continued, "Don't be upset! Just think, once we get back, every minstrel in Plagiar will want to hear the tale firsthand. Won't be any trouble at all to talk them into giving ya one."

"I'm counting on it." Karla sighed.

Aldric glanced at me as if to ask if he'd said something wrong. I mirrored his shrug and kept on walking. I had enough going on with figuring out dragon-slaying to try and deal with relationship stuff. Although I suppose in my case there was a fair amount of overlap.

We started getting close to the outskirts of the village, which was pretty hard to distinguish from the center of the village. Hadn't spent a lot of time on this side of town, so I made sure to take note of it for later. Some would've questioned if they would ever return here, to the homey little town of Hammerk, with girls-next-door charm in each of its hookers and our recent discovery of its mouthwateringly good bread. Some would've questioned if they would survive a fight with the most dangerous monster to ever live, but not me. I figured the odds were pretty good we'd never make it there to begin with, so I wasn't too worried about the fight itself. Was Marisa being abducted terrible? Yeah, it was horrible, but you know, no sense in dwelling on the negatives, right? *I'm taking a leaf out of Aldric's book.*

Aldric endured the silence for about half a minute before piping up with, "Where we headed, Hark?"

"Hm. Well, I'll level with you. I wasn't really clear on that myself." I hitched the wineskins at my shoulder, lifting them up and putting them down in my satchel. I wasn't walking halfway across Plagiar with those things bumping into my chest every other step. "But, if I am remembering correctly, there's a river some miles thataway." I pointed to the west-ish area of the horizon. "And down that river, or maybe on the other side of it—I can't remember—there is a city called Drowduss. Assuming we can get to the river and find a boat, or maybe some really friendly fish, we can hitch a ride to Drowduss." I paused. "Or if it's on the other side of the river we can just cross. I just remember there's a river in the picture somewhere on the way to Drowduss."

"Why are we headed to the city?" Aldric asked, either ignoring my quip about the fish or perhaps buying into it. You never knew with that kid.

"Well, I think they have a…what do you call it? The place where they watch the stars…"

"Outside?" Aldric asked.

"Observatory?" Karla asked.

"Yes. That. Observatory. It's a part of that temple they have, the one dedicated to Remos." If you've forgotten our fairy tale already, he's the one in charge of the seasons. That dick was the reason we were all sweating bullets right now. His Seasonally-Oriented Divineness just goes and changes the seasons, and seems to like making our winters nightmarishly cold and our summers hellishly hot. Not much you could do. He's a god. We're people. *Suck it up and keep on trucking.* "So, I assume somebody was watching the skies when the dragon attacked. They saw which way it went, and we follow."

There was silence, which was telling. They didn't want to voice any criticisms, but at the same time….

"Okay," I relented. "It's not the *best* plan, but I don't know what else we got. I haven't any idea where that dragon flew off to, let alone where the magic sword—"

"Layana's Blade," Karla corrected. "*With a heart of love that ne'er will fade, with a lover's hand that cannot be stayed, so may they find Layana's Blade.*" She smiled, pleased with herself. To be fair, Karla knew more songs and stories than anyone else in our village. She would've cleaned up on trivia night at Sorro's pub. If, you know, Plagiar had trivia nights. Illiteracy does a number on your hometown's quiz bowl team after a while.

"Ah, yes, thank you. *And when he becometh sick of the dragon's sass, Harkness shall go forth and kick his ass.*"

Karla glowered at me.

"See, Aldric, she gets jealous if other people do it. Now, more to the point, there's supposedly a decent fortune-teller in Drowduss. Maybe she can do some crystal ball malarkey and point us in the right direction."

"Crystal ball's not malarkey," Karla said. "The knuckle-bones are the ones they make up."

"No, the knuckles are the real thing. That's all up to the gods which way they turn out. Why would you even see anything in a glass ball?" Aldric said.

"Hey, let's debate the merits of psychics later and walk now. Sound good?" My voice was a little quicker than was perhaps warranted—I thought I'd heard another faint echo of a laugh. We were almost out of Hammerk, the bunched-together houses growing more and more spaced out. Stray dogs and lean cats were being replaced with roped up cows and grazing sheep.

Aldric clapped me on the back *(gods, stop it already)* and grinned. "Ready to save his Marisa! I like that! Shall we put this debate off for a later time, Karla?"

"Huh? Yeah, sure." Karla was staring back at the hill we'd crossed to get into town. Hammerk sat in the bottom of a small valley, and we'd begun ascending the hill leading out the other side. None of the buildings in town were particularly tall, which meant you could make out the way we'd come in. "Oh, sorry, thought I saw somebody else from back home crossing it. Just my eyes playing tricks on me. Onward!"

"Excuses," Aldric said, speaking in that taunting voice that never fails to irritate whoever you're using it on. "You're just covering up the fact you lost."

Karla rolled her eyes and the two of them followed after me, struggling a bit to keep up with my quickened pace.

All three of us were constantly glancing around, looking at the rather shoddily constructed homes. There isn't really such a thing as "the ghetto" in medieval-era Plagiar, but there is a definite vibe of "oh-hey-walk-faster-I-think-that-guy-has-a-knife," which makes it essentially the same thing. While you may have been equally likely to get harassed in any part of Hammerk, the outer edges did have the risk of no witnesses. Lot easier to be bolder when there's no Goody Two-shoes law enforcement to come along and stop you. Although, come to think of it, "law enforcement" in Plagiar was also a pretty vague term.

The path segued from dirt to grass that was as downtrodden as Hammerk, and we slowed a bit as we accommodated the constant changes in the terrain. Walking through the hills made for a nice view, but we had to keep glancing down to make sure we didn't trip. The sun just kept crawling up higher, sticking my tunic to my back and reddening my neck. When we stopped for the night, I was going to be peeling off half my skin.

About a minute after we'd cleared the last house in the Hammerk outskirts, gazing out over the rolling hills and crooked trees, we all started to breathe a little easier.

Which, of course, is exactly when we got jumped.

The bushes around us exploded with movement and three guys burst in front of us. *Oh, gods, talk about out of context.* I stopped suddenly, nearly falling—my sudden braking made Karla yelp and bump into me, but Aldric must've grabbed her before she could fall. I felt them back up a few steps, giving me a little space. The muggers stared us down, one of them grinning like a psycho, rubbing his uneven, yellowed teeth back and forth over each other. The others just looked indifferent, and that messed with me a little worse—this was no big deal for them. The tallest was Aldric's height, but thank the gods not as big—they were all as scrawny as me, their clothes hanging baggy on their bony arms and legs.

Scratches and scrapes (somehow, with adrenaline coursing through my veins, my mind found time to notice all these little details) littered their forearms, and I wondered how long they'd been camped out in the foliage waiting for someone to come along. These guys had, well, not much. One of the bandits was using a knife, but it wasn't even the sort of knife you'd use to fight with. It was something you'd find in a kitchen. Another guy had a length of rusted chain (*maybe we are in the ghetto*) two or three feet long, and the last, poor son of a bitch just had his fists. Only the knife-wielder had shoes. The others just had layers of dirt thick enough to pass for socks. They must not have been very good thieves—no shoes, gaunt eyes sunk back into their heads, skinny as Aldric was tall. The knife-man—the yellow-toothed psycho—stood in the center, with fists to his right and the chain guy to his left. He raised his arm, twisting the blade at us as he jeered. As he did so, his shirt came up, and I saw his ribs press against the skin of his chest. "Give us all you got!" he hissed. Their eyes danced between my sword and Aldric behind me. The guy with the chain snarled in agreement, but the man with only his fists did something strange—he opened his mouth to shout some other threat, but no voice come out. He stopped and closed his lips again. *Weird, but there are more pressing issues than his apparent mutism.*

I'd rather not fight these guys—not because I'm a pacifist—but because I have a very healthy fear of having my ass kicked, even by scrawny, B-list muggers. Judging by how poorly these guys were outfitted, I didn't think they were pulling a lot of coin as highwaymen. But in a way, that just made them more dangerous—they were desperate, and a hungry dog bites a lot harder than a fat one.

There was a second or two of dead stillness, with none of us knowing how to react, and them trying to decide if they could take us or not. I saw the knife-man stare over my shoulder at something, and I started to put two and two together.

I'd like to think of myself as a pretty clever guy. I mean, I'm not like super smart, but I kinda sorta know how to read, and I'm not dumb enough to believe that Plagiar is round. So when I see this asshole staring at something over my shoulder, I knew what was going on.I drew my sword like I knew how to use it and spun, thankful that Karla and Aldric had given me space. I was pretty sure there was another mugger behind us, who was going to sneak up and shiv us once we were good and focused on those three. Knife Guy's eyes had given him away—he'd have to be a lot smarter than that to catch me off-guard. I turned, sword wobbling in my hands—

No, wait. There was no one behind us. My sword sliced cleanly through the open air. *Aw, man. That would've been so badass if somebody had been there.* I spared half a second to make sure there was no one behind Aldric or Karla—they seemed torn between watching the muggers and watching their friend who had apparently gone entirely insane, slashing through empty space and turning his back to the muggers.

Yeah, I look like a total dumbass right now. I may have been giving these guys too much credit. Thankfully, I managed to cover it pretty quickly. Mid-swing (Even in the middle of being shaken down, I felt my cheeks burn with embarrassment. *Smooth, Harkness, smooth.*) I drove the sword down, embedding it into the soft dirt of the path beneath us. Aldric let out a barely audible *"What?"* and I spun back to the would-be muggers. Everyone was staring at me—no more looking over my shoulder now—and it looked like I'd thrown off their plan. Granted, I was then realizing that "plan" was a strong word for the little heist they were pulling off. They weren't looking like hardened criminals anyway—a little crazy and dumb, but not *hard*. Maybe freaking them out would make them scatter, and we could get out of here without having to throw down with them.

So I roared like a demoniac with a drinking problem, slammed my hands on the ground (surreptitiously getting a handful of dirt in each hand) and stood, half-hunched, glaring at these three guys with all the craziness I could muster. They were maybe five, six feet away—close enough that if they came for us, I wouldn't be able to grab my sword in time. I saw Aldric subtly inch closer to it out of the corner of my eye, managing to position himself between Karla and the bandits in the process. I vaguely heard the shuffling of feet and the rustling of a bush, and Karla grunted. Must've been doing something, I couldn't see what. "You!" I shouted, pointing at the one with the chain, on the left. Immediate confusion washed over his haggard, wispily bearded face. "You know what I'm going to do to you with that chain?"

There was more silence. Just absolute, total confusion from all parties involved. I'm pretty sure even the birds in the trees around us were wondering what the hell was wrong with me. *My plan is working.* This wasn't even bluffing with a pair of twos. This was like bluffing without having any cards. I forced myself to keep a crazy face and not a terrified face. *Gods, if we get our asses kicked three hours into the adventure because I overestimated the worst muggers in Plagiar.*

"I asked you a question, bitch!"

"I...uh...what..." He looked to his other muggers to try and figure out what the protocol here was.

"You're gonna like it, too!" I stepped a little bit closer. A smidge more was all I'd need. They were confused, but not total idiots—they still had their weapons (or fists) ready to go, and were watching me very closely.

You have to remember, in this day and age we didn't really have things like "mental health treatment" or "diagnoses." For all these half-starved thieves knew, I was possessed by demons or something.

I mean, after all, no one who was sane would throw away their sword at the start of a fight.

All I had to do was sell these guys for a second or two longer. Dirt in the eyes, I shout for Aldric and Karla to break, and we turn and haul ass back into the village, then find another way around. A gentle breeze—the first I'd felt all day—moved the branches of the trees around us just a bit, shifting the shadows on the faces of our muggers. They were glancing between me and Karla and Aldric, trying to figure out what was going on. I thought of Dirk the baker's cat, tail flickering back and forth as it waited to lunge at a mouse.

I took another half step closer, growling. I licked my lips, staring at the guy with the knife, watching the other two out of my peripheral vision. One of them twitched, but none of them did anything. Knife's brow furrowed, his mouth opened to say something—

Out of the side of my vision, I saw Fists' mouth open up, his eyes seize shut with pain—he clawed at his throat, keeling over. And out of the woods nearby came a voice.

I would've sworn it was his, but it sounded...off. I couldn't tell you how or why.

But I didn't think it was human.

"*It's a trick. Kill them.*"

Well, shit. There went my plan.

I screamed as loud as I could, mostly because I figured it would at least disorient them a little, and definitely not out of terror, and I threw the dirt at Knife-guy and Chains. They flinched back, and I didn't stick around to see how effective it was—even if I only made them stagger for a second, Fists was preoccupied clutching at his throat, and we had our escape. I whipped back around, jumping over my sword as Aldric swooped under to rip it out of the ground with seemingly no effort.

"Aldric, Karla, Run!" I shouted, reaching out to grab Karla. She'd pulled a branch off the ground and nodded, turning and throwing it into the woods where the strange voice had come from. Aldric backpedaled quickly, but the muggers were still recovering—he turned and sprinted after Karla and I as we thundered back down the road.

Adrenaline took over and my brain started running as fast as my legs. *Were Aldric and Karla's shoes going to hold up? What was with that voice, and that guy's throat? Were my friends even still behind me?*

I kept turning my head around to make sure Aldric and Karla were with me—we couldn't afford to slow down. The muggers started to follow us, but we were trucking it—after maybe thirty seconds of giving pursuit, they started wheezing and staggering, falling or simply giving up the chase. *Maybe hungry dogs can only bite so hard.*

The ramshackle houses and meager farms blazed past us as we took down the road, stumbling on the uneven ground. I heard Aldric grunting a few times, maybe catching Karla as she fell. I turned back one more time and my foot promptly connected with a rock. The world flipped sideways and I hit the ground, moving too fast to outright stop. I bounced, rolling down the hill (with each impact, my satchel and sheath shifted and smacked me somewhere else—stomach, groin, legs—everywhere took a beating). I finally managed to dig my arms into the ground and slow myself to a stop.

Ow.

Karla got to me first, shaking me (*sweet merciful gods, Karla, that does not feel pleasant*) to make sure I was good. "Hark? Harkness!"

"I'm fine. Agh, Damnit." I pushed up off the ground and stood up, legs feeling like…well, really, I didn't have a frame of reference. I'd never gotten smacked around that badly before. The world was still spinning a little bit, and I patted my head to make sure I hadn't caved in part of my skull or something. *Nope. All good up there. Relatively speaking.* My arms were a patchwork of scrapes and dirt, but I didn't see any bones sticking out, so I figured I was okay. Aldric slid to a stop, his slightly uneven blue eyes wide and apprehensive. "I'm all right," I said, wincing and rolling my shoulders a bit. *Walk it off, Hark, walk it off. Not about to let a hill stop your kick-ass adventure.*

"I think we're far enough along we can walk back to town," Karla said, helping steady me for a second as we began again, much slower. "You sure you're okay?"

"Nothing fifteen minutes' rest and a pint of mead can't fix," I said. Well, their concern was nice at least. Aldric grinned and clapped me on the back (*Damnit! I just fell down a hill! Stop it already!*) and brought up the rear, hanging back by seven or eight feet to keep an eye on the path behind us. Thankfully, there wasn't really anywhere to hide—aside from the occasional shack, it was open grassy patches and the occasional lonely tree. We'd be able to see them coming, but I had a feeling they'd given up a good ways back. I didn't know how far we'd just sprinted, but it was far enough to qualify as "you'll be sore to the bone tomorrow." Myself doubly so. *Freaking hills.*

There was also a profound awkwardness over the absolutely moronic stunt I had just pulled, but I think the sympathy for getting beaten up by a hill kept them quiet. I was grateful.

"We shouldn't stay in Hammerk long," I said. "Need to get back on the road."

"Are you out of your mind?" Karla said, staring up at me. "We almost got killed and you want to head back?"

"We did not almost get killed," I said. "Nobody even got hurt, barring the tripping and falling." The voice whispering out of the woods came back to me, and even in the summer heat I felt a chill run down my spine.

Karla was right.

But we...we couldn't stay in Hammerk, regardless.

"We came close," Karla said. We walked past a collapsed, one-room house, which a few tired-looking men were trying to piece back together. *Rough all over.* "Not so much from the muggers."

I dropped my voice down so Aldric wouldn't hear—he was busy offering to help the guys with the house, but they were graciously declining. "What was that? The voice in the woods?"

Karla opened her mouth to reply but stopped, eyes narrowing. "No. Tell me what that laughter by the bakery was, first. Why we took half an hour longer by going down side roads instead of the main street."

"Karla, if you're so worried about us getting hurt, now is not the time to start holding secrets."

She glowered at me for a full ten seconds, and then checked to make sure Aldric was far enough behind us. "I...I think it was a hollowthroat. Can't be sure." She hesitated. "I don't want to be sure," she added.

Oh. Oh shit.

"Wait, then—"

"Hush," she said, giving me a pointed glance as Aldric closed the distance. We were back in Hammerk proper, now—if you could call any part of Hammerk "proper"— and the bustling crowds of people going to shops or work meant that the muggers couldn't outright pick a fight with us even if they had bothered following us back here. None of us had entirely calmed down, but I forced myself to relax. *Deep breaths. Deep breaths.*

"You two all right?" Aldric asked, his usual smile gone. I wasn't sure if he was totally aware of the danger back there.

"Yeah. I don't think those three assholes are following us anymore." We stopped near the end of the main street, which would eventually curl out and loop back onto the road we'd taken. We had an okay view of the path out of town from there, and couldn't see any movement on it at all. Over the crest of the hill, a few puffy white clouds floated by, but for the most part the Plagiar sky was blue and empty. When the breeze occasionally came through, it was tolerable, but otherwise the heat was annoying—especially after sprinting as much as we just had.

I glanced around and saw a man walking by on the street, who gave the three of us a very strange look before moving on. I guess we did look kinda weird, in ashy, messed up clothes, still breathing hard as we stared off into the distance. Karla sat down on the porch of a butcher's shop, clenching her hands together. They were still trembling. Aldric crossed his arms and watched the hill with me, chewing on his bottom lip.

I looked between the two for a moment.

"Neither of you…you've never left home, have you?"

There was silence for a minute.

Huh.

"Thanks," I said. It wasn't often that I heard sincerity in my voice, but it was there that time. "We're going to be all right, understand? I say we linger around here for a little while, then…maybe at nightfall, we sneak right past those pricks. I don't know of another way to the river. We could ask the locals, but I'm not sure how reliable they might be." They'd know the path, sure—but those muggers had to be living in Hammerk. That meant they knew people in Hammerk. That meant people in Hammerk might like them, and might side with them over us. All it would take is for them to direct us off on a dead end path, then send the muggers—and their friend the hollowthroat—along after us.

"Sounds good," Aldric said, giving me a fleeting smile. None of us were entirely confident in our plan—in fact, going in the dead of night seemed even *more* terrifying, but I didn't see what other choice we had. As drained as those guys were, I didn't think they'd last all day in the heat. Maybe they'd return back here for the night, and then we could go on through. As for the voice in the woods, well, there was a chance we were wrong.

Wasn't sure what the plan was if we were right.

"All right." I paused for a moment, considering the roaming group, the laughter I'd heard earlier. No rest for the wary. "What do you two say to us heading off to the other side of town, somewhere out of the way, just catching our breath for a while?"

"That," Karla said, eyebrows raising at *out of the way*, "Sounds absolutely lovely."

IV

There comes a time—a first time—in every man's life when he must run from a town in the dead of night. This was not that time for me, but I was pretty sure it was for Aldric. I don't know if women have a similar rite of passage, but if so, it was for Karla as well.

We traipsed down the main street of Hammerk, eyes too busy glancing at all the suspicious types around us to pay attention to the wide open, starlit sky above. I'm not one to marvel at the beauty of stuff, but it really was breathtaking—and a lovely distraction from our current predicament. If I was a rugged, hardcore type, I could've used those to guide me instead of making wild guesses and running with them, but alas.

Some may not enjoy Hammerk's rustic, illegal charm. If you don't enjoy the risk of mugging or stabbing, then it's not for you. That being said, if you're not totally lame, it has some serious perks. Lanterns lit up the busy streets, and open windows let the sound of black-out drunk laughter (men laughing—nothing to worry about, nothing at all) escape into the night. At least four or five people staggered out of a bar/brothel, furiously throwing punches at each other as we walked by, but they courteously didn't involve us in their drunken scuffle. One of them yelled and jumped at another, missing him entirely. We picked up our pace and let them beat each other senseless.

After sundown, everyone in Hammerk became shady, because no one clean was in Hammerk at night (with the one-time exception of Aldric and Karla). Everyone watched you with a sort of pragmatic gaze, trying to determine how much valuable stuff you had on you, if you were any good in a fight, how many weapons you had. Between my sword, Aldric's size, and Karla's boosting our numbers, nobody messed with us outright, but there were plenty of eyes on us the whole time. Aldric, for once, had his game face on—he was glaring everyone down, mostly because quite a few people were looking over Karla.

We stepped around a fresh splatter of vomit on the ground and Aldric piped up—and stuff like this is what made me enjoy being around Aldric. Regardless of the situation, he would find an off-the-wall question to ask. He was curious, but never about stuff that any rational person would really wonder that much about.

"Hey," Aldric said, keeping his voice low. "How come there aren't any...you know..." he shrugged.

"No, we don't know," Karla snipped. Someone was feeling cranky. Granted, if every mugger in Hammerk was giving me the once-over, maybe I'd be a little testy too. *See, I can be sympathetic sometimes.*

"Prostitutes. Like, Dad always said this town was crawling with those. And drunks. And I see the drunks, but none of the, uh...women of the night."

"Glad you're so interested in hookers, Aldric," Karla said, a touch of venom to her voice.

Aldric blushed—visibly, even in the sort-of dark. "No, no, it's not like that. I just hadn't ever seen one and—"

"Relax, you big oaf," I said. A breeze came by and made me shiver just a bit. *It was the breeze. All the breeze. No other reason.* "Prostitutes hang on the other side of the village. Now you two stop bickering like a married couple and hush up? We've got to stay quiet so we don't get mugged again."

"We don't bicker like a—" Karla protested.

"I mean," Aldric said, his voice quick, "a *little* like a married couple, but not like—"

"Hush, hush."

We took the main road—the side roads would just be more dangerous this time of night, and we were pressing our luck enough as it was. We'd done a bit of casual scouting in the afternoon and realized that trying to trailblaze out of Hammerk was going to be a teensy bit trickier than we thought—tall grasses and shrubs grew off to the side of the road for a real good ways, and attempting to get through them would leave us wide open to a knife in the back. Going off-road would've meant even more treacherous terrain, and if one of us fell and broke a leg—or, even just rolled an ankle, it'd make things a lot easier for our friends lurking in the shadows. Our best chance was to try slipping through quiet-like, in the night, and hope that those rather inexperienced muggers were too busy getting wasted to be out in the night stabbing people.

And to hope the hollowthroat was feeling merciful.

We began to move a little slower—Aldric had proposed just sprinting down the road and minimizing our time there, but Karla shot that idea down by asking him how he planned to run in the dark on a bumpy, uneven dirt road. Aldric's not the best guy for long term stuff, but you can't fault him for enthusiasm.

Something flickered in the distance and we bit back shrieks.

The three of us stopped and dropped low, straining our eyes to see what it was. It was…well, I actually didn't know how far off it was. Really hard to tell in the dark. It seemed to be where we were (almost) mugged earlier, but I'd give thirty yards' margin of error on that. Part of me wondered if this was some elaborate ploy to distract us before we got jumped, a flash of razzle-dazzle to stun us before something snatched us right up. I forced that thought out of my head, the same way I'm sure Karla was forcing the hungry eyes of Hammerk's nightlife out of hers. We just needed to get through here and keep going. We'd walk for a few more hours and when we found somewhere safe for the night we could get some real rest. Chilling in Hammerk had let us recover physically—my legs were fresh and ready to go for another round of running away—but staying on high alert for one thing after another had me feeling dull. Staying perceptive is hard. Staying perceptive for an entire day is harder. We were gonna need real sleep, sooner or later.

I stared as long as I could but didn't see anything move. We crept forward, crouch-walking at a painfully slow pace. My back began throbbing after about two minutes of being hunched over, and my thighs started burning up after that. *If their criminal scheme is to wear us out, it was working.* We saw a flicker again and stopped cold. I let my fingers close around the sword, eyes focused on the flash in the distance and ears focused on the grassy hill around us.

This time, we realized what it was—they'd started a campfire. The light danced up occasionally, just barely visible past the thick brush around it. We rose, moving cautiously, and stayed entirely silent. No quarrels over hookers or nighttime sprinting were had. Even Aldric was doing his best to walk quietly. And, hey, they were doing it in new boots—they must've had some nasty blisters from all this. We moved in tandem, staying close. The wind started up every few minutes, the tall grass *shhhhhing* around us. We'd freeze at any movement, eyes straining in the dark to see if there was anything other than slumbering sheep and the distant farmhouses behind us.

On paper, we weren't far from the campfire—but when you factor in walking slow, pausing a lot, and trying to move quietly on uneven ground, it was taking us a while. *Fine by me. Fine by me.* Running from these guys would be a lot harder in the dark, and while they didn't seem to be very successful in mugging, they had to have had more experience fighting than we did.

There were a lot of silent prayers between the three of us.

Minutes dragged on and we were moving up the incline, trying as hard as we could to make our feet fall without any noise on the grass. We were close now, close enough to make us hunch back down, the pain in our lower backs forgotten. Maybe twenty feet from the fire, there were several short, crooked trees, and a few gnarled, thick bushes. We couldn't see the fire—or the thieves—directly, but the glow of the firelight lit up the trees' upper branches. We stopped and scanned our whereabouts, trying to see where we could move that would keep us out of sight. I caught Karla's gaze, her face barely visible in the reflected light, and we shared the same dark thought; if there really was a hollowthroat out here, those muggers were the least of our worries. Over the crackle-hiss of the growing campfire, we began to hear their conversation.

"How's your arm, Frederick?"

"Still 'urts pretty bad," Frederick—the one with the chain—replied, his voice laced with a thick accent I couldn't place. Of course, I wasn't exactly well-travelled, so not being able to place an accent wasn't surprising. "Ah'll kill the bitch if I e'er see 'er 'gain."

"Mm. Need me to run to town for you, get anything?"

"Yeah, two 'hores and a bot'le o' whiskey."

These prompted muffled laughter from the first voice—who I think was the Knives guy, the maniac with the yellow teeth. It was all high and reedy, the sort of slippery sound that made your skin crawl. *Wouldn't let that guy alone near my kids, you know? Or near me, for that matter.*

But the third guy—I think it was Fists—he made a very, very different noise. We stopped, crouching behind the cover of a thick bush, trying to see where we could step in the shadows. He...wheezed? Coughed? It was dry, hollow, totally empty of *voice*—like his throat was seizing up in some weak imitation of laughter. The other two fell silent fast at the sound of his "laugh," and I could sense the mood in the grove shifting. Hmm. Maybe they'd get preoccupied with each other and not pay us any attention.

We were now real close to where we'd been when they'd tried to mug us. If one of them stood up, they'd have a clear line of sight over the bushes, and things would probably get awkward. I started to draw out my sword—to be ready, but I felt Karla's hand grip my arm. I made eye contact with her and she shook her head, pressing a finger to her lips. I wanted to tell her it wouldn't make any noise—the sheath was oiled and stuff—but she pointed to my left. I glanced and saw my elbow about to touch the bush. *Oh. Yeah, that would've made, like, a lot of noise.* I nodded and slid the blade back, trying to keep my breathing quiet and shallow.

"You all right, man?" It was Knife Guy. "I don't like thinking about that thing. Your throat, you good?"

There was silence, but Fists must have signaled something. They muttered agreements.

We'd reached an impasse—we were spaced out a bit, hunkered down behind cover. They couldn't see us—I was in the lead, behind a thick shrub of some kind. Karla was pressed flat against a tree, and Aldric was behind a much smaller bush, flat on his belly. *Please don't let any of them stand up to take a piss right now.* I ran through a couple ideas.

We could rush them. It might work. It sounded like they were hurt—from what, I have no idea, but it might give us the edge. Especially with the element of surprise. I drummed my fingers against the hilt of my sword, gulping down a feeling of nausea. I didn't know how to fight. They probably did. And if so, we...well, that option either ended really well or really badly. Plus I didn't really want to kill anybody. I mean, I wanted to kill Aldric sometimes, but that was different.

We could go back to Hammerk. Try to find a new way. But there were problems with that, too. If they heard us, they might've been smart enough to follow us quietly. In the dark we'd have trouble outrunning them, and we'd only have to trip and fall once for them to catch back up with us. Then, we'd be fighting them, but they'd have the upper hand. *Not really my cup of tea.*

That left sneaking by them. I turned my head and saw another bush, foliage thick enough to hide us. Problem was, it was two or three feet from where I was, and there was nothing but wide open space in between. If they were looking up, they'd see me plain as day. I had no way of knowing which way they were facing, so it'd be a gamble. Either they'd see us tiptoeing by or they wouldn't. There was no other way around, not that I could see. We'd have to move and skirt the edge of the hill, or pass back along the other side. With some luck, they'd have their backs to us.

Regardless, this wasn't my idea of a good plan. At least if we got caught, we'd still have a bit of surprise—enough to hit 'em hard once or twice, catch them off guard, and scamper. I didn't know who'd wounded these guys—or just Frederick, maybe—but I'd buy him a round if I got the chance.

"Don' like what tha' thing did t'yeh," Frederick muttered. He must've been talking to Fists. "S'not natur'l."

"Hush!" the Knife Guy hissed. "It might be here."

"Naw 'ere. Naw righ' now," Frederick said. "Got tuh sing isself a lullaby. Them the rules."

"Still. Can't be too careful. We don't hurry up with our—"

The breeze came and made the trees rustle, their branches creaking just a bit, the bushes trembling.

It clicked. I waited, made sure the gust would last—and before I lost my nerve, rolled forward into the cover of the next bush.

The half-second after that was the longest of my entire life. I ripped my sword out, holding it with shaky hands as I pressed flat against the dirt, ready to turn and—

"It's gonna want yours or mine, too, and then what do we do?"

"Ah dunno."

There was a strangled cough of pain, and I got a mental image of Fists clawing at his throat. They were occupied. I caught Karla's attention—she was mouthing furiously at me. *What are you doing?*

I beckoned her closer with my hand, and she shifted, a half-step at a time, to where I'd been. I held up my palm, waiting. Waiting.

Five or six seconds passed before the breeze began again, and I beckoned her closer. She hesitated, mouthing a silent curse, and then dove forward, rolling behind the bush and knocking into me. I started to grunt but caught it in my throat as the wind died out.

A half second. Then another.

"Sure I can't get you two something? It's not a long walk."

That's not good.

Aldric had been watching what we were doing and scrambled as quickly and gently as he could to where Karla had been, crouched and ready for the next noise-dampening gust of wind. *Hurry up, hurry up.*

"You nee' enething?" Frederick asked.

Fists must've been "saying" something, because the rapt silence of the thieves filled the clearing once again. The fire crackled as a branch snapped, and all three of us jumped. Thank the gods none of them heard us. I snaked an arm around Karla's stomach, making her tense up, and nudged her toward me. She caught the message and we quietly moved back a few feet, still behind cover, but allowing enough space for Aldric to slide behind the thicket. I turned my head and saw the crest of the hill begin to drop down. I elbowed Karla and tilted my head toward it. She nodded, then looked over at Aldric—he gave her a reassuring smile and she started moving over my chest as quietly as she could, getting down behind the cover of the hill.

"All right, let me grab my boots, and then—"

The breeze came back and Aldric rolled forward, moving fast enough to slam into me. I grunted as the wind got knocked out of me and then rolled over the hill *(Freaking hills!)*, smacking down onto Karla (who grunted in turn). I tumbled over her but dug my legs in, stopping myself fairly quickly. We waited, backs pressed against the slope. Aldric scrambled over, joining us, mouthing *sorry*. Had they heard us?

The wind was working against us, now—we couldn't see them at all, and as long as the bushes were shaking, we couldn't hear them either. I gripped the sword, holding it at the ready.

"*Where do you think you're going, gentlemen?*"

The almost-human voice came from the clearing, and even over the wind I swear I heard the three of them draw in their breath.

Oh gods. We didn't have to talk. We didn't even worry about being quiet. We started moving down the hill, their voices fading as quickly as we did. *Fine by me. Fine by me.* Once we'd gone maybe twenty yards, we found a path cut into the hill, one that must've gone around the side. *Figures we find it now.* We moved at a quick walk, each of our necks craned back watching the ridge of the hill, fearing any of them would stand up close enough to the edge to see us. Their firelight was gone, and we walked as best we could see in the starlit dark. We ducked along the road, finally breaking out into an outright run after about a minute of walking.

It was the same as when we ran from the thieves the first time. I don't know how far we went. This was slower, not by choice—the road twisted and the trees were thicker here, not sparse as they were on the path up. The curved roots under the road (if you could call it a road) and the branches that hung down low kept us side-stepping and swerving, unable to keep up a straight run. Soon the sound of their campfire was gone, replaced only by the steady hum of cicadas and the frenzied panting of our own breath. Even through the fear, I felt the day's travelling catch up to me—my feet throbbed with every step, and it was getting harder and harder to push my legs at the same pace. My shoulders were chafing where I'd been wearing the satchel, and I finally ripped the stupid thing off and just carried it against my chest as we ran.

Under the trees, there was hardly any light to go by, but even if we'd had a torch we weren't about to light one. The road continued as it was, shifting from grass back to worn dirt. We hammered along for maybe thirty minutes before we were too tired to run for our lives any longer. We stopped, Karla falling back against a tree as I leaned over and clutched at my knees. Aldric stood, facing back the way we'd came, but all of us were breathing too hard to even hope of fighting those guys off.

Three teenagers, sweaty, hot, and out of breath in the middle of the woods. I felt wronged, almost. *There are a lot of far more enjoyable circumstances that our current state of being could apply to, ya know?*

"Who do you think they ran into?" Karla asked, her words coming out broken with pauses for air. Damnit. That got me thinking about what was around us. Cards on the table, Karla was beyond useless in a fight. She'd spent her life practicing troubadouring and not much else. *Maybe we'll run into a serial killer with a crippling fondness for folk tunes.* Aldric was a big guy but without a weapon he could only do so much. And I'd got my sword (*that still felt good to say*) today, so I wasn't really a master of the art yet. Give it another week.

So if there *was* someone out there, strong enough to fight off three bandits—crappy bandits, but still bandits—what chance did we stand?

We started on the trail again, but walking this time. Running was…out of the picture. Oof. My legs and—well, everything really—were still sore from falling down that hill. That was a great start to the heroic journey.

"Before or after we got there?" Aldric asked, squinting as he peered back the way we came. It was no use—what little light the stars gave off was gobbled up by the trees above us, and they would either find us or they wouldn't. We needed to keep moving, but the fact they hadn't come for us yet was a good sign. I'd been on edge for eleven or twelve hours straight, and I was burning out. Aldric still had some alertness left in him. He'd have to watch out for us for a while.

Oh, gods help us.

Aldric stayed quiet for a while, and we followed suit. Nothing made any ominous noises, relatively speaking. When you're paranoid about being stalked and murdered, everything's kinda scary, but there weren't any outright branches snapping. Just frogs croaking and those stupid cicadas chirping nonstop. The breeze had stopped—figures, doesn't it? Once we get all hot and sweaty, that's when High God of the Seasons Remos decides to kill the summer breeze. *The gods are dicks.* I was keeping that thought to myself, but I was thinking it nonetheless.

Well, I got used to it. Karla flinched, eyes darting about. I felt kinda bad. I mean, she clearly wasn't enjoying this. At all. Aldric wasn't really enjoying it per se, but he had that mentality of "this is going to make a kick-ass story one day." Karla was really just here because she wanted to be there for me. A part of her wanted to go questing, to be a part of those stories she'd always sung, but reality was setting in. I had a pretty good grasp of what adventuring entailed—and it was the exact reason I didn't want these two with me, and the exact reason I didn't want to be doing it. Was I sad about Marisa being abducted? Yeah, it was terrible and all. But there comes a time when you've got to look at the facts, and Karla and Aldric still had their eyes shut tight.

The part of me that wasn't focused on not tripping on the rocks and twigs as we began walking again, thought about how I was planning on getting out of this mess. There didn't seem to be a really clear-cut solution. Look, a dragon shows up and takes your girl? Sometimes you gotta know when to admit you've lost, and I classify anything that can wipe out a village single-handedly as "above my pay grade."

But figuring out what I was going to do with Aldric and Karla was the real problem. See, had my two devoted tag-alongs not accompanied me, I could've wandered Plagiar to my heart's content, seen all the sights, figured out why everyone was always so amped up about the ocean (it's just a bunch of water!) and, you know, been a tourist. We hadn't been given a ton of money, but enough to last a little while. For one person. With three, we were going to burn through it pretty quickly, especially after Karla and Aldric went shoe shopping earlier. And with my sidekicks with me, I couldn't do all that—I'd have to, more-or-less, go off questing for my (probably dead) betrothed. Otherwise, they'd tell the village I was the world's biggest pussy ever, and Old Man Granger would be talking crap about me at every town rally for the next hundred years.

Or…however long he had left. Probably not a hundred years. But who knew? We all kinda figured he'd just be around until the End Times. *And the End Times will probably involve more dragons, too.* I guess I could cut and run—leaving town, ditching Aldric and Karla, well, it was a possibility, but…not really one I wanted. I wasn't exactly attached to my hometown—I mean, c'mon, it got burned to a crisp and I was making jokes about funeral urns—but still. I didn't want everyone to think I was a giant coward.

Our walking slurred into stumbling and our stumbling got slower and slower. Two desperate bouts of running for our lives had left us pretty winded, and my legs were literally dragging in the dirt. I thought I saw Karla start to nod off once, but she caught herself before she face-planted.

None of us wanted to stop—no matter how far we went, it didn't feel far enough, but my recently-buried horse was better suited for travelling than we were at the moment. Everybody's got their breaking point. We cut out to the side of the path, moving through the woods until we found a clear spot. The road was maybe twenty yards away—nothing terrible, but enough to give us a little comfort. Unless those bandits were really looking, they'd miss us if they walked on by.

Of course, this meant we couldn't have a campfire. That flint and steel in my pack would go unused. It was warm enough we wouldn't need one, and cooking wasn't a priority since we were all too tired to eat, but gods if it wouldn't have been helpful for keeping the bugs away. We spread out blankets and tried to get settled—Aldric attempted to rig a blanket hammock-style between some trees without any luck, and Karla, heavy-lidded and stumbling, tried to lay some dry, brittle-looking branches around the campsite. I guess her thought was if somebody snuck up on us, we'd hear the branches snap, and then…well, I guess we get to die awake then. I'd rather just go in my sleep, honestly.

Unfortunately, we'd all greatly underestimated Mother Nature's capability for making sleep impossible in the wild.

As soon as Karla had finished laying down sticks, Aldric's oversized foot made friends with a giant pile of fire ants.

Limping and questioning which god created the fire ant, Aldric angrily insisted we find another spot to sleep. I was too tired to argue, and didn't really enjoy the idea of ants crawling over me while I slept, anyways.

After a bit more walking, we found another clearing. After a thorough fire ant examination, Aldric deemed it an acceptable stopping place. Karla kinda half-assedly threw some sticks down and then flopped onto her blanket. Didn't bother taking off her boots.

I didn't want to think about what kind of nastiness was going to slither over my face as I slept—or what might, even more terrifyingly, just sit and watch us instead—but of course that's the first thing my mind jumped to. I squirmed on my blanket, my body torn between near-comatose exhaustion and how freaking uncomfortable the ground is with only blankets for cushioning.

Nature sucks.

A deep, guttural noise came from my left, and I muttered for Aldric to stop snoring so I could try to sleep.

"It's not me," Aldric said. Oh God, that was Karla. *You go, girl. Break down those feminine stereotypes. Shatter that glass ceiling with your godawful snores.*

Huh. That was weird. Not Karla's snoring—I mean, that was weird. She sounded like an asthmatic grizzly bear after a marathon—but Aldric's tone of voice. Not a trace of weariness or sleepiness at all. Just quiet worry and tension. The dark woods around us continued their constant noise, the breezeless night interrupted only by Karla's breathing.

Eh, screw it. He's probably fine.

I tried to roll over and go to sleep, but I now had guilt prodding me in addition to the gnarled tree root under my ass. "Uh, Aldric, something up?" *Please be an easily resolved emotional problem. I want to go to sleep.*

There was a moment's quiet, and I wondered if the big guy had just drifted off himself, but I heard that lip smacking people make when they're about to speak but don't know what to say. I heard it a couple times. I couldn't see him, but I could picture him—clothes sweaty and grimy, hair clinging to his forehead, eyes staring up at what few stars we could see.

"You and Karla, earlier, you were talking about—"

"Oh, no, it wasn't like that man."

"No," he said, abruptly stopping. *Oh, crap, I think I just gave him more to worry about. Gods I'm bad at this.* "I mean… you mentioned a…a hollowthroat."

It…it was my imagination, I know, but I swear the world went a little quiet for a second, all the nocturnal creatures stopping with bated breath. Even Karla's snores paused for a moment.

"Yeah, we, uh, might've. What about it?"

"You think that's what it was? That voice?"

When my words came out, they were wide awake too. "I dunno. She's the expert on myths and monsters and stuff."

"Not a myth," Aldric said sharply, and I could hear that there was no grin on his face, just a scowl that he wasn't used to baring. "One got my mom."

"Oh. Oh, gods. I…I didn't know." I mean, I knew the kid didn't have a mom, but like I said, Plagiar didn't have the best life expectancy. I just figured it was the plague or food poisoning or not bathing for three weeks that did her in. "You…you saw it?"

"No. Found her by the river. It must've taken its tongue and, uh, it got her on the arms. Up and down. There was a lotta blood. I was little. I don't remember it a lot. Dad said it was a hollowthroat. Lured her out down away from everybody and…"

"Damn. I'm sorry. I didn't know."

I…I wasn't entirely sure what the cause of Aldric's mom's death was. Didn't sound like a hollowthroat's MO. Granted, I didn't know much about them. From what I'd heard—and I was sure as hell asking Karla in the morning if we were really going up against one *(and, for the record, we were fighting them* only *if we couldn't run away)*—that wasn't how they did things. Stuck that razor tongue of theirs down your throat and just…ripped. Ripped your voice right out of you. Didn't know if it killed you—that mute kid sure seemed to be alive and kicking, enough to try to shake us down.

I guess it was possible it could've slit her wrists.

A few other options were possible, too, but I wasn't about to break that to him.

"It would've been me, I bet. Or maybe Dad," Aldric continued, and he spoke the way water seeps through a dam. Little trickle at first. Then flooding out. "She wouldn't have just walked away for anybody. Maybe it took mine. Or his. Made it sound like I was drowning, I bet. Then it…"

"It's not you, man. Don't…don't think that. You, uh, were a kid."

Gods, this wasn't what I wanted. Firstly, and, yeah, selfishly, I wasn't going to be sleeping anytime soon, which sucked, but I also wasn't really the most in touch with my emotions. I didn't know how you respond to crap like this. I'd known this guy for gods knew how many years and never heard a peep about this.

"Not a kid now." There was another long pause, and I politely pretended that the raucous, mood-killing snores of

Karla masked the muffled sniffling. "Look, you hear me crying for help or something, you don't come, all right? It's not me. Don't...."

"Course I'll come. 'Cause either your dumb ass is hurt, or there's a hollowthroat with a death wish. Either way."

Aldric chuckled. "Thanks."

"Don't mention it."

"I know we're gonna find her, man. Marisa. You're gonna be the one."

I didn't say anything back. A few more seconds passed and Aldric started to drift, I think. His breathing got deeper and slower. I shifted and twisted a while longer, even once I got comfortable.

I wasn't so worried about the hollowthroat anymore.

V

ventually, sleep came. I was immediately woken up by harsh, bright light that was rabbit-punching my eyes. So, even in my dreams, things were pretty much par for the course.

I issued a string of curses that I won't repeat here, 'cause honestly I thought they were pretty impressive and I'm holding onto them for another occasion. I blinked my eyes open and looked around, immediate panic rushing through me as I figured those bandits had followed us.

But there weren't any muggers. No, it was sunlight. Had I just woken up? I glanced to the side and saw Karla and Aldric were both absent—as was everything else I'd seen when I put my head down.

I was in an endless, grassy plain, stretching as far as the eye could see—and then some. Everything was pure. Something about this place had taken my eyes and scrubbed them clean, tweaked with my vision and let all the colors come in brighter, fuller. The grass radiated energy, the clouds rolled with quiet warmth. *I swear if this is some residual wise man's willow, I cracked my spine too hard and now it's all flood-*

ing my system at once situation. The grass was maybe knee high, and a soothing wind sent it all swaying one direction, then the next, no rhyme or reason.

"Beautiful, isn't it?" a voice asked.

Okay, I've gotten black-out drunk in my time, and on one rare occasion—maybe my coming of age ceremony, I honestly don't remember, 'cause, hey, that's the point of getting black-out drunk—I had this really, really good stuff. I never caught the name of it but it was so damned sweet going down, like honey was just kissing your throat every inch of the way. This voice sounded the way that tasted, smooth and gentle, warm and flowing. Images started flashing through my head, disjointed, yet connected. *Clear, clean water bubbles over smooth rocks. A shooting star glitters across the fullest night sky. An old dog curls up by the fire.* I blinked and rubbed at my head, making the visions fade away, but the feeling stayed, that buzzing in my chest and gut like the sweet voice was echoing down inside me. In a way, it was almost like… like the voice was another language, and these images, the feelings, they were the few words of it I could grasp, the way you only see the bolt of lightning that strikes the ground, but not all the ones above the clouds.

The tension—the literal muscle-ache of being on edge for one thing after another all day long, of sprinting from danger and walking for miles, it all started to…melt. The nagging fear of the hollowthroat, the bandits, it was growing harder and harder to access—it just seemed silly the longer I stayed here. Maybe there were things waiting in the dark, but this place was full of light. This place was warm and gentle. There was no blade at my hip, no dragon in the sky. Just quiet grasses, idle clouds.

I turned and saw nothing. Just more endless plain. There was no one there. But I knew I'd heard something. I could *feel* it, like I'd swallowed one of those fat white clouds and it was tickling me with lightning. Whoever could figure out how to put this chick's voice into a bottle and sell it was gonna be Plagiar's next tycoon.

"Who's there?" In hindsight, I should've come up with something wittier. *Who's there?* That's what every asshole says when they wake up. Should've gone with a pick-up line or something smooth. *You like beautiful things? Well then I guess you must love yourself. Name's Harkness. Let me buy you a round.*

There was a pause for several seconds, during which I figured I'd finally gone entirely, blissfully insane. Maybe the dragon attack hadn't even happened, and I was just imagining this whole trippy scenario from the inside of a cell in one of Plagiar's esteemed mental hospitals/prisons. Maybe my happy little wise man's willow birth defect was on "medium" before, but got dialed up to "real trippy." I'm not sure the village would put up with any more weird references from me, so that was going to be a pretty problem if that was the case.

"Oh, child." The heavenly voice came again, and where the thrum of energy, the vibration like literal butterflies were in my stomach, had started to fade, it picked right back up as she spoke again. Definitely a woman's voice, although I guess since she was calling me "child" it was good I didn't open with the pick-up line. *Nothing like accidentally hitting on old ladies.*

"Who's there?"

"Someone who wishes very much to help you on your way."

I paused, mulling over this whole thing.

"In that case, thank you." I have very rare moments of being polite—I had a real strong feeling about what this was—an encounter with the sort of being that's a few weight classes above "human." If that was the case, I was going to smile real pretty and talk real sweet. If this…whatever it was, could get my bones shaking with just its voice, I didn't want to know what it could do when it got pissed. But despite that, her voice was still so gentle to listen to. I felt my muscles loosen and sag as she spoke, just naturally reacting to her presence.

And I had another real strong feeling "it" was the sort of thing people built temples and sacrificed calves to.

Which is to say the voice was ranking pretty high up there on the list of Things Not To Be A Dick To, next to "the mass-murdering dragon" and "well-armed ex-girlfriends." "Any aid you would give is appreciated by, uh, your humble servant." *Yeah, I'm laying it on thick. Goddesses eat that stuff up.*

A great wind began to tear through the plains, physically pushing me back a few inches. The clouds above burned past faster than anything I'd ever seen. The idyllic feeling began to melt away, and I felt the ache in my legs set back in, the rattling in my chest grew faster and more violent. The grass flattened, roots ripping from the earth as the wind drew to its full force, knocking me down to one knee with it. Dust and pollen felt like they were tunneling into my eyes and face from the force of the wind. *Yep, very good thing I was not an asshole to her.* The sun surged down below the horizon, and the moon came up the other side to replace it. "The gift I offer thee is that of wisdom. The prophet Granger pointed you on your way—"

"What the hell?" *Well, crap, there goes being polite. I tried. I really did.* "Granger is a prophet?"

There was another pause, and the voice was a little more disdainful. She sounded like my mom answering one of my many stupid questions as a child. The grass and moon and clouds were frozen, as if she had to stop the demonstration to deal with this interruption. "Little one, how do you think he's managed to live so very long, and know so very much?"

Huh. Good point.

The world resumed its blur around me, night fading back into day and continuing as the sun arched up over the sky, reaching noon in a matter of seconds. For some reason, seconds didn't seem like the right term for measuring time—not in this place, wherever it was. Seconds and hours didn't matter here. Maybe heartbeats would be more accurate, or maybe it was just a place without time. *Look at me get all philosophical.* "What the prophet was unable to tell you, as the crowd interrupted him—was that your quest cannot be completed at your leisure."

It took me a moment, but I realized that we weren't just zipping through time on this trippy little dream of mine, we were covering actual distance. Given that there were no discernible landmarks in the never-ending grasses, I think it was excusable. We reached a mountain and...

As sweet as the woman's voice was, this mountain was awful. It was trying to go to sleep after killing a roach and knowing others could fall on you as you dozed off. It was staring into a fire and wondering what it was like to be roasted alive, immolated an inch at a time. I felt it deep, in my gut and bones, the gentle peace her voice had offered quickly shredded. My throat burned with acid as my stomach started to eat itself. I felt small, not just standing against the black rock that tore those clouds apart miles above my head, but...spiritually. There was nothing I could do to this place. They were fields without end and stone that could not be broken. This place would continue for centuries after I was dead and would not remember me. The skies above were violence, all black, streaks of eye-blinding lightning ripping across the dark. They swirled at the summit, and I wondered if the mountain was corrupted from the storm, or if it was the other way around. Barely visible at the top was a sort of…emptiness, the sort of thing I felt more than I saw, and I instinctively knew that's where the dragon made its den. That was the only place on Plagiar that could make a human feel so utterly…worthless. It was nothing, but it was a *hungry* nothing, and the longer she kept me there the more hollow my bones and gut and thoughts began to feel.

The visions trying to force themselves into my mind had changed now, and this close to the mountain I couldn't shut them out. *A candle burning to the wick in a starless night. A bloodsoaked calf, newborn and feeble, nuzzling at its dead mother. A songbird with a broken wing screeching as a hawk settled before it.*

The sun, above us, barely visible through the dark clouds that swirled and stormed across the horizon, began to sink steadily, falling out of the sky and plunging the world into night. The sun and moon, spinning above. How many times had they passed over? It must've been—

"Three days?" I whispered. "We…we have to get there and…"

"Yes, child. Three days' time after the eve of the Reckoning. The first of which has already passed. Recover my Blade. Find the lair of the dread beast. Do you comprehend?"

It's not often my smart-ass can't think of anything to say. I just sat there feeling like the hollowthroat had ripped out my voice and not that mugger's.

The vision around me faded, running like watery paint, until we were back in the grassy field, serene, a thousand miles away from that terrible place. I took a few deep breaths, knowing that in a dream my hands shouldn't be shaking, cold sweat shouldn't be running down my face.

"You...you don't think I can...."

"The beast must be stopped. When time runs out, it will devour the two it has taken."

"H-how are we even supposed to find your stupid Blade? Let alone find where the damned dragon is?" My voice wasn't mine. It was breaking and shaky, a little kid spitting out excuses to a drunken father. "I can't.... That thing could be a thousand miles one way, your temple a thousand miles the other. Granger didn't exactly hand us a map!"

"You do not need a map to become lost." The voice— Layana's voice—was gentle, but just as insistent.

What does that shit even mean?

"But where do I go? What direction and...I don't...this wasn't even..."

The skies around us, perfectly, peacefully blue, began to fade, far off at the horizon, but then slowly around us. The grass began to lose its immaculate quality, feeling more and more like real grass, and the dream nirvana slipped further and further away...

"Three days, child. Three days."

VI

very few seconds, I felt another glare from one of my tag-alongs. It was a lovely reminder that I'd interrupted what few hours of sleep they'd managed to get. *We are Plagiar's least happy campers on the world's worst camping trip. Woohoo.*

"You talked with Layana?" Aldric asked, his voice dripping with jealousy.

"You have a deadline?" Karla asked, her voice dripping with panic.

Yeah. None of us were really happy about that.

News of our quite literal deadline got my ass up and moving a lot faster than the other two.

This…altered my plans significantly.

Very significantly.

I was busy cramming our belongings back into my satchel while Karla and Aldric, bleary-eyed and their hair somehow even more messy (I'm sure mine wasn't looking great either, to be fair, but I could pull off the messy look.) from a night of sleep on the ground. My back groaned and cramped up, and judging from the stiffness of Aldric and Karla, they hadn't fared much better.

"You sure it was three days?" Karla muttered, staring longingly at the blankets as I punched them down into the satchel. *How did this stuff fit so easily when we packed it to begin with?* We'd only *lost* stuff as the trip went on, eaten food and whatnot. But now it was taking up *more* space. *If there is a dark god of mishandled luggage, he's on the dragon's side.*

"Yes, Sleeping Beauty, I'm sure. Two days, come to think of it. We burned up one running from bandits and the hollow—"

There was an awkward pause and Aldric winced.

"And the, uh, whole trying-not-to-get-mugged-in-Hammerk thing," I recovered, perhaps not very smoothly. "So we have to double-time it. Or triple-time it. Or…" I rolled my hand, not sure what came after triple. *Quad-something? I dunno, we don't really have the best educational system.* "Haul ass, basically."

Aldric got up, shaking his head like a dog getting rid of water. He rubbed at his eyes and began stretching out. Huh. He was surprisingly limber for somebody as tall as he was. He hummed one of the songs Karla had been singing yesterday as he leaned down to grab his toes.

"You're off-pitch," Karla snapped. "It's *'Past the branches gnarled and dark, where lie silent the singing lark….'*"

Aldric frowned, which was a pretty rare thing to see. "Sorry, just trying to, you know—"

"Hey," I said, not willing to listen to forty-eight more hours of this crap. "Not to hurt anyone's feelings, but we need to get moving. Those bandits are still out there," I added. What else might be out there could stay unmentioned. It wiped the smirk off Karla's face and the frown off Aldric's. We finished cleaning up the campsite in relative silence—although there hadn't been much to pick up. We were travelling pretty light, and within about fifteen minutes of getting up we three happy adventurers were back on the road.

Not only that, I wasn't sure what the goddess had meant. The Reckoning's eve…three days after. The dragon had struck early in the morning two days ago. So was it still night when it had attacked, or morning? Did she mean eve, like, the night before or the night of? Did we have until sundown tomorrow, or sundown tonight? How late was the eve? Was it at sundown, or if we made it by midnight, was that fine? Regardless, how in the *hell* were we supposed to accomplish anything in so little time? It would have been better if the stupid love goddess had just told us nothing. Damned vague prophecies. Why could no one tell us straight up where we had to go and what we had to do?

We ate as we walked, which I've heard is bad for your health. But you know what else is bad for your health? Trying to kill dragons.

I gnawed on some of the bread, divvying it up between the three of us. We'd burn through the rest by nightfall, especially with the way we were hoofing it. I don't know how many miles we'd covered, but it'd been a fair few. Well, with the heat, it probably wasn't that many, but it *felt* like a lot more.

"We," Karla said, her voice still a little tight, "should probably try to cover as much ground as we can while it's still pretty cool. Then we can slow down in the afternoon."

"That's a great idea, Karla," Aldric said.

I raised an eyebrow at him. Karla huffed and walked a bit ahead of us, missing it, but he returned my skepticism with a frown.

There was no need to bother the silence—Karla needed time to wake up, and Aldric needed some time to mellow out. Me, I was just perfect all the time, but I guess you can't hold everyone to my standard.

The hike really wasn't bad—sans the temporary tension in our group of world-savers, it was a nice change of pace. Farthest from Sorro I'd been was, well, Hammerk, so it was pretty cool to see anything that wasn't a total cesspit. Sure, the birds were shrieking a little too loudly (the sun was barely inching out over the horizon—it was too early to be doing anything, let alone singing), the road was a little too uneven, and the wineskins were a little too devoid of actual wine, but it wasn't *terrible*.

After a while, Karla started humming again, and occasionally sang to herself a bit. And after a little while longer, it felt like she was singing to *us* moreso than just herself. Aldric's tone of voice got less artificially bubbly and Karla grinned once or twice.

My conflict-resolution skills are great.

"Where lie silent the singing lark…I'll come for you if you will not wail…." her voice drifted off as she stopped and paused, head snapping up and eyes flickering around.

You know when you miss a step, and your stomach drops down past your legs? I got that. My hand settled on the hilt of my sword as I turned around, walking backward a half step at a time. I bumped into Karla and checked the road behind us—empty. The side of the path was clear, too, just woods. Nothing there.

"…and we'll fly to the stars on nightingales," Aldric finished, a tone of pride to his voice. Somewhere, vaguely, I realized he must've listened to Karla sing a lot, 'cause there weren't any other troubadours in our village. Weird how your mind seizes up on little details when there's way bigger stuff to be focusing on.

There was silence.

And something hiding in it.

"Wait, that's the right verse, isn't it?" Aldric asked.

"Aldric, hush up a second," I muttered, not sure what Karla thought she saw or heard. My mind immediately jumped to the hollowthroat. She had been singing, after all. I wasn't 100 percent sure on how those things worked, but a song seemed like the perfect bait.

And as if that wasn't tempting enough, there was just, you know, one weapon between the three of us.

"Thought I heard something," Karla said. She turned around, flipping some split-ended brown hair back behind her ear with a puff of air. "Sorry. Just nerves." She met my eyes, and I couldn't tell if she was trying to tell me something or not. It was always tough to gauge that with girls. Mostly because they're *always* trying to tell you something, but you never have any idea what. I wasn't sure how to understand women, but I knew those kinds of generalizations would help me.

"You sure?" Aldric asked.

"Yeah, I'm good. Lack of sleep's getting to me. When it gets hot later, maybe we can find someplace cool and crash for a while."

I nodded and we started going again, but my stomach was taking a while to unclench and wiggle back down to its normal spot. We broke free of the treeline, which was real nice—no matter how alert we were, something still only had to make it four or five feet to get at us there.

Slowly the thick oaks gave way to sparser, thinner pines, and those came fewer and further between until it was just grass. Ahead, the path led straight up a hill, which seemed like our best bet for the short-term. Even if climbing another hill made my aching thighs scream in protest, it'd let us see around a pretty good distance. Might be able to get a glimpse of some landmarks—what few landmarks we knew of.

Like I said, it was the farthest away from home I've ever been. Most people never even left the village—I knew Drowduss was relatively close, but that was about as specific as I could get.

Aldric's boots had come undone, so he told us to go on ahead while he laced them up. Normally, I wouldn't have left a guy behind like that, even in broad daylight—I mean, hey, have you ever heard a horror story? That's how they get you—but I did need to talk with Karla, because gods know I was never going to figure out what she meant just by looking at her eyes.

We went up along the path, walking quickly and shooting frequent glances at Aldric, who was still humming, but significantly closer to the right pitch.

"Hollowthroats," I said, and the word came out as quiet as I possibly could. Didn't feel right, saying it. Made it *real* when I said it. "Give me the rundown. Quick. Did you know they…Aldric's mom…?"

Karla grunted and clambered up onto a ledge with more effort than I'd needed. I forgot the height advantage, sometimes. "Stories say they rip your voices out."

If you hadn't known her, you might not have picked up on it. Her eyes didn't go wide, she didn't piss herself, she didn't turn pale and start stammering and shaking.

But that was the most terrified I ever saw Karla.

"How?" I asked, not wanting to be a dick and push it but legitimately unsure. I had some idea, but our resident fairy tale fanatic knew more for sure, and I wanted to know as much as possible in case…well, just in case.

She stuck her tongue out and rolled it around. "Tongues. Theirs are sharper than that sword you got. They weasel down your throat and...." she shuddered.

Ugh. I was kinda glad we had a light breakfast.

"That's...pleasant," I said.

"Yeah, they don't show up in a lot of kid's stories." She blinked. "Well, they show up in stories for kids who wander off into the woods."

I hopped up a step and offered Karla my arm. She grunted and tugged herself up with a silent nod of thanks.

"That's just how they...they hunt. Tales all differ a little, here and there. They do on most things. Usually they get you hiding by the wayside, luring you out with somebody's voice. Somebody crying for help...usually somebody you know."

Well, the good news is that I don't try to help people anyway.

"How do you kill one?" I asked, feeling the sword weigh on my hip, almost hungrily. I'd rather not cross paths with it, but if we had to...

"Legends are a little less helpful on that front. Don't think it's easy though. They're mean. And clever. Don't like a straight fight, though. They hide and trick you, tease you."

"And," Aldric said from right behind us, "they usually know just what to say."

I hadn't heard him come back up—Karla and I both yelped (I'll admit it) and it made me stumble. I fell and hit the ground.

"No!" I shrieked, thrusting my elbows down and digging in hard. *Damn hills!* I stopped pretty much immediately. Karla snorted, but screw her, I wasn't falling down another one of these things. My forearms and legs were a lovely mosaic of blacks and blues from that tumble yesterday. Aldric—even with the sobering topic of hollowthroats being discussed—cracked a smile, and hoisted me back up to my feet.

Well, uh, let's hope those bandits were a little noisier than Aldric was.

"I appreciate it," Aldric said, the usual cheeriness and pep sapped right out of his voice, "but you don't have to hide it from me. I know what it is."

"Sorry," Karla said.

"It's okay. It was a nice gesture." He smiled, a little half-heartedly, and squeezed her shoulder, which made her smile.

Then I, was, ya know, over by myself, doing my own thing.

I wanted to ask one more question—what the deal was with the lullaby I'd heard that one bandit mention—but I didn't want to press it with Aldric there. I mean, it seemed important or whatever, but I also was just tactful enough to not ask with Aldric standing beside us. We changed the subject, somewhat awkwardly, and kept on pushing up the hill, managing to clear it about as quickly as Karla can start snoring after she lies down to sleep.

I'd been right—we had an excellent view. I don't know how tall the hill was, and even though it wasn't bright enough yet to really see a long way, the terrain sloped down below us. Sure enough—some distance I didn't know how to gauge with the naked eye—there was the river, a surging blue snake that cut through the valley below. *Maybe two miles away?* Everything sloped down toward it, so the perspective might've been kinda screwy. Like I said—new to this whole adventuring thing. There was never any use to guesstimating distances when you lived 90 percent of your life within a three-mile radius. We felt safer, too—we could see everything, and there was nothing.

"I really, really, *really* want to shout and see if it echoes," Aldric said, staring out over the basin.

We both turned and looked at Karla.

She gave us a very mom look.

Screw hollowthroats.

"Echo!" Aldric howled, his voice bouncing out over the woods below.

Totally, totally worth it.

"Sorry," he said, grinning like a dog who stumbled across a paralyzed cat. "That was irresponsible."

Karla sighed, but Aldric's eagerness was infectious.

"Well, where to from here?" I asked.

"Wait, we're not going to the river?" Karla asked.

"No, no, I mean how do we get there?" I pointed at the landscape below. The hill ended somewhat abruptly, like the gods got bored and left halfway through making it. Scaling down a rock face was not my idea of a fun morning activity, mainly because crawling with broken legs towards civilization was not my idea of a fun afternoon activity. The other sides were a little more accessible—the left sloped down gently, dropping an inch at a time as it bent around. That was the way the path kept on going, faint and easy-to-miss as the road had become. Back near Hammerk, it was wide enough to pull wagons across, maybe even to trade on. Here, it was pretty clearly for solo travelers, or maybe somebody who knew how to ride a horse.

"We should've stolen those horses," I said under my breath.

Aldric left looking ahead to Karla and me, returning to the side where we'd come from to make sure we hadn't been followed by the bandits. I figured if they hadn't caught us by now, they probably wouldn't. Those guys had been in pretty rough shape, after all.

The problem was, on the left it sloped down gently—we'd have no trouble getting down at all. But it was going to take some time—just from what I could see, there were switchbacks and winding curves all the way around to the river. I wasn't sure how long it'd take, but it was going to be a while. Maybe half a day. Maybe.

We didn't have much food—or more importantly, water left. I think we had enough to get us through the day if we were smart about it, but it was only getting hotter, and we were only going get more tired.

Then…the right side.

The right side was steeper, sharper. Trickier. Cut straight down to the basin. It wasn't as much of a suicidal incline as straight ahead was, but it wouldn't leave a lot of room for error. *Good thing we're so freaking experienced with climbing down rock walls.* Once we got down, it looked like we hit a kind of swampy area—it was about even with the river, maybe a little below it, elevation-wise, and I guess there was runoff or something. I was *not* looking forward to mucking around in the swamp, and from the look on Karla's face, she really wasn't either.

"Okay, team meeting."

Aldric came back over and stared out around us, generally taking in the sights. He eyed a few billy goats strolling over one of the other hills, watched the early morning clouds drift on by. Guy was hard to rattle, unless you brought up a hollowthroat, or were Karla.

"Way I see it, we have two options. Left looks easier, but it's gonna take a lot longer. Right looks…little harder. A lot faster though. You two agree?"

Karla nodded, and I had the feeling she'd come to the same conclusion. Aldric meandered over to the edge in front of us. "And we can't go straight down?"

"You kidding me? You said it yourself. It is *straight* down."

"Yeah," Aldric said, kneeling down and peering over. "I think we can do it. Doesn't look too bad. Definitely faster than the other ways."

Karla shook her head. "Nope. I'm not. You two can, but I'm not going down that way."

Aldric looked back over his shoulder, raising an eyebrow. "What, you afraid of heights?"

"No! I'm not. Just—ah!"

Aldric jerked himself toward the edge and Karla yelped, darting forward. He laughed, falling backward, completely safe. She smacked him across the back of the head and stormed back over to me. Aldric lay back on the top of the hill, chuckling and nursing his newest bruise on the morning dew.

"Idiot," she huffed. "What do you think, Hark?"

"I really, really don't want to. But I think we're going to have to go through the swamp." I stared out over the valley, trying to see if there was any other way to go. The hills on the other side of us were equally sharp, more baby mountains than the grassy lump we'd climbed over to get to Hammerk. Those mountain goats might've been able to tap dance up and down, but we would be doing our best to get down without literally busting our asses.

"Not," Karla said slowly, "the biggest fan of swamps."

I turned and raised an eyebrow at her. When had she ever even been to a swamp before?

"If you don't want to swim, it's not like Hark and I really know how to either," Aldric piped up. *Oh, gods, we have to get across that river later. One thing at a time.*

"Not that," Karla said. "Lot of bad things in swamps. Snakes, alligators." She chewed on her lip for a minute. "That's not even getting into the creepy stuff. What fairy tale witch or goblin or something *doesn't* make their home there?"

"Karla, a dragon just glassed our hometown. I kinda think we've endured the worst as far as bad things go."

Both Karla and Aldric shuddered a bit. Oooh. Yeah. I forgot, you know, I hadn't been there when Sorro became Plagiar's biggest campfire. Might've stirred up some emotional trauma with that one.

"Still," Karla insisted, "no way we're getting through there quietly."

I glanced over at Aldric, half a foot and fifty pounds bigger than me. He caught me looking. "What?"

"Nothing," I said hurriedly. "Okay, swamp-plan is definitely more risky. But it's quicker than the long way 'round."

"Assuming none of us gets hurt—getting through that swamp's gonna take a lot longer if we don't."

Quiet fell as we mulled over the decision a while longer. Part of me was almost *itching* with how much time this was eating up. I wasn't sure how much time we had but it wasn't much longer before we were the biggest cowards anybody in our village knew of. We had to find a freaking magic Blade and then kill a freaking dragon before…I started trying to figure out what Layana had meant again and pushed it out of my head. We had to just assume it was midnight tonight. That was the only thing that gave us a chance. If she was even being literal, or not trying to trick us.

I wasn't even supposed to be doing this, damnit.

And we were up here, worried about splashing through an oversized pond. The brown water, some indeterminable distance below us, looked pretty still. It wasn't even that big of a swamp, although to be fair it *was* the only one I'd ever seen.

I sighed, getting up. Either way, I was tired of waiting. "Can't believe I'm doing this, but Al, you're the tiebreaker." I turned my head back around to glance at him.

Karla glanced at him and—*damnit, she's doing puppy-dog eyes.*

"Well," he muttered, looking like a wishbone right before it snapped, "uh, you both make good points...."

Karla sighed, somehow conveying disappointment and damsel-in-distress-ness all at once.

"I would hate to get these new boots wet...."

As Aldric stood up, I glared at Karla with everything I had. She stuck her tongue out at me, and we started walking down the stupid left side of the stupid hill.

VII

The river was wide and fast, much like most of Hammerk on Half-Price Mead night. The water was pretty clear, all blue or whatever, smashed on the rocks and spitting up white foam—also like most of Hammerk on Half-Price Mead night. The river was loud, too, and I hadn't quite expected that—I mean, I knew what a river was, but they never tell you about the noise. Steady rushing, thousands of gallons of water and thousands of pounds of tasty fishies all coursing on by, with no regard to you. Aldric carefully removed his shoes and sunk his dirt-caked feet into the water, rolling his head back and sighing with relief. I debated whether or not the cool water was worth the effort to unlace and then re-lace my shoes. It was well past noon, and taking the long way down had taken that much more out of me. The closer and closer to the ground we got, the more I saw how much faster the swamp path would've been.

That being said, I could've sworn I saw something moving through it, coming down the hill right after we did. But... you know, we hadn't gotten much sleep, and I was hungry, so it was probably just that. Nothing more.

I shook my head clear of weariness and paranoia and returned to the river, enjoying a moment's rest.

I'm not a particularly well-read man, or even a very smart man, but I have heard from a scholarly type that wandered through once that rivers are the go-to thing in tales. I mean boring tales, not the cool ones Old Man Granger tells. Like they're a symbol or something. He was going on and on about how the river was life, coursing on through and such. Mostly I listened to him because to be able to sit on your ass and read books all day in Plagiar, you have to be loaded, and he was buying the drinks. But, that hours-long, drunken lecture of his stuck with me, and I ruminated on his teachings as I pissed into the river.

Aldric yelped. "Aw, c'mon, Harkness, go downstream!"

I heard somebody walking closer and turned my head slightly, seeing it was Karla. "Hey, Karla, maybe give me a sec? Nature's calling."

Karla's glare went from "hungry, tired teenager" to "mother bear without her cubs." *I am Karla, hear me roar.*

"What? Don't give me that look. I know girls piss too."

Aldric gave me a look that was either telling me to knock it off with the "juvenile" humor, or perhaps he was merely expressing amazement at the fact that girls do, in fact, piss. I try to keep him up to date on the goings-on of the world like that.

"Not in the river we have to cross." Karla waited until I was done and came up to the shore, looking down at the water. It was...well, I don't know how deep, but deep enough for somebody who couldn't swim. She fumbled in her pocket for a moment and came up with a pebble, throwing it underhanded into the swift current. It *plopped* before getting ripped downstream at an alarming rate. She didn't have to say anything—I felt that awkward, pins-and-needles weight of people's expectations slithering up around my neck and face. Cheeks started to burn a bit.

I don't have time for this crap. "Look, honey—"

Aldric's scowl deepened. *Well, I guess he does know girls piss, then. He's just annoyed at me.*

"I never claimed to know how to get across the river. Sorta like everything else, we have to figure this out as we go along. Maybe it gets narrower upstream."

"River gets wider upstream," Aldric muttered, kicking at the dirt. "I remember seeing that when we were up on the hill."

"Well, fine, we go downstream then."

"That's not the point," Aldric said. "How far to Drowduss, after that? We don't have that much time. If we're not sure this is gonna work, maybe we come up with something new, or...."

"First off, we'd have a few more hours to work with if we hadn't taken the Old Man Granger-accessible route down."

"Don't try and—" Karla began. I didn't stop.

"Second, Aldric, if you have a better plan, I'd would *love* to hear it." As soon as the words spilled out my lips, I realized it had come out harder than I meant—but it still needed to be said. I wasn't going to get second-guessed for the rest of this trip. *Whose fiancée got captured? Mine.* This was my thing, and I needed their help, not their bickering.

"Ease off, Harkness," Karla snapped. *Ah, and the Three Musketeers fall apart.* "He wants to help save Marisa just as badly as you do. We just"—she paused, trying to choose the most diplomatic phrasing—"want to be sure we go about this the best way we can."

"I'm open to any other ways if you two have them. Currently, the plan is, find a way across this river, get to

Drowduss, find someone there who has an idea of what's going on, and then try to find all the stuff we need to kill that dragon." I paused. "By…tonight, most likely. Maybe tomorrow. I'm not sure." *Maybe yesterday*, I wanted to say, but that wouldn't help us. Marisa and Elaine's betrothed could both already be marinating in that dragon's belly by now for all I knew.

"No, stop thinking big-picture for a second. We've gotta focus on this," Karla said, pointing at the rocks jutting out from under the surface of the water. "What's our plan for getting past that?"

"Look, we did get visited by a goddess, okay?" No. Not we. I did. They didn't put Granger the prophet in *their* hometown, they put him in *mine*. "She's on our side. I think we should bank on that."

There was a moment of laughless quiet, which is the worst kind of quiet.

"Get it? *Bank* on that? Because it's a river?"

I'm not trying to cope. Not even a little. This is anything but that.

"Harkness, shut the hell up, just—shut up," Karla said, crouching down as she massaged her temples with her hands. "Do you even know where the nearest bridge is? Do you have any idea of how we'll get a raft, and if we do get one, how we'll even manage to get around those rocks or-or—" Karla sputtered, losing steam and stopping for a moment. She took a few deep breaths and looked relatively calmer, but her face had only gone from a more passionate fury to a more restrained irritation. She grabbed our wineskins from us and walked away a bit (upstream from where I'd pissed) to refill them in silence, cooling herself down.

A few moments passed, nothing but the churning water to fill the quiet. "Look, I'm sorry. I don't have some brilliant scheme to get us through this. The river thing was the best idea I had and I honestly was hoping something would enable that to happen along the way. I didn't know about us having a deadline to save Marisa—"

"To find the Blade," Aldric said, his voice quiet but firm. His blond hair was stuck to his forehead. Walking with a slight hunch, he didn't seem quite as tall as he had before. "Then to get to the dragon. Then to save her."

"I'm aware the odds aren't exactly in our favor, Aldric!" My voice came out loud and harsh, overpowering the roar of the river for a moment. Karla flinched—Aldric shifted slightly, putting himself between me and her, standing up a little straighter. "None of this was supposed to happen, okay! None of this was exactly what I had planned!"

Karla was studying my face, her eyes dissecting mine. I could almost hear women laughing. I turned away and walked to the edge of the riverbank, staring at the water perhaps a foot below my toes. I watched everything surge by, hoping an answer would come rising up over the surface, that something could magically come along and fix all this. Another vision, or, or somebody from the village catching up to us and helping us or *something*.

I don't know how much time passed, honestly. Couple minutes of precious daylight, a small fraction of the hours we'd wasted walking that morning. Sweat had soaked through my shirt thoroughly now, and the satchel weighed heavy on my back, even though we'd been steadily burning through food and water the whole trip. We were all messed up by sleep deprivation, and not much food or water, and I didn't want to be doing any of this. I don't know how everyone thought I could manage to pull any of this off. This was a dragon we were talking about. Something nobody had ever or would ever be able to kill, and here the lackluster tanner's son's supposed to go adventuring and cut its head off? In three days? Or eves, or whatever the hell Layana had meant? My fingers rolled up into fists and I bit down hard on my tongue, trying to hold back a long series of curses at the gods that would not have endeared them to our cause.

I felt Aldric's hand clasp me on the back and I just…snapped.

"Will you all stop doing that?" I turned and shoved him. Gods, every single damned person in our village, every single one!

Turning, of course, on the edge of the riverbank.

I felt my ankle start to roll and Aldric's eyes widen as he reached to grab me, but I'd pushed myself back more than I'd shoved him. My arms spiraled in the air, trying to grab onto empty air as my weight slipped backward. My heel began to tilt back, my toes pointing up, and there was a subtle but unmistakable feeling of going past that point of no return.

"Oh," I whispered, closing my mouth tight and falling into the river. The current ripped me immediately away and under, muting Aldric's shouts and Karla's screams. I didn't think I'd miss the damp, humid heat we'd been trudging through all day, but being submerged in freezing water quickly changed my mind. My bones shook and my muscles seized and cramped as the coursing water slapped me along the floor of the river. I tried to push up, off of anything, but I was curled up in a ball, spun senseless. I couldn't get an idea of which way was the surface and which was below. My lungs split open and started to take the rest of my chest with it before I got thrown back up to the surface. I wheezed, sucking in as much water as air as I tried to breathe as hard

I could before going back under. *I can't swim. I can't swim. I can't swim.*

People were screaming and I think they were Aldric and Karla but there was cold force and no air and a low buzz at the back of my head and a burning emptiness in my chest.

One of those big rocks that spiked out of the water smacked into the side of my head.

The burning stopped. In fact, I didn't really feel bad at all—everything slowed down, Karla and Aldric started running upside down and the river swerved up sideways beneath me. They must've been going backward because they just sounded farther and farther away—I clutched at the rock, but my hands weren't closing up so well, and it was wet and slippery. *Red, too. Water's not supposed to be red.*

Have I been drinking? I feel...drunk.

A couple seconds later, I noticed the river was sounding really distant too, and as the water pulled me loose from the rock and down the current, my waterlogged brain came up with a really, really good-sounding idea.

Sleep....

VIII

I would've preferred to open this chapter with "I woke up spitting out money and also a bunch of sexy chicks were rubbing me down with oil, throwing gold coins all over the place."

Who knows? There's an idea for the sequel.

Instead, I woke up spitting out enough salt to preserve an entire slaughterhouse. Also, someone had lit my arms and the back of my legs on fire, which seemed like an asshole thing to do to someone. I hoped it hadn't been the dragon.

My entire body coughed, which sounds ridiculous if you've never half-drowned. I spent a solid thirty seconds trying to get the sand out of my mouth, and that's really, *really* hard when everything else around you is also covered with sand.

Wait, what? Sand?

Adrenaline exploded through me and I scrambled upright, the soreness of my whole body *(and especially my head, sweet merciful gods who stabbed me in the head)* melting away rather quickly.

I stared at the smooth, silky sand. I reached my hand down into it, feeling how warm and soft it was. I mean, take away the total disorientation, unbelievable pain, and this wasn't too bad. I'd never seen sand before—and, come to think of it, I hadn't ever tasted salt water that often. Even the air was salty. How? We had salt, like, once a year back in Sorro, and that was usually only if a salt trader felt bad for us and cut his prices down. I stared around, trying to get a sense for where I was. The sand, maybe fifty paces from me, gave way to a forest, but it was like no forest I'd ever seen. It was vibrant greens and yellows, visibly teeming with life even from this distance. There was the constant chatter of birds screeching at each other (I saw one, huge and colorful, swoop down and dance back behind some trees) and vines hung from branches, thick foliage swaying in the cool air. Behind me, there was a rhythmic roar—sorta like the rush of the river, but not constant.

I slowly hauled myself up and turned around, bearing witness to more water than I'd ever seen in my entire life. The satchel's straps had begun to rub sores on my chest and shoulders, which was literally the only thing that kept me from diving in, unable to swim or no. I just…I can't describe how much water there was. It stretched as far as I could see in every direction, going on forever. Can you even imagine? I'm not lying to you, it…the…the ocean, oh gods, this was the ocean—it swirled and frothed, white-crested waves breaking the surface and coming back down.

I'm not a really touchy-feely, let's-sit-and-look-at-how-pretty-the-flowers-are type, but it was objectively beautiful. So, naturally, I assumed I'd died when my head smacked against that rock in the river—and, thanks to a cosmic screw-up of some sort, I'd been mistakenly thrown into one of the nicer afterlifes. Pretty soon some celestial bureaucrat was going to figure out I belonged somewhere way worse and rip me out of this little paradise.

At least that was the theory I was operating on—my short-term memory was kinda (read: totally) fuzzy, and I wasn't sure all of me was working at 100 percent. As if on cue, the entire world started to compress on my skull. Colors blurred to grey as my legs decided to go on strike. Oof. I half-sat, half-fell back onto the sand, where I figured I'd stay for a good…ten years or so until this headache passed. *Standing up was a very poor choice*, I thought. Or maybe I said it. Or maybe someone else said it. I blinked a few times, grogginess settling into my skull and weariness seeping through my arms and legs. I predicted one hell of a nap in my immediate future.

I looked around, checking to make sure there weren't any…whatever predators lived near a beach coming to snap off my fingers and toes. A few feet away, there was a body-sized imprint in the sand, then…footsteps. They led off into the woods, disappearing out of sight. Somebody else was here. Or had been here, at any rate. I peered at the treeline, trying to see if there was any movement—but there was too much to pick out any one person. Leaves and vines swayed in the ocean air, birds darted in and out of branches, and a red crab sidestepped its way across the sand. This place was…this place was pretty cool. This was what I'd signed on for, this sort of sightseeing. Not climbing (and falling down) hills for twenty-four hours straight.

"Wondrous, isn't it?"

The voice was a woman's, which, generally, are nicer to wake up to than men's voices. I scooted myself around, not trusting my limbs to hold me if I stood up again, and looked at its source. The cadence and weight to her voice was vaguely familiar. Not her voice itself, but the…the poise, the force of it.

The woman was…well, I guess she was pretty, but it was in a really eerie way. She was completely symmetrical. Not a single imperfection, not so much as a single hair that didn't mirror the other side. She walked slowly, her grey hair parted evenly down the middle, her flowing half-white, half-black gown split in two halves. She stopped a few feet away from me, dark eyes surveying me closely. Her face was round—almost circular, but I didn't know for sure because I had a feeling it wouldn't be wise to stare at this woman. Letting my eyes linger on her, I felt a strange pressure in my head, a buzz entirely unrelated to where I'd hit that rock. As I looked upon her, there was an equal amount of glare in both my eyes, even though the sun was behind me.

The strangest feeling, though, was that…hm. I don't know how to describe it. You know how sometimes, with huge bonfires, you can feel the almost-painful heat from ten or eleven feet away? It was like that, but not as immediate. I wasn't close enough to get roasted, but there was no doubt in my mind she could go from "peacefully admiring the beach" to "disemboweling Harkness" in about two seconds.

I decided to choose my words very carefully.

"Indeed it is," I murmured, not making eye contact. I found the patch of trees over her right shoulder to be particularly intriguing, even as I felt the weight of her gaze. That's not one of those "she was glaring at me so hard I felt it" type exaggerations—I could literally feel her staring at me, the force of her will bristling against my skin.

"Know thee who I am, little one?" her voice was monotone. Never rising or falling. Steady.

I'm beginning to pick up on the motif, here.

It wasn't the gentle stream that Layana's voice had been. This was a still, quiet pond, and I was going to try my hardest not to make any ripples.

I paused for a moment, letting the ocean crash against the shore behind me. The sand was warm and, altogether, not the worst thing to wake up on. I mean, hey, they could've had me wake up in a pile of horse manure. Or in bed with Aldric.

"You," I said slowly—the same way you talk to a drunk with a knife—"are Lady Aurea. Goddess of Fate...Lady of Balance."

Her face betrayed nothing, neither confirming nor denying it. "What dost thou knowest of Lady Aurea, should I be her?"

Man, the one good thing about goddesses (in my observation) is that they were pretty awful at hiding the fact they were divine. I mean, c'mon. You're telling me average people appear out of nowhere with literal perfect features and start chatting you up? Wolf can only wear sheep's clothing so well, you know?

I said this next part slowly—the same way I'd talk to a drunk with a knife to my throat. "You...I am told you are a woman of...justice. Equality. An even hand." *Nice, neutral statements. Nothing controversial from me. That's Harkness, ever the diplomat.*

She stared at me, her face impassive, her emotions unreadable. She could've been about to wave her hand and scorch me clean off the face of the earth, or maybe she'd just send me on my way. "Mmm. What shall become of thee, then? That is the question that needs answering."

I said this even more slowly—the same way I'd talk to drunk with a knife to my dick. "Um. I...." my voice trailed off, and I thought for a good ten seconds before answering. Another rarity coming from me. "I...I suppose you'll do what balances the scales?"

There was about a minute of the longest silence in my life. The ocean waves seemed to quiet down, as if they were trying to make sure they heard what happened next. The birds hushed themselves as well, the way they do when there's a grizzly or a wolf in their midst. That crab was power-hobbling across the sand, desperately trying to get away from Aurea.

I don't know if you guys have gods, but they're a pretty big deal with us. They're not on the same plane as humans, obviously. No matter what you do, they can swat you down with pretty much no effort. There are no stories of humans going against them and coming out on top—occasionally, they can eke out a draw with trickery or charm or beauty, but even then, it's rare. We're blind mice thrown to some real hungry tomcats, and our only hope's that they go for the fatter, blinder ones before they came for us.

And Aurea? Well, she had a rep as a hardass. The woman was behind everything—sure, the other gods and goddesses handled specific stuff, like nature, or war, or whatever, but she fit all the pieces together. She wove prophecies, dealt out good luck and bad. She kept everything in balance.

Let me put it to you like this. You miss the census, you don't pay your taxes. Who should you fear more, the tax collector or his enforcers? First thought is the enforcers. Big, tough types that come knock your door down and ever-so-kindly incentivize you to pay up. But that's not it. You can run from them, or hide, or maybe even beat them if you're bigger and tougher. But that tax collector? A hundred miles away, you're just ink on a page. Doesn't matter what you've done—your name on that list is just as liable to get scratched through as anybody else's. That was Aurea. The other gods, they were partial, for better or worse. You could hope to win their favor—or hope they were too irritated with somebody else to focus on you. Not her. Not Aurea. She didn't care—you got what was coming to you. No running, no hiding. Can you imagine talking to a mountain? Trying to reason with something as vast and powerful as the ocean? That was her.

But to more immediate issues…balance.

I didn't want to show fear, but I couldn't help licking my lips (more sand choked up my throat, which didn't make it easy to keep a brave face, because it's really hard to look fearless when you're coughing and sputtering), letting my eyes wander to the mark in the sand where someone else had been.

And the footsteps where they'd walked away.

Two people had been on this beach, if those footsteps were any indicator.

Balance.

Even scales.

One had left here alive.

Now I guess we figure out what happens to me.

My throat became very, very dry, and I pressed my hands down into the sand. Aurea wouldn't have the pleasure of seeing them tremble.

At least I'd die somewhere pretty and not that horrible place Layana showed me.

"That would be correct," Aurea finally spoke, her eyes never once leaving me. I couldn't keep straight which gods made which animals—unlike Karla, I'd stopped listening to nursery rhymes and old songs many years ago—but I think Aurea had something to do with the hawk. Harsh features, constant glare…she could've sat there until the next Reckoning came around, just sizing me up. *Hey, maybe it's just 'cause she thinks I'm cute. Optimism, people, it's all about optimism.*

"And," I asked, very quietly, my voice closer in pitch to Karla's than my own, "What…what does balancing the scales entail?"

There was another long silence, this one a little less terrifying. Her presence was just…regal. She carried herself with such confidence that you knew it wasn't an act. It was nothing conscious on her part. She was just innately better than me, in every possible way, and the way she stood and the way she looked reflected that. Some instinctual part of me recognized that, wanted to bow my head—and, hey, you may have picked up on this, but I'm not really big on respecting authority figures, so that was saying something.

There was something my subconscious recognized, something that overwhelmed the animals and every aspect of the natural world around us. The trees swayed in perfect unison, mirror images on either side of her, even the clouds above had ripped and shifted to match her symmetry. That buzz in my skull, the gentle crushing I felt when I stared at her—that was her sheer presence trying to do the same to me.

"One has already left this beach alive, unharmed. It would be balanced to strike down the other, perhaps."

"P-perhaps." My hands dug a little deeper.

Her dark eyes never blinked. "But that is not the case. Both of the souls brought here were not wholly alive when they came."

There was another pause, and I realized she was yielding the conversation to me, not just doing it for dramatic effect. Gods are big on theatrics. Unfortunately, I was confused by what she meant. "You mean…I was dead?"

I don't know if you've ever been through a scenario where you came pretty close to kicking the bucket. You probably don't think about it often, or if you do, you try and rationalize it, joke about it…you try to put some mental space between it and you. Nobody really likes admitting "Yeah, I almost transitioned from being a person to being a memory that one time," but, hey hey, it's coming for everybody.

Having someone who very, very easily, could end your life, tell you that you *should* have died, well…it's a step above making it out of something narrowly. The ocean sun didn't feel quite as warm anymore, and the salty air almost chilled me. It burned in a few places, searing the many scrapes and cuts I'd earned over the last day and a half.

"Not dead. Rendered unconscious, in the river. Wounded. Not mortally, but…severely enough. The current was going far too fast for thy friends to possibly reach thee in time. The chances of surviving, in any condition to continue thy quest were…" a brief scowl tugged at either end of her lips at once. "Minimal."

Well. Guess that was 0-1. Scoreboard, Dragon.

"And the other person here?"

"Collapsed of exhaustion, owing to several days without sleep. It's unlikely they would've awoken, given the rather… dangerous…creatures that roam Plagiar."

I shuddered, thinking of stolen voices and murky swamps. Love how she said that like, you know, we should've known better. Last I recalled, the gods were the ones who put all those dangerous creatures out there for us.

"Well, if we were both half-dead, then…"

"Then by permitting the both of thee to live, it is fitting that another—one whole—should die."

It didn't take me long to decide what I'd do.

You know, I'm sure a lot of people would have felt a lot of remorse over this choice, tried to offer themselves up and be all "No, Aurea, I can't condemn someone else to die."

But you know what? Screw those people. They're liars. Not a single damned person, freshly awoken after almost drowning, having gone two days with very little sleep and food—and, during those days, having hiked their ass off, brushed paths with painful, messy deaths a few times over, would've looked at one of the most powerful things in existence and said "No, I can't. Just go ahead and kill me."

Aurea would've done it in about half a second. Snap of her fingers and Harkness' head gets sent a few hundred miles away from the rest of him. She would not have thought twice about it, no time for last words, no "I'll pass along news of what happened to your loved ones." Anybody who tells you they would've is trying to impress whoever's around them.

End.

Of.

Story.

It's real easy to have a messiah complex until somebody wants to nail you to a cross.

Besides, whoever came before me? They already killed half of one dude. What did that equate to? Leaving somebody crippled? Maybe just giving them a life so unbearably bad they wished they were dead? Was me dying to give somebody else that kind of existence really any better? If my choices were live a half-life or just kick the bucket, I'd probably go with number two. I was doing whoever this was a favor, really. Besides, much as I didn't consider myself the heroic type, there was the whole "stop the Reckoning from ever happening again" thing going on. I just casually met with two goddesses within twelve hours. I think that's a world record. And now I was supposed to do a one-eighty and off myself so that dozens of other people could die in the future thanks to the dragon? Losing one guy, or losing how many people over the years because of the Reckoning? I wasn't really that confident in my abilities to stop it, but you know, with two immortal, possibly omnipotent forces breathing down my neck, I kinda had to try. Or at least wait until I could find somebody who could and pass this whole stupid adventure off to them.

So, I moved my eyes over to make contact with Aurea's, instantly feeling like someone's thumbs were rammed through my eyes to the back of my skull. A staring contest with her would probably make my head explode. "I understand."

Aurea nodded and snapped her fingers—in, of course, both hands. Instantly, something warm and fiery ran through my body, obliterating the pain in my head and my arms and—well, I'll save us both some time and just say the pain everywhere. I felt...good. Really good. I bounced up, surprising myself with how quickly I moved. My forearms weren't pocked with reddened scrapes and hideous bruises. All clear and clean, not a trace of ash or dirt or dried blood to be found. Something like smooth lightning raced through my chest a few times, and I was ready to take on Aurea, the dragon—hell, just throw all of Plagiar at me and let's see who came out on top. I guess if two of us were walking out of here alive, we were walking out fully alive. Some poor bastard was getting fully dead, but that wasn't my problem.

I took a few deep breaths before I looked back up at Aurea, who was clearly waiting for me to finish—a slightly impatient look was on her face, and I quickly focused back on her. Repeat: I did *not* want to piss the goddess lady off.

"Know thee where we stand?"

"Uh, near the ocean?"

Another flicker of irritation. She may have misinterpreted my utter ignorance as smartassery. *Fair enough.* "Not incorrect, but...not what I..." she stopped for a moment, then started again. "We have brought thee to the shrine. The weapon you seek lies in wait."

Well, this is turning out to be a pretty great day. Fifty percent of saving the world taken care of in about fifteen minutes. Something even more infectious and energizing than whatever supernatural pick-me-up Aurea had shot me up with began to flood through me: hope. Yeah, I know I sound like an after-school special saying that crap, but, honestly, I hadn't even considered the possibility of pulling this quest off as, you know, a possibility. It was a vague afterthought, like cleaning your room or stopping after that next drink.

But actually doing this? I filled my lungs up with air, slow and steady, then let it out just as gentle. *Don't get cocky. Don't get crazy. You're still making small talk with an incomprehensibly deadly force of nature. Happy thoughts. Good vibes. Celebrate when her Divine Equanimity has left to go vaporize someone else.* "Isn't...isn't it supposed to be really hard to find?"

"Not for those who know how to find it."

What kind of fortune cookie bullshit is that?

I figured since I was already here, I couldn't mess it up by saying this. "But, Lady Aurea, I...I didn't know how to find it."

"By falling head over heels, naturally. Layana, fittingly, has a taste for the romantic." There was a pause, and I got another sense of annoyance. In Aurea's form I got images similar to the visions I'd felt near Layana. She was more than just a person, she was an essence, a concept. The symmetrical woman I saw may have been how she showed herself, but it wasn't *her*, per se. *A tribunal. One man walks free as another walks to the gallows in a dark hood. A fisherman drowns while another stumbles onto shore. Twins, naked and innocent, grapple and wrestle, no victor, no loser. Mountains. Stone. Strength, uncompromising strength.* That was Aurea. What I'd done—getting here by a technicality—upset her. It threw her world-view off. She wasn't angry at me personally, not that I could tell. Maybe annoyed with herself, disappointed that there had been a Harkness-sized loophole in her karmic lawyering. "Perhaps…more literally than any of us had anticipated," she admitted, "but the requirements were fulfilled nonetheless. Through the jungle—" (So that's what those woods were called!) "lies the Shrine itself. Should thee survive the guardian, Layana's Blade is thine to wield."

I nodded my head. "Thank you, my lady."

She bowed her head in polite acknowledgement. "There is one final matter that we must settle." Aurea extended both her fists to me and opened her hands (I noticed her palms were devoid of any lines). She was clutching a small—and I mean tinier than my pinky—glass vial, inside which a clear liquid bubbled, changing colors occasionally. "When thy time on this island comes to an end, thy need only imbibe this."

I didn't know what imbibing was, but I used context clues to figure out that it more or less meant "chug." *And they say Plagiaran education needs to be improved.*

"Thank you." I reached out to grab it, clutching the cold glass container in my hand. A last-second thought popped into my head and I stilled my hand. Before I picked it up—thereby officially taking the gift, I asked, "Wait…will this cause someone else to become lost, since you're helping me find my way?"

Aurea grinned wickedly, and there was a manic sort of look in her eyes. Yeah, forget what I said earlier. She was definitely pissed at me personally. "What, little one, makes you think I'm helping you find your way?"

There was a sharp breeze, buffeting me from both sides. As the sand kicked up, Aurea's dress rippling and flowing like crazy, she rose a few inches off the ground and vanished in a blast of light, a second sun that left a blind spot in my vision for a full minute. Immediately, the wind settled, the sand falling back down.

Even after my vision cleared, I wiped sand out of my eyes for a few more minutes. I considered getting ocean water to splash my face with, but I didn't know how well the salt would get along with my eyes. It would really suck to go blind after getting all fixed up. Or in general. *I'm no expert, but I think having swordfights with dragons becomes a lot tougher when you have to use a cane in the other hand.*

I very quickly tucked the vial inside my satchel, wrapping it up in one of the blankets. No way was I letting this thing get broken. I very strongly doubted Aurea would show back up to give me another one if my dumb ass dropped it and shattered my get-home potion all over the rocks.

Trying to breathe slowly enough to keep my heart from exploding out of my chest, and also trying to not dwell on the single most terrifyingly ominous thing I'd heard in my life, I walked toward the jungle. My shaking right hand drew my sword from its hot-to-the-touch scabbard (I'd been in the sun longer than I thought) although gods only knew if a sword could even help me against the guardian in there. Given that no one had ever managed to get Layana's Blade in the history of all Plagiar, it, uh…it was probably going to be a real pushover. *Totally easy to take down. Really, it was like I'd already gotten the Blade. No need to be worried. Nope.*

I sighed. I was getting real sick of this kinda stuff.

It's all about optimism, people.

IX

The part with the jungle and the Blade and the Shrine... you know, it's, uh, kinda boring. We're skipping ahead. We'll cover it later if we have time. Don't question it.

So, yeah, if a divine being ever gives you a drink, go ahead and expect it to taste like ass.

For the second time in a day, I woke up spitting, frantically rolling over and trying to cough the nasty taste of that vial's contents out of my mouth. It was like I'd been kissed by the devil. I guess I had been. I felt something hard and sharp press into my hand and looked down at the little glass bottle, entirely empty. Heaving, I picked up the stupid thing and threw it as far as I could. *Gah. Blegggh.* I curled up onto my knees, panting from the rather sudden change in scenery. I was a little too close to the river for my liking, so I nudged a few inches away and stopped to catch my breath. Rivers were not like the ocean. Rivers were fast and had sharp rocks.

Well, uh, I guess since the getting-the-magic-Blade half of the quest was taken care of, that left the killing the dragon half. I don't know if there's a word for nostalgia over things that were around maybe three hours ago, but I certainly had it.

My clothes were soaked with sweat from the jungle, and there was a faint echo of mosquitoes buzzing around my head. *Gods couldn't have warped me back dry and cozy, oh no, they had to be pricks and drop me back all tired and wet.* I guess your sense of humor gets really warped when you live forever. I pressed myself up into a squat, and quickly realized where I was: downstream. Same river I apparently should've died in, which was a mildly terrifying thought.

"Ow, damnit!" wheezed Aldric, coughing as he spoke. That's how good my aim was; I nailed him with that bottle without even knowing he was there. I stood up, eyes peering into the brush.

It…it was nice, you know, to know they were looking for me. But, and I'll be honest, the rest of this quest…prospects for survival weren't looking so hot. That dragon was, you know, *that dragon*. Aldric and Karla had been helpful thus far—or, at least, entertaining—but I felt bad bringing them along too much further. It'd…be better for all parties if I did this solo. Telling them that was gonna be really awkward.

I turned and found the sun, halfway to the horizon. Almost to sundown. I could make it to Drowduss before then, but I'd need to figure out just which way it was. I didn't know how far that river had carried me, but I was hoping the gods had warped me back to a convenient location.

Since, you know, my luck had been so wonderful thus far.

"Huh? A bottle? What…" Karla's voice was hoarse, a little strained. I figured she'd been yelling for me, trying to find me.

Okay, that did make me squirm a bit. Hoofing the rest of this solo seemed like the only opportunity to have a shot at this, but, I'd also feel like a dick leaving them out here trying to find me when I was alive and well. Mostly well. *Sure, my life expectancy is now down to hours and not years, but I'm doing well for the moment.*

I sighed, hoisting my satchel across my chest and walking toward the thick bushes that grew alongside this part of the river. It was secluded, real wilderness—the hill we'd come over was off in the distance, although there were a few more pretty close by. I pushed some of the branches out of the way, keeping an eye on both the prickly thorns and the fat red berries hanging from them. *Probably poisonous. Probably poisonous.*

My stomach growled.

"Stupid poison. Stupid stomach," I muttered, ducking my head down and managing to slip through the hedge with only a scratch or two on my—

Something solid connected with my forehead and I went down hard.

I grunted, vaguely aware of the slash one of the thorns had made across my cheek. I noticed it mechanically, unconsciously—my hand was fumbling for the sword at my belt, but it was too slow, I couldn't get the clasp undone—

I looked up in time to see a knee slam into my gut. I heaved. If there was any water left in my lungs, that took care of it. Whoever this was, who the hell was in the bushes to—

"Do you have him?" Karla asked, her voice…a little… not…not human…

"Yeh," came the guy above me. "I got 'im." I tried to push him off. *Frederick, wasn't it?* Death staring me down and my brain was trying to remember names. He drove his knee down further into my gut, smacking me in the head again with that cudgel. Well, at least they'd gotten better-armed since we'd last seen them. Before I could react, another pair of hands had grabbed my own, thin, lanky arms from my side. I pulled as hard as I could, but their combined weight was too much. The other guy was the one who'd had the knife, giggling softly as he slapped a pair of manacles on my wrists. I squirmed and kicked, thinking if I could get back through the bush I could roll into the river and maybe hope to get away. Swimming with my hands bound would be next to impossible, especially given that I didn't know how to swim, but I had to try and—

Something wet and slimy and painfully sharp pressed against the side of my throat. I felt a dull thudding in my head, the steady pounding of my heart. My fingers went numb, and I swear all the colors in everything I saw faded a bit.

Oh gods.

The two bandits were talking but I couldn't hear them, I couldn't make out any words. Frederick scrambled off me, eyeing me with cold indifference. The other guy, he was enjoying this, the sick bastard. Frederick just needed the money, maybe, or at least he wasn't getting off on it like that yellow-toothed prick was. I slowly turned my eyes, not daring to twist my neck at all. Before I could see where it was, the Knife Guy scrambled back and slipped a black hood over my head. I had only a second's relief from the sharp pressure before the hollowthroat put its tongue back against the cloth. It wouldn't have slowed it down. I could still feel the edge. I had a very nauseating suspicion that it had split open enough kids' throats to know just how to do it right. I trembled, the chain between my wrists shaking and clinking. I couldn't see. I couldn't see. All I could feel was the hungry spit of that *thing* soaking through the hood and getting onto my skin and—

I screamed. I screamed like a little kid.

The hollowthroat's tongue shivered, an almost orgasmic shudder. It laughed, sounding just like Karla, but…cold. It was her voice but it wasn't her, there was something empty and cruel and dead to it.

"Delicious," it purred. "He will be enough for tonight, I think."

And hands, filthy and rough, grabbed my ankles, hooked under my shoulders. The razor tongue left my throat, and I nearly whimpered with relief, the hood clinging to my lips as I struggled to try and get air.

Then they hoisted me up and carried me off.

They ripped the hood off once we got back in the cave, but I was still shackled. No chance of that coming off. I realized very quietly that I was going to die with that steel around my wrists, and I began pulling and straining again. The Knife Guy held his wicked little blade under my chin, stopping my shaking real quick. His hungry eyes bored into mine (I refused to look away) as Assface Frederick tied up my ankles with rope. Must not've had two sets of manacles. Worked out better for me. *I have to get out of this place before that hollowthroat decides to—*

I gulped, uncomfortably aware of my throat.

I had to get out. And if they were going to tie up my ankles with rope, that was better than steel. Unfortunately, this guy bound me like he knew what he was doing. They may have been pretty laughable at mugging us the first go 'round, but I could hardly feel my toes by the time he was done stringing up my ankles. I flexed tentatively, but it was no use. They took off my shoes and threw them next to my satchel, across the cave. Frederick grabbed a rag—some nasty, grimy thing.

"Open up," he hissed.

I kept my mouth shut.

He paused for a moment, and then slapped me as hard as he could. I gasped, at which point he unceremoniously stuffed the rag into my mouth, wrapping it around my head and tying the gag shut. I tried to spit it out but couldn't. *Ugh. Blegh.* I at least tried to keep my tongue off of it. I didn't want to know where that rag had been. How many other mouths it'd gotten stuffed in before…

Gods. This was…this was terrible. I…no. No, I had to focus. *Okay, surroundings. Deep breaths. Deep breaths.*

We were in a cave—I guess these hills must've had a few tucked away. It wasn't a very big cave. No, that's not accurate. This cave *was* pretty big, it just sloped down and back— we were near the front, so it seemed relatively small. A few feet from me, a small campfire had been started, and it was quickly gnawing through the branches they'd tossed onto it. I looked around, doing my best to move my head slowly and subtly, not wanting to draw any more attention. My back was against the wall of the cave, hard and rough and wet with trickles of water. I glanced up. Little droplets fell from the ceiling from time to time. *Great. I'll get marinated before this thing eats me.*

To my left there was just darkness. The fire's light carved a path through it, sending shadows flickering along the walls, but the dark was impenetrable after a few feet. I didn't know how far back it went, or what was down there. A cold, quiet little instinct told me the hollowthroat was in the dark some-where. If I was going to get out I needed to start moving. To my right I could see sunlight—it was impossible to gauge how long or how far they'd carried me, but if there was still light coming in, it couldn't have taken long, couldn't have been far. The light was a faded orange, so I figured the sun must've been nearing the horizon. Sundown wasn't far off. So that was good—if the river was relatively close, then maybe my escape plan could still happen. The memory of my skull smashing against that rock was still fresh in my mind, but I'd dive in there head-first with the chains on if it meant getting out of this cave.

Knife Guy sat across from me, partially obscured by the dancing fire. He grinned, cleaning his fingernails with his knife. "Not the heaviest, is he?"

"Been better if we'd snagged the girl," muttered Frederick.

"Which one?" Knife Guy asked quietly. *He's got some balls on him for calling Aldric a girl.*

Frederick shot him a venomous glare but didn't reply—he was too busy running through my satchel, going through my belongings. *Ass.* He picked up my sword, and I felt a strange sense of territorialism—I mean, I was pissed about being abducted, and I wasn't the most reverent guy, but damnit, that was my dad's. I strained against the ropes, the manacles. Nothing budged.

He pulled it out and eyed it, his face even more gaunt and hollow in the dim light. These guys looked - well, I almost managed to feel bad for them.

Almost.

Knife Guy lifted up his shirt to wipe his face clean of sweat, revealing his ribcage pressing against his skin. Frederick was a little better off, but not by much. His chin was covered in a beard, the untamed, haggard type. Their skin was pale, almost yellowed in a few places. Frederick had a little more weight than Knife Guy, but they were both lanky, deathly thin.

My sword wobbled in his hands, and he needed a few tries to get it back in the sheath.

I frowned. A cave...in a hill. They must've carried me a ways—a ways *uphill*. And these guys didn't have much muscle to work with from the start...I was no powerhouse, but if they were that tired, that hungry? I might be able to take them. I didn't dare to hope—living through this seemed too good to be a possibility at the moment, but there was a chance.

I flexed one more time, testing the rope. Nothing but hurt ankles. I couldn't undo the knot without them noticing, and I didn't think I could get that gag out either, much as I wanted to. The manacles weren't coming off without a key. *One of them has to have it. Right? Right. Of course.*

There weren't any sharp rocks around me, although I did see one decent-sized stone. I started to nudge towards it, but Knife Guy turned towards me, a wild, bloodshot pair of brown eyes boring right through me.

"Move another inch and I'll cut your eyes out."

I promptly stopped moving. *Okay. There...there goes that plan.* There had to be something else. Anything. I scanned the cave one more time, and saw he was still watching.

"Heh. There's nothing. You know there's nothing."

He tilted his head to the side, a quiet grin tugging at his lips and stretched cheeks, like he was entertaining some morbid fantasy. He twirled the knife in his hands and turned to Frederick. "He have any food?"

"Not much," Frederick sighed, tossing him the last bit of jerky I had. Knife Guy gnawed on it, chewing and wincing a lot. *Should've brushed those yellow-ass teeth a little more.*

There was a rustle to my left, and all three of us turned toward the darkness.

The fire crackled for a moment. Then there was the most convincing imitation of birdsong I've ever heard. An entire symphony of redbirds and bluejays came out of the back of the cave. All three of us exchanged glances, equally unsure of what was going on.

One fell for the trap. A bird, small and red and clueless, fluttered inside, landing by the fire. It turned its head quizzically, unsure of what was going on. It tweeted, singing back to its brothers deeper in the cave.

Something grey flashed out of the abyss, latched around it, and wrenched it back. A few feathers and some blood fell to the floor of the cave. There was crunching, chewing, snapping. Then quiet.

"Yeh 'bout done?" Frederick barked. He stared into the dark, trying to keep his gaze steady. He had my sword back out, clutched in his hand. It swayed back and forth in his arms, the veins popping in his arms as he held it up. *This is some kind of deal gone terribly wrong and they know it.*

A songbird and a set of thieves. I prayed its stomach couldn't hold any more.

Then it spoke—it really did, not some imitation or echo. Its true voice was raspy, steel grinding on rock, rotten wood bending and bursting to splinters. *"I will take as long as I want. And you will wait."*

Frederick turned and looked at Knife Guy, who nodded his head. Knife Guy asked, real soft, "Where's Johann?" He gripped the knife in one of his hands, ready, waiting.

Johann? Must've been Fists, the mute.

I kept pulling against the ropes around my ankles. *Break already. Please break. Let the knot come loose.*

There was more silence, and the heavy shuffling of slow, careless walking. Then the voice began again, much quieter.

"Past the branches gnarled and dark, where lie silent the singing lark…"

The thieves exchanged looks, trembling but sure. The air in the cavern had gotten colder, and the fire seemed to flicker, weakening and fading. Some draft pulled toward the back of the cave, and the faintest—just barely perceptible— echoes of noise started up. There were children giggling and a songbird crying.

"The 'ell's Johann?" Frederick said, taking a step toward the fire, toward the hollowthroat. Knife Guy stepped up, edging his way around the fire, skirting the edge of the darkness. He'd pass right in front of me, then make his way around toward Frederick. That was it. That was my chance. When he got in front of me, I'd kick out with both my legs and knock him into the fire. Lights go out, I squirm for freedom, try and slice the ropes on something and…run. Not a great plan but better than nothing. Better than what was in the dark. Slowly, I edged closer, making sure I'd be able to knock that son of a bitch down.

There was a pregnant silence, the cold, the draft, the *void* stopping for a moment—it was only when that thing sang the lullaby. *"I don't like interruptions. Hold your tongue, or I will hold it for you. I shall be done soon, and then I will answer all your many questions, Mister Frederick."*

"No," Frederick said. "You killed 'im. 'N soon as yeh finish tha' song, yeh're gonna try an' kill us."

Silence. Knife Guy was shaking. Not even trying to hide it. At least Frederick was putting on a bold face.

Knife Guy was a little more than halfway around the fire, now, and he'd pass in front of me in just a few seconds. He'd been stepping with his back to Frederick, but he turned, looking at Frederick about what to do.

He froze.

Completely paralyzed.

"Wha' is it?" Frederick growled, lifting the sword up.

Knife Guy trembled, and blood started to leak out of his lips. His eyes were wide, bulging. The knife fell out of his hands and clattered on the floor. It bounced toward me, and my gut surged with hope for a moment.

Just one moment. Then it remembered I was still next in line.

The cave was totally quiet for a moment or two. Then the outline of *something* just formed halfway out the shadows, pressed up against Knife Guy. It hunched over behind him, like some monstrous shadow cast by the fragile campfire. Knife Guy's mouth started to move, a grey tongue sticking out of his mouth and hanging out a few inches too low to be his own.

"I thought I told you," hissed Knife Guy, still alive, a puppet with only one long, bloody string, *"To hold your tongue."*

Frederick screamed, I let out a muffled shout, and Knife Guy tried to do—something—but couldn't. There was a quick snap and he went limp, the hollowthroat's tongue pulling back out of the back of his throat. Knife-guy crumpled and went limp fast, blood gurgling out of the hole and running down into the dark of the cave.

I....I had never seen anyone die before. I'd never seen a dead body before. Maybe in passing, back in Sorro. I'm sure there were a few people who'd kicked the bucket in the dragon's attack, but most of the time there wasn't much left. Just urns and piles of ashes.

So what I saw was...traumatizing.

But I don't remember that so much as I remember what came after.

When Knife Guy dropped—*like the curtain falling before the real show begins*—I saw the hollowthroat. It was…wrong. There was nature and a natural order and a way things should be and then there was *this*. It was hunched, tall enough to brush the top of the cave with its shoulderblades. Its skin was mottled and jaundiced, stretched too thin over too many bones. Its knees were bent in backward, jutting out behind instead of in front, and I realized that was why it dragged, why it made that shuffle when it walked. Gods, its feet— there were no toes, just rounded nubs that scuffed across the cave floor (but, apparently, could still move nightmarishly fast when it had to). Its ribs matched Knife Guy's and Frederick's, bulging against its paper-thin flesh, wearing the thing's hunger for everyone to see. The monster was almost fetal—the hollowthroat's claws, four times bigger than my own hands, were curled up around its chest, six-fingered talons twitching and squirming, dripping blood from where they'd caressed Knife Guy. Its muscles and skin were taut with veins and tendons and gods know what else, all running up towards its throat, where there was a big hollow, a depression that curved too far back. It breathed shallow, heaving and pulling in the twilight air.

Then, of course, that thing's face. Its head was too small, maybe half the size of mine, and there was…there was nothing. No eyes or nose or ears or…or anything. Just a mouth, wide and full of dagger-teeth. That tremendous grey tongue slithered in and out, swaying like a tail before the pounce. Its jaw opened up and it spoke in Knife Guy's voice.

"Scream for me."

Frederick backpedaled toward the front of the cave but even he knew it was futile. The hollowthroat's tongue lashed out, too fast to be seen, too fast to react to, and sliced across the back of his legs, making him drop to the ground, calves bloodied and useless. He fumbled, trying to stand back up, but his legs refused to work, muscles split open too badly to hold his weight. He held up the sword valiantly, cutting the air in some wild attempt to strike back. The hollowthroat staggered toward him, and I felt pity for the guy. I mean, yeah, the asshole had tried to get me murdered and fed to this thing, but…gods.

It was just toying with him.

It had been a ways back in the cave, judging by the sound of the lullaby. That thing had covered a good fifteen feet in half a second when it lunged up to Knife Guy. Now it took its time, shuffling with each methodical step, inching around the fire (it went around the far side—I very quickly debated kicking it into the flames, just as I would've the other thief, but the chance didn't come to me. It might've killed me for it, but…what did I have to lose?). It wheezed and coughed, stopping once and letting its tongue drag across the floor for a moment. Then it moved in for the kill.

I turned my head and closed my eyes.

At some point, the screams stopped.

This was all real.

This was totally real.

I was gonna die wearing filthy rags in the back of a cave in some pissant part of this damn place. I was gonna die slow and painful and alone and forgotten.

I shook, pushing with everything I had against the ropes around my legs and the chains at my wrists. Nothing. *Nothing.* The hollowthroat hadn't heard my commotion, and I scanned the floor, trying to see where that knife fell. If I could get to it before him, I might—just might…

I squirmed, moving as silently as I could, my eyes locked on that monster the whole time. It knelt—which made it look even more unholy, its hunched spine inverting further as its legs bent more. It dropped its face *(if you could call it that)* down to Frederick. There was a low, rasping noise, and a bitter cold bled through the cave. Except this time, it was toward the mouth of the cave—toward the hollowthroat.

I moved a half-inch at a time, praying it was too pre-occupied to see what I was doing. A few more feet. A few more feet.

The hollow noise picked up, the air growing staler, the flames thinning. Nothing I could see came out of Frederick's mouth, but I heard his voice. That thick accent came spilling out his dead lips, a hundred different words and sounds and shouts and screams all at once. The hollowthroat trembled, its needle-point teeth feasting on something invisible.

I started moving faster.

If it turned around, it was going to see that I was nowhere near where I'd been a moment ago—and it probably wouldn't be very happy about that. I kneeled, getting my ankles back behind me as I grabbed the knife off the cave floor. I forced myself to take a second—one whole, precious second—to take a deep breath, just trying to tell myself how cool this part would seem when Old Man Granger regaled the village with how we escaped the bandits, got away from the hollowthroat, how I, uh, killed the dragon. All of that would happen because I was going to live. I was going to live.

I glanced over at my satchel, thoughts of Layana's Shrine and my little island detour flashing to my head. It hadn't noticed the satchel yet. *Okay, good vibes. Optimism*, I thought, looping my bound hands under my knees, keeping my eyes on the hollowthroat. *It's all about freaking optimism.*

The voice coming out of Frederick got louder and faster, sentences and words I couldn't make out—it was one giant blur, like he was singing every song and saying every word he knew at once. My hands tightened around the knife as I groped back, feeling out blindly until I was sure the knife was on it. I started sawing as fast as I could, arms jerking back and forth awkwardly to try and get a good angle.

You ever cut something behind your back? It's hard. Really freaking hard. Especially when death is about thirty seconds away.

The thought occurred to me that it was probably going to eat the second guy's voice—the guy who'd so courteously loaned me the getaway knife after trying to shank me with it—after Frederick's. If I moved back to my original spot, it might not notice, it might buy me a few extra—

My hands, sweaty and shaky—shuddering each time my heart squeezed out another beat at its feverish pace—slipped with the blade. I sliced through the flesh of my ankle. It wasn't deep; it wasn't anything serious.

But before I could stop myself, I yelped, the noise only partially muffled by the gag.

The hollowthroat stopped eating, its head twisting slowly and totally around, its grey, stretched-too-tight skin shadowy from the campfire. It faced me, staring for just a second. I didn't know how that thing got around—it didn't have eyes, so maybe it was all noise? I froze up, not sure if I should keep on trying to saw my way free or stay as still and quiet as possible. My breath caught in my throat, and I stopped with the knife. Warm blood trickled down my ankle, running onto my feet. Frederick's voice—and the beast must've been hungry, because his voice was down to abstract noises, like laughter—petered out, and there was just the crunching of branches getting devoured in the fire.

"Did you think you were going to live?"

I started sawing at the rope as fast as I could, now holding that gag as tight as I could with my teeth. I didn't really think it would slow the hollowthroat down, but it had to count for something. I just…I would've driven that knife through my own throat before I let that thing touch it again. My frenzied sawing got most of the rope, straining against the fraying knot. It split, thank the gods, and I scrambled back into the shadows of the cave, trying to loop my manacled hands back around my legs so I could have a chance of…of…something.

The hollowthroat began stalking forward. Frederick's laugh, now perfectly mimicked, started coming from its lips.

Rocks dug into my ass and thighs as I shifted back.

The fire was getting low. It'd go out in a few more minutes.

The way the rocks in the ceiling were dripping water, the pattern of it almost sounded like a song Karla sang sometimes.

I was noticing tiny little details because they were going to be my last.

I wondered what kinds of nasty things Knife Guy had done with the knife that made a nice little cut in my ankle, and what kinds of nasty things I'd gotten in my blood as a result.

A very weak laugh bubbled up my throat. *That's* what I was worried about.

The hollowthroat's laughing withered, and I fell backward down into the slope of the cave. I fumbled with my legs, getting my arms up and in front of me at last, but knew it wasn't going to do any good. It moved closer—no more than nine or ten feet, now—and I tried to get my feet under me, ready to run. I'd seen how fast that thing's tongue lashed out, I knew I couldn't outrun it, but—

"'*And Karric's voice wavered not even a note…as he brought low that vile hollowthroat.*' I was always fond of that one, even before all this."

The hollowthroat seized abruptly, and I realized that it hadn't said that. It was a girl's voice—a very familiar girl's voice—but I didn't know if….

"Turn around. I've got a deal to make," Karla said.

The hollowthroat giggled, not using an imitated voice, but its own hideous screech. Gods, if I sounded like that, I might think about taking somebody's voice too. It twisted its head back around, facing the front of the cave. Karla stood defiant, one hand curled into a fist at her side, the other gripping my sword. She stepped over Frederick's body, eyes never leaving the hollowthroat's face. She moved close enough for me to see the brambles and twigs in her hair, the newly-acquired dirt smudges across her face. I realized the sun was close to sunset, if it wasn't past the horizon already—the hollowthroat's shadow grew longer and longer as it faced the mouth of the cave.

"*They just get more desperate. Speak, little girl. Soon, I will do it for you.*"

"I give you my voice. You let us walk away."

My stomach turned over. *No…Karla…don't….*

The hollowthroat didn't wait to laugh this time—it guffawed, the noise rebounding back inside the cave and drowning out everything else. Its laughter broke after a moment—it coughed furiously, curling up for a second, and then it steadied itself, growling. *Weird.*

"*Cute. I'd rather just kill you both.*"

Karla raised my sword, rested it against her own throat. "You can try," she hissed, "but I'm the best one you'll ever get." To some, it might've been arrogant, but I guess it really wasn't. The girl sang all the time and stuff, took notes from every bard who had the misfortune of wandering through Sorro. She practiced what she did more than anybody I knew practiced anything. She held my blade right up against the lump of her neck, and I was pretty sure she knew just how to mutilate it, keep it out of that thing's claws. "If you don't want to deal, you'll have to live without." She grinned, forced confidence in the face of...something a lot worse than death. "If you can call that living."

The hollowthroat snarled, wheezing and growling as it moved closer to the fire. *"Insolence. You think your voice that precious?"*

Karla took a few steps back, calm and steady, keeping herself out of the hollowthroat's reach. She wasn't going to have it catch her off-guard. Karla took a breath, lifting the sword off her neck just a hair, and sang, sweet and slow, *"Past the branches gnarled and dark, where lie silent the singing lark..."* The hollowthroat twitched, and I could see hunger in its alien features, its muscles coiling and claws dancing. Karla knew she had it, the echo of her voice lost down the back of the cave. "You want to deal or no? I don't have all night."

Wait.

All night.

That lullaby it was singing....

What was it that those bandits had said? Back at the campfire the first go 'round? My mind raced, a hundred different thoughts bouncing around my head, but none of them were the ones I needed.

"Your voice isn't that sweet. You should never have come here."

"Bullshit," Karla hissed, a touch of pride amongst her words. "You're just getting by on these half-starved bandits, guys who've drunk burning liquor for decades straight, haven't you? You need this. You're not looking too healthy yourself."

The hollowthroat shook, something distinctly angry, and its claws hungered at its side, fingers twitching back and forth. Karla was pressing her luck, and I could see it in her eyes—she was running the numbers, trying to figure out if she'd made a mistake, if she could sell this thing on her gambit. It was faster and stronger than she was by far. She only had to slip once. Karla was almost to the edge of the cave's mouth now—behind her, there wasn't much space left to go. She stood silhouetted against the setting sun, waiting to see what the hollowthroat would do.

Then it clicked.

I dropped the knife out of my hands in a panic—it fell and bounced back into the darkness behind me. I barely noticed. I was already reaching up and yanking the gag out of my mouth. "Karla! It hasn't sung the lullaby tonight!"

The shadows on the cave darkened a bit more, and Karla's eyes went wide, a smile stretching across her face.

"Lies!" wheezed the hollowthroat, whipping back around to me.

"No," Karla whispered, the sword falling forward. She held it out toward the hollowthroat now, stepping in closer. "It's true, isn't it?" She stared up at it, holding her ground. "No lullaby. You can be killed."

The hollowthroat turned back, drawing itself up, shuddering once again. It turned its head towards the mouth of the cave, its shadow growing longer and longer as the sun dipped down further. It had missed that deadline. It hadn't sung the song. It coughed, clearing its throat enough to spit out another sentence. *"Enough of this. I've still heard your voice. I can still rip that little melody right out of you."*

Then everything slowed down, so that it could all happen all at once.

The hollowthroat lunged forward, but it was slower—much slower. Its movements were choppy now, that unnatural speed replaced with an almost drunken lack of coordination. It slashed out at Karla with its whip-like tongue, but it was sluggish enough for her to dodge. Karla dropped to the cave floor with a grunt, holding the sword out awkwardly so she didn't impale herself on it. Its razor tongue was black and rotting, and it lost control for a moment as it swung over her. It stumbled, another whooping, racking cough coming out of its throat.

It wouldn't matter. Karla was on the ground, and this thing could still take her out, no problem. She twisted with the fall, landing on her back. She held it up in a vaguely defensive gesture, eyes shooting back and forth, desperately looking for some other way out.

There was a thump behind me, and another, and then Aldric jumped over me, landing for a step before he jumped over the fire and threw himself onto the hollowthroat's back. The knife I'd dropped was firmly clutched in one hand, the other curled tight around the monster's neck. It shrieked, thrashing and throwing its disjointed elbows back. Its arms were too long—it couldn't get a good angle on him. Aldric twisted his weight, getting it facing back toward me—*what are you doing, Aldric? Other way!*—and I saw his face, red and contorted with strain as he held on with just the one arm. Their blankets had been crudely tied around his neck and mouth, giving him a gag of his own—an improvised shield against that thing's tongue. It was the best Aldric and Karla could throw together at a moment's notice, I figured.

The hollowthroat howled. It kicked one of its back-jointed legs out to try and knock him off-balance. Aldric held on. It nearly took off Karla's head as its tongue flailed, and instead sliced a lock of her hair clean off. She shrieked and rolled back, the hollowthroat standing straighter as her scream filled the cave. The thing swung Aldric out to the other side, but he held on, bringing the hollowthroat back with him. He jabbed the knife down into its side, getting it right under the armpit. It screeched, like steel grinding on steel, and Aldric didn't waste any time in ripping the knife back out, finding someplace new to stab the damn thing. Every wound he left was gaping, but no blood oozed out. Instead, voices started to flood the cave, starting with Frederick's, and Knife Guy's, and then onto a half dozen others. The hollowthroat twitched and convulsed as Aldric let go, stumbling for just a second before slamming his whole weight against its legs. It tumbled, tripping forward and landing in the fire. It wailed, rotting tongue slashing up against the top of the cave (it left foot-deep gouges in the rock) as it wailed trying to get out of the fire.

Aldric went in to finish the job, but Karla grabbed him, pulling him back. "No! Stop!" She shouted, barely audible over the thousands of screams bleeding out of the hollowthroat. "We have to get out now!"

Huh? I looked around, and realized I'd been focused on the hollowthroat—and ignored the cave. Everything was shaking—not just our mortally-wounded monster friend. That thing had been screaming a lot louder than I'd thought, and the roof of the cavern above us was trembling and screaming back, the rumble louder with each deep wound the hollowthroat's tongue left in the rock. I scrambled up, running over to Knife Guy's body and frantically padding him down for the key to the manacles. Water drops fell in earnest, but I doubt they did anything to help the only son of a bitch who needed it. Karla and Aldric disappeared out the front, Karla slowing only to pick up my satchel. I shoved my hands into the asshole's pockets, fingers finally managing to grab the little copper key out from it. Something wet and warm started to soak into my legs from Knife Guy's corpse and I forced down the urge to throw up, forced myself to focus on getting out of here. A piece of paper, colored and marked up, fell out as well, and I snagged it up quickly. I did my best to ignore his lifeless eyes as I stumbled out around the convulsing hollowthroat, being sure to give the monster a wide berth.

My legs were cramping and stiff from being bound under me for so long, but they woke up real quick when the whole cavern began to groan and tremble behind us. I staggered to the cave's mouth, where the still-muffled Aldric grabbed me and pulled me outside. There was a deep rumble—something beyond the hollowthroat, part of the earth itself, and a bone-rattling tremble underneath our feet. I curled up and covered my head, the roar of falling rocks drowning out any curses I might've shouted.

After about ten seconds the rumble had stopped entirely, and the hollowthroat went silent forever.

I blinked my eyes open.

We…we survived that. I…was not expecting that.

Aldric ripped off the blankets around his mouth, dropping the knife at the ground beside him. He heaved and fell back against the rock, wheezing for air. He stared at the collapsed cave, looking through the dust and fallen rocks, listening.

There was nothing.

It was dead.

I stumbled over and clapped him on the back. "You good?"

He turned to look at me, his mother's blue eyes twinkling just a bit in the hazy twilight. "Yeah," he said hoarsely. "I'm good. Real good."

XI

We sank our feet in the river and made small talk to avoid thinking about how close we all came to dying horribly. Our boots and all our gear—actually, all our stuff, but saying gear makes us sound way more organized than we really were—sat well away from the water because the last thing any of us needed was more blisters.

Given that the river was a constant reminder of "Hey, Harkness, old buddy, guess who can't swim and likes to head-butt boulders!" it was less comforting for me, but it seemed to help Karla and Aldric calm down.

I think I'd just reached the point where my body had resigned itself to whatever came my way, where I was both completely stressed and entirely non-stressed at the same time. I stared at the satchel in my lap, thinking about how the last trip in the river had wound up. Wondered if it would've killed the gods to bring me back a hundred yards upstream, away from the murderous monster and bandits and whatnot.

Never easy. Never easy.

"We spent most of the afternoon walking downstream," Karla continued, me only half-listening. They saved my life, so yeah, I probably should've mustered up all of my attention, but I had world-saving responsibilities weighing on my mind. Dragons and…whatnot. The thought of how to politely ask them to let me finish this solo after they just saved my ass was tough to put into words. I noticed her voice was rough, winded. Aldric sat next to her, periodically starting to droop towards the river. Eventually he settled for Karla's shoulder, which was probably a wiser place to sleep. The water gurgled and splashed against the (stupid, dumb, painful) rocks as Karla went on. "Just calling out, trying to figure out where you were. We got the feeling something was…wrong." Aldric squirmed on Karla's shoulderblades, perhaps unable to find a comfy place. Snoring and sharp shoulders are apparently the way to a man's heart. Karla stared at the water for a minute, taking deep breaths.

Aldric sighed, resigned to the fact he wasn't going to get horizontal for a few more hours. "Yeah, there were a couple spots in the river where it got all narrow, and there was no way you could've floated on past. One or two really shallow spots, we could walk right across. We didn't know if you…" Aldric's voice drifted off, and I tried to roll the lump in my throat out of the way.

"Uh, I was thinking more about the rustling," Karla said. "We kept hearing voices. A girl's voice, a couple times. Familiar-sounding. We—"

Lump got bigger.

"But, anyways, eventually we heard you—right when you got caught by those guys," Aldric said, covering for Karla's rather abrupt stop. "We wanted to bust right in, but we thought we should wait a bit."

"It was all Aldric, really," Karla said, giving him a playful nudge with the elbow. He grinned, and there was something weird about his smile—the kid smiled all the time, but this was layered. There was the superficial grin of just Karla messing with him, but there was deeper joy there. He was at peace, which made (if Karla's bloodshot eyes and rapid-fire speaking were any indicator of her mental state) for exactly one of us. "He saw some of the caves going into the other side of the hill."

"We didn't know if it would connect through…we got lucky."

"Real lucky," Karla agreed. "Gods had our back on this one."

"But, hey, we figured one of us had to work, right? Karla takes the front, I try and sneak up through the caves. And as it turned out…we both did!"

I paused, letting the water wash over my formerly filthy feet. How's that for alliteration?

"You guys searched all afternoon?" I asked, staring down at the water.

"Yup!" Karla said, rubbing at her eyes. "And, uh, if we could camp sooner, rather than later, that'd be nice."

"And then you split up, to come get me? Outnumbered three-to-one?" (And counting the hollowthroat as one seemed generous.)

"Yeah," Aldric said.

I felt their eyes on the side of my cheek. My fingers rolled over the satchel's strap a while longer.

"Guess…guess I'm really not getting rid of you two, huh?" I asked weakly. Aldric and Karla chuckled, and silence fell on us for a moment or two. The horizon above the treeline was a blend of pink and orange, soft fading light giving way to a handful of stars. "Serious, though, you guys want to head on back home…now…would probably be a good time. I really appreciate everything, but…"

"Hark," Aldric said. "We're with ya, man. We're gonna get Marisa back."

"All the way." Karla nudged me, somehow exactly the same and entirely different from the way she nudged Aldric.

"Huh," I said, splashing my feet in the water a bit. The rest of me felt colder than my feet. "Thanks."

We just sat, bone-weary—and, wow, they must've been even more tired than me because I'd gotten that little refresher from Aurea back on the island. Well, to be fair, I also got kidnapped, which is pretty stressful, so I guess we were about even now.

"You know," Karla said, "I don't want to be a killjoy, but…we've still got to find that sword. And the dragon. By sundown tomorrow."

Aldric grunted disapprovingly.

"Well, I have some pretty good news on that front. First, uh, I can get us to Drowduss." I held up the rumpled piece of paper I'd snagged from Knife Guy's pocket. I flicked my wrist and it unfolded into a map. Karla squeaked and snatched it out of my hands, nearly ripping it. She scanned it with her eyes a few times, the weariness gone.

"We're…we're not far at all!" she said, out of breath. "Guys, we could get there *tonight!*" She blinked, finding Sorro with a finger then tracing it across. The three of us combined could read enough to figure this out. I mean, after all, those moron bandits were using it to get around. "Oh gods, we walked a lot today."

"Well, you know, it's getting pretty late, and uh…" Aldric began.

"They have beds in Drowduss."

Aldric grunted approvingly.

"Glad to hear you guys are down for a little more walking, because we actually kinda have to go tonight." I began standing up, walking in the grass a bit to dry my feet off before I sat down on a rock—a dry rock, which is my new favorite kind of rock—and began to put my boots on.

"Why?" Aldric asked.

"You guys were right about the river being…kinda weird. Like, divine intervention weird." I paused, mulling it over. "That's about as weird as you can get."

"Layana?" Karla guessed.

"Nah, Aurea." I remember that feeling of her nuclear-heat gaze. "I mean, uh, Lady Aurea. I'm gonna give you the shortened-up version, because honestly, not totally clear on how it went down myself." I pulled tight on the laces, standing back upright. I grabbed the manacles off the grass next to where I'd been sitting and hurled them as far as I could. They disappeared into the trees. *Hope you're roasting in hell, Knife Guy, Frederick, and Johann.* "Long story short, I got pulled to the Shrine, which I'm guessing is why you couldn't find me."

"*The* Shrine?" they both asked at once.

"With *the* Sword?" Aldric asked, bouncing up and staring at me. He started looking me over, trying to see where I must've hidden it.

"Blade," Karla corrected absentmindedly.

He wasn't even fazed. "You…you got it?" he asked.

"Yup," I patted the satchel. "All in here."

"Holy shit," Karla breathed, running a hand through her hair. "This…I…What was it like? What did it look like? Aurea, was she…they say she has lightless eyes, and that—"

"Let me see the Swo—Blade! It's that small? I thought it would be huge, like, I dunno, just, huge! Is it heavy? Do you have to—"

"Guys," I said, laughing a bit. "I really hate to be that guy, but the rules are I'm not really supposed to talk about it."

They both gave me that look of "...*but you* are *gonna talk about it, right?*"

"Sorry, it's gotta stay tucked in here for now. But they did say Drowduss was the right way to go. So, scoreboard, Harkness and friends." I held up my hand and Aldric high-fived the ever-loving hell out of it, sending pins and needles down my arm. And you know what, I didn't even mind this time. "But we've got to make it to the temple in Drowduss before sunrise. So, I'm thinking...we haul it over to Drowduss, get an inn—"

"And food," Karla said.

"And beds," Aldric said.

"My thoughts exactly," I agreed. "Get a few hours' rest, and then head to the temple. They can get us to the dragon from there, but only at night." I anticipated Karla's follow-up question. "I don't know why, gods like arbitrary rules is the best I can figure out."

She nodded, and Aldric started picking up stuff the way a mother does before family comes over. Oh, hey, mothers. Wondered how my folks were doing. And the rest of Sorro. Hey, you know what a really dick move would've been? If they set up the Reckoning so every few centuries, the dragon attacked the same village twice, but the second time was only a week or so after the first attack. Man, I would've made a *great* deity.

Mulling over reassuring thoughts like those, we were ready to head out in about five minutes. We wanted to cover as much ground as we could while we still had a little sun-light. Aldric got us back to one of those shallow places and— nervously, hands locked around each other tighter than those manacles—we edged through the six-inch-deep water, not breathing easy until we made it to the other side. I'm telling you, a swimming instructor would've made a killing in our neck of the woods.

We consulted the bandit's map (In a way, those muggers had helped us. *Optimism, people, it's all about optimism.*), straining our eyes on the faded parchment. It was only about ten minutes of "please let this be the right way" trailblazing before we stumbled onto a road. It was dirt, and it was bumpy, but, man, it if that road wasn't the most beautiful thing.

We started down it, trudging south. It was wide enough for us to walk side by side, and even as the sun bottomed out completely (*time's running out, Harkness…*) we didn't feel that uneasy. It was bright enough with the moon and stars to see an okay amount, and with the hollowthroat dead, the night didn't seem quite as scary. We all got these dumbass grins, like bartenders during happy hour (I mean, in Plagiar, pretty much every hour is happy hour. Have I mentioned there's not much to do here?). It was one of those times where you were tired, but you didn't really seem to notice—whether it was Karla trying not-so-subtly to get more details about the Shrine out of me, or Aldric cyclically looking up at the stars, stumbling, almost falling, and then looking back up to start it all over again, none of us felt that winded anymore.

"Hey," I realized suddenly. "It was actually probably good we didn't go through that marsh."

Karla raised an eyebrow at me, her surprise visible even in the twilight.

"Shut up. I bet there were leeches and stuff."

"Aren't those good for you though?" Karla asked.

"Yeah, probably, but it's still nasty to think about. I go to Hammerk whenever I want to get latched onto and suc—"

"Oh, hah, very funny," Karla said. Aldric grinned, which was all the consolation I needed. *Thank you, thank you, I'll be here all week, folks…or maybe not, we'll see how tomorrow goes.* "So…this Shrine's guardian…are we thinking more of a…'fierce and vengeful' type, or a…'answer me these riddles three' type?"

I missed a step, but in the dark they didn't notice. "Karla, I kicked its ass all the same. What does it matter?"

Karla rolled her eyes, shoulders sagging a bit. Yeah, I was sorry I couldn't provide material for a cool new ballad or story or whatever. I should've just made some ridiculous crap up for her. *Yeah, it looked just like Old Man Granger, weirdly enough, and it could only be defeated by tap dancing.*

She probably would've preferred that to the truth.

My mind drifted to Drowduss, and stuffing ourselves with cheap food and cheaper mead. After that winning nutritional combination, we'd figure out where the observatory/temple was then go right along and kick that dragon's scaly ass to the curb. Be home by the end of the week, be world-renowned heroes by the end of the month. Done and done.

For the first time this whole journey, there was a good sense of what we were doing and how to do it. With the sun down, we were even free of having to worry about skin cancer. If things kept up like this, I might take up questing as my new yearly vacation. *Just keep thinking these happy thoughts, Hark. Easy to sleep with your head in the sand.*

It was perhaps a solid hour (as opposed to, say, a liquid hour) later that, in the distance, the thriving metropolis of Drowduss came into view. I say that not wholly sarcastically—it was certainly bigger than Hammerk and our hometown of Sorro combined, and probably the biggest city in this corner of Plagiar. A lot of the food we grew or trees we cut down wound up here, so it felt gratifying to see the results of our labor. I mean, well, not from me, per se, but in general. Needless to say, we backwater wood-cutters and sheep farmers didn't venture much into the city.

Even from a few miles out, its size was impressive, the city glowing with...gods, I don't even think I know a big enough number for how many lanterns they needed to shine bright from that far. Beds. Warm food. Warm *meat*. We all started walking faster, and I considered dropping the bags (well, not the satchel, I guess, I, uh, kinda had to keep that) and running. We started throwing questions back and forth to pass the time, anything to take our minds off blistered feet and empty stomachs. We were all staring at that city of gold tantalizing us from afar, like the mirage of an oasis in a desert, or a cruel burlesque dancer.

"Okay, Harkness. Favorite food?"

I mulled over Aldric's question, cursing how he'd reminded me of being hungry. "Anything that's not cooked enough to burn my mouth and not raw enough to run away. Uh, Karla, worst way to die?"

There was a pause. "Hm. I guess being stabbed, or shot with an arrow...fighting in general. At least dying in your sleep or something is peaceful."

Aldric frowned. "What? No. What if you were in the middle of a really good dream, and then—nope. Dead. What about that?"

Karla started to say something and just stopped cold. She turned and stared at Aldric for a second, a look of absolute wonder on her face. "You...you can't...that's...that's the stupidest thing—"

Aldric broke up laughing, not able to keep a straight face any longer.

"He totally had you sold on that," I said. *Outplayed by Aldric. Damn.*

"Oh, hush. Okay, Aldric, fine. Favorite story?"

Aldric took his time, giving it a full quarter of a minute before he piped up. "The one about the girl and the woods."

"Aldric, that's, like, every story," I said.

"Well, I can't remember the *exact* one," he said.

"You must set the bar pretty low for favorites."

"True. Okay, Hark, favorite feature about Marisa?"

"She has a pulse."

Karla slugged me in the shoulder. "Oh, c'mon. Why is it every guy is so afraid to open up just a bit. You guys are no fun."

"No fun? Woman, we just killed a monster and are half-way toward killing another." I tripped over a rock and righted myself. "I've got fun out the ass right now."

Aldric frowned, perhaps considering the imagery of what I'd said.

"No, not like that," Karla said. "Well, I wouldn't call this fun, you know. Exciting, terrifying, definitely memorable, but not so much fun. I bet you two wouldn't answer any really hard questions."

"Try me," Aldric said. "Anything you got. Go."

"All right," Karla said, taking her sweet, sadistic time. "Biggest fear."

"Oh, that's it?" Aldric asked. "Dogs and the dark."

I chuckled. "Dogs? What, did you fall down a well as a kid?"

Aldric shook his head. "Don't like dogs. Don't like the dark. I can handle just about anything else."

I thought about crawling through the caves, and the hollowthroat, and watched Aldric walk, glancing up at the stars.

My stomach twisted.

"Well, since Karla's sexism just got shut down, let's keep on going. Drowduss is getting closer but hey, let's make that time pass a little quicker. Whose turn?"

"Mine," Aldric said. "I answered last. Hm…Harkness, I know. What was going through your head the night… you know?"

I frowned, waiting for him to explain. "The night…?"

Aldric raised an eyebrow. "Uh, the night the dragon attacked? The Reckoning?"

"Ohhhh, uh, that night. Eh, pass."

Gods, I could feel them staring into the back of my head. Not as bad as Aurea's glare, which was my new benchmark for how uncomfortable a stare could be, but still pretty high up there.

"So…where were you?" Karla asked.

"Hey, I said pass."

"See, exactly what I was talking about. You two are all talk when it comes to hunting down dragons, but you have to reveal one little thing about yourself…"

"Not taking the bait, Karla."

"C'mon, Hark," Aldric insisted.

"I'm not answering the question, all right! We're almost there, anyway. Just…ugh."

We marched out the last quarter mile or so in relative silence, all too weary and hungry to really keep much of a conversation going. Drowduss was mind-blowing. The three of us had never been that far from home, and here was easily a city bigger than any we'd ever seen. Candles flickered in the lights of most of the windows, lanterns hung throughout the streets. We pulled out the candles maybe once, twice a year— and I had a feeling nobody would be messing with them for a while in the wake of a dragon attack. Here…I couldn't even wrap my head around how many they must use up in a month, let alone a whole year. The houses were all built better, too. I know that sounds stupid, but they were a damn sight nicer than the thrown-together shacks of Hammerk or the small, hunkered-down cabins we called houses. Actually, all of Sorro's real estate just got turned into cinders, so really anything was better than what we had. *Oh gods, what if we become the next victims of gentrification.* These houses were built up, eight or nine feet at the shortest, some brick, some wood. Smoke rolled out the chimneys and we heard laughing and talking through open windows—along with the smell of food.

Cooked food.

I think all three of us considered breaking in and stealing whatever was cooking in those houses right then and there.

We walked deeper into the city, following the dusty road (which eventually—I kid you not—turned into cobblestone. It was an actual road!) and grouping closer the tighter it got. Buildings were seemingly built right on top of each other as we went further in. They were clustered as tight as could be, and the alleys and roads started making weird switchbacks. *Guess Drowduss hasn't invested much into city planning.* Wagons were pulled by horses (who went clip-clop, clip-clop on the *cobblestone* roads), the drivers shouting at each other to get the hell out the way, questioning the sanctity of one another's mothers, and speaking in all kinds of weird accents. Well, I definitely had career options here if dragon-slaying didn't amount to anything. There were people yelling at us from all around, trying to get us to buy stuff they presumably thought we could afford: food, drinks, some weird cloth thing called a tapestry.

We got cursed at a few times for walking so slow, our obvious little group of out-of-town peasants stumbling through the middle of the road, staring at all the booths and lights with slack-jawed, touristy grins. There were people everywhere, more on that single street than all of our hometown, all going about their business seemingly indifferent to the others around them. People bumped and jostled against each other, and if I'd had anything of value in my pockets, I would've been concerned. Well, they weren't totally indifferent—we were getting some weird looks, what with our ash-covered, burnt-at-the-edges wardrobe choices. Everyone else was wearing slightly less ragged tunics, a few women had dresses, all of which were considerably nicer than our getups. Karla absentmindedly ran her hand through her hair a bit, and even Aldric glanced down at his legs (which, hilariously, were caked in dirt and ash except where he'd sunk them in the river).

"Get a job, street rats!" some passing old guy shouted at us. *Whoa, do we really look that homeless?*

"Get a grave, Grandpa! Tick tock!" I shouted back, prompting Karla to clamp her hand over my mouth in a rather maternal fashion.

Aldric started to bristle up for a fight, his wide shoulders coming down as he stood up straighter and glanced around. Fortunately, Gramps merely gave us the most withering old-man-stare of all time before turning and going on his way. Man, Drowduss' old guys were way less cool than Old Man Granger. Still, we three half-starved street rats probably didn't have very good odds in that scuffle, especially if the town guard showed up. We saw them pass by occasionally, surveying the crowd around them. They had on armor: I think chain mail's the right term, with iron helmets and spears. Or maybe they were steel helmets. I never really knew the difference or the metallurgy behind it. You may recall that our hometown's blacksmith was not particularly friendly, which made learning about these things tricky. Most had swords and shields, and I recalled a few on the wall around the city toting bows and arrows. All in all, they had that general, authoritative look of "don't do anything stupid and I won't have to kill you."

Bad news for them—I specialize in doing stupid stuff.

Still, Sorro didn't even have town guards. And, well, I think Hammerk had a couple bouncers, but they were too economically dependent on chaos to try to regulate crime too much. Seeing guards, bored but alert, mulling around, walking up and down the streets, hands close to their swords…it was sorta cool. Terrifying, but cool.

We continued through the city, and I forgot about being hungry for the first time this whole trip. Karla's eyes nearly burst out of her skull as we walked past a man selling lyres and flutes; Aldric saw that fortune-teller peering into a crystal ball and was determined to prove he was right. Much as I would've loved seeing that argument flare up again, we didn't have money to burn, not on anything other than the bare necessities. I'm pretty sure the vendors picked up on that, too, because after they eyed us up and down, they were a lot less enthusiastic about trying to sell us stuff, and a lot more preoccupied with making sure we hadn't palmed anything. *Profiling's not cool, guys.*

It was impossible to get a grasp for how big this city was—around us, two or even three-story buildings made seeing off into the distance impossible. There was so much racket, all hustle and bustle, and all the noise—back home, when the sun went down, you went to bed or to the bar. The streets of

Sorro were quiet and the houses quieter. This was insane—it had to be two hours past sundown, easily, and everyone was still going strong. A few chickens burst out from an alley and raced across the street, followed by a panicked guy a few seconds later. They screeched in their mad bid for freedom, and the guards just kind of lazily watched. I sorta hoped they responded with a little more force to serious crimes.

"Well," Aldric said, breaking us out of our consumerist stupor, "we should seriously get some food before it gets too much later."

"Good point," Karla said, stretching up to her tiptoes and trying to see through the crowd. "Hmm. I see a bakery down the street. We could try that."

"Oh, c'mon, we just had bread for lunch yesterday. Let's branch out a little."

The three of us meandered through the crowd, which proved to be a lot harder than we thought. Everyone was trying to get somewhere, and that made it hard to, you know, try to get somewhere. Eventually, we had to force Aldric into being assertive, and once he put his game face on and stopped pausing to let people by, we started to move more quickly. I readjusted the satchel as we turned down a side alley. Coming out the other side, the crowd was significantly lessened. We started walking down the cobblestone *(Do you not grasp how awesome that is? They had cobblestone, like,* everywhere*)* road, eyes peeled for an inn. Or at least a house we could squat in or something.

There was a familiar flash of pink somewhere up ahead of us, and I craned my neck to try to figure out who was distracting me from getting food, but the crowd was a raging sea and I was but a mere fish. See, I have my moments of being all poetic.

We stuck to the side of the road, ignoring vendors and homeless beggars alike (hey, I don't want any judgment for not helping out the poor—if I didn't stop that dragon, there were going to be a lot more homeless people in ten years' time, right?) Karla was clinging onto Aldric's hand to keep from getting separated. I raised an eyebrow at her and she pretended not to notice. I kinda tagged along, not really willing to hold his hand in exchange for safety from the mosh pit surrounding us. Some things in life are worth a bruise.

Walking through the streets of Drowduss was awesome in the original sense of the word. Definitely a high point of our little journey (almost drowning was what we in the hero biz call "a low point"). After another ten or so minutes of aimlessly walking up and down the streets, we spotted an inn—two stories tall, rickety wood, and the sign hanging out front had splintering, faded paint that really reassured you about the maintenance standards it had. Two stories. Huh. Well, it dwarfed anything back in Sorro, but judging from the looks of it, the pub's architect spent more time at the bar than the drafting table. *The Dancing Goat.* Certainly lived up to its namesake in terms of smell. We all looked back and forth at each other and had pretty much the same thoughts: there's no way it's not cheap, there's no way they don't have food, and there's no way we'll be here long enough for this shack of an inn to collapse on us.

We slipped inside, sizing up tonight's abode. Eh. A hole in the wall, but not unbearably bad—the tavern was open, a bar lining one side and tables haphazardly scattered about the floor. There was barely enough space in between to squeeze around them with the mismatched chairs wedged in so tightly. They'd tried to fit as much tavern into as small a space as they could, but none of the three of us really had high standards. I don't even think Aldric and Karla had spent the night somewhere else before, so we're talking almost no standards here.

People moved about, but it wasn't completely crowded—the bartender was wiping down a mug, waiting for another customer, and I saw a few people disappear upstairs to head to their rooms. After a moment, some waitress—no, wait, I'm squandering a perfect opportunity here—some *busty tavern wench* approached us and split her attention between our clothes and my sword.

"Um…may I assist you?" she asked, a subtle hint of *may I assist you in getting the hell out of here?* lacing her words. Gods, even the people in this cesspit were giving us the staredown. We were looking worse than I thought.

"Indeed you may," I said, reaching into the satchel and pulling out a fistful of coins. Granted, it was about all we had, but she didn't know that. And, hey, given that we were going to be done in twenty-four hours, I didn't see any need to continue being thrifty. Get some food and some sleep in us—whatever it cost—and we could figure out how to get back home when that time came. If that time came. Heh. *Glass half full, Harkness, glass half full.*

Her eyes widened at the sight of our money, and her posture quickly shifted to one of *oh, they're actual customers*. She took us to a table in the corner and we sat down, Aldric groaning with pleasure as he took the stress off his legs. Karla lucked out and got the seat in the corner, slumping back against the wall pretty much immediately. I stared at the table, taking my satchel off and resting it on the chair behind me. We got some mead—which is good, because after that whole mess with the drowning and the island and The Shrine, I *needed* a drink. We idled, watching people around us move around, enjoying being able to sit and do nothing for a little while. I wonder if that's what it's like to be really old.

She came back by, taking orders.

I nearly cried when she said they had meat, and we could actually afford it. I'd been waiting for so long.

The busty tavern wench scampered off to do busty tavern wench things (*Yeah, I know, I'm failing the Bechdel test pretty bad right now.*) and we sat in silence, contemplating how mouthwateringly super-delicious that food was going to taste in a couple minutes.

I looked at Karla and Aldric. Our clothes had been bad at the start, coated in ash and cut in a few places from the chaos of Reckoning night (well, their clothes, at least), but they were even worse now. Thorns and briars (and a dunk in the river for me), makeshift camping, abductions, monster slaying…it'd taken its toll. Even if I couldn't see it, I could feel the sweat and dirt caked into my face. We looked like we'd tried to wrestle a schizophrenic bobcat in the middle of a coal mine, and only narrowly won. Scrapes and cuts littered our arms and legs, and I legitimately lost count of the number of mosquito bites. They itched. A lot.

The bar brimmed with noise, a dozen half-buzzed conversations all at once. I got the feeling most of Drowduss sounded like that, no matter what hour of the night it was. Unlike Sorro, which was pretty much silent unless a dragon was attacking.

My mug went still in my hand, slowly going back to the table as I realized something.

I probably never would've made it here if a dragon hadn't destroyed our hometown and abducted two of our own. In a macabre, horrible way, it was a good thing. But still, we were out…on an adventure. Karla was the only one with a half-decent idea of what that entailed, given her seemingly endless mental library of odes and ballads, but Aldric and I had learned very quickly what this kinda stuff really meant. A lot of walking. A lot of pain and hunger and sweat. No changes of clothes. Little sleep. We all looked and felt like hell, which is, as a rule of thumb, not a good way to look or feel.

And sitting there, sipping occasionally on mead that honestly didn't even taste that good, we thought about how much we actually kinda missed home. Even me. I never thought I would've said it—what I would've given a week ago to have this. Now?

I mean, were these my options in life? Be a tanner's son until one day dysentery or the bubonic plague or something liquefied my internal organs, or go on an adventure and die young, half-starved and sleepless? Was that really it?

I looked at Karla, who had fully embraced the wall behind her as a pillow (thankfully she wasn't sleeping hard enough to snore), and at Aldric, brushing some of the hair out of Karla's eyes. We had been on the same mental page for a little while, yes—but it was only because *I* had been on *their* mental page. They…they looked to have things figured out, as beaten up and generally bad as they looked.

The waitress returned with our food and I didn't even try to savor it. I wolfed it down. Maybe you've never thought about that word—*wolfed*—I mean I abandoned all pretense of civility and chowed down. Not that I gave the flavor much time to sink in—it went from mouth to stomach like a hollowthroat at a choir practice. Karla woke up and muttered a few quick but nonetheless genuine prayers of thanks and began to dig in, Aldric quickly following suit. We didn't say a word, just ate and ate.

At the end, my plate was clean, but I still felt empty.

I figured we needed to hurry up and get a room—we were at risk of falling asleep at the table, what with the general lull of the restaurant's conversations, the warmth of the fire, bellyfuls of food…who could resist? We blew nearly all our money on a room for the night and slinked upstairs, doing well to put one foot ahead of the other. I rolled over the five or six copper coins we had left, enough to get us a loaf of bread if we haggled a bit. *Well, here's to people willing to buy us drinks once we got this mess over with.*

We were halfway up the stairs when Karla's face turned pale and she whipped around (I could almost hear her neck cricking). "Harkness," she stammered, out of air, that kind of panic that chokes up your throat and mangles all your words. "The…the satchel! Did you leave the—"

I padded myself down for it, which was pointless, because I could immediately feel it wasn't on me. "Oh, this is just friggin' wonderful," I said, turning and moving back into the bar.

Look, I hate to get your hopes up for some exciting chase scene or whatever but it was right on the chair where I left it— the aforementioned busty tavern wench was actually holding it, scanning for where the three of us (not easily mistaken with anyone else in the bar) had run off to. I moved over and graciously accepted it, thanking her. And just, because I'm so nice, I tipped her with the last of my coins. Whew. That could've made things awkward, had the satchel been lost. You know, what with the whole…only weapon in existence that can kill the dragon thing. Might've been bad.

I slipped the ever-important bag over my shoulder, fastening it securely, and swung out toward the entrance of the bar, squeezing my now-bulging gut between the tables as I headed toward the stairs, where Karla and Aldric were watching me with visible relief.

"Any idea where the thief went?" A gruff voice came from just outside the door.

"No, sir. The temple's only about a half mile from here, so—"

"So get every damned guard we have surrounding the place in a circle two miles wide. I'm not taking chances. We ruin things with the priests, we're going to be lucky to get jobs changing bedsheets in Hammerk."

What a lovely mental image.

"Y-yessir." Presumably, a younger and very-averse-to-housekeeping guard shuffled off to go rally the other guards. This did, admittedly, raise a considerable bit of concern. If there was going to be a small legion's worth of guards surrounding that temple—and, you know, if the temple was our ticket to finding that stupid dragon—how were we going to get in? Suddenly craving another drink, I went up the stairs and found our room. There was no lock on the door.

Karla glanced at the lockless door, then back at me.

"I'm too tired to give a damn," I said, walking in. "And there's not really any furniture to brace it with, anyway." We'd be here for all of five hours before heading back out. My drooping eyelids were saying we should just roll the dice on this one.

There were only two fairly small beds, but they were sizable enough for the three of us. Aldric had sprawled out over one, seemingly comatose. He moved over to his half pretty quickly when I asked him if he'd rather slide over or have me sleep in Karla's bed.

The room was barebones, but so were we. We bought the only room we could afford, and it was just big enough for both beds to fit in. There was a small nightstand, rather hastily constructed with uneven boards, on which a candle rested awkwardly. For our purposes, it would work just fine, but I would never consider taking any *busty tavern wench* of merit back to a room such as this. I rested my head on the straw, sighing. I was reluctant to take off the bag again, so I settled for using it as a pillow. In theory, it would be harder to lose that way. *Theory, yeah. In theory, I shouldn't be here right now.*

"Don't know how you can sleep on that thing," Aldric said. Oh, yeah, the sword. Sword with a capital S. The Blade. My father's sword sat leaning against the wall near Karla and Aldric's bags.

"Eh, you know. I'm that kinda guy."

Aldric chuckled. "Yup, that's you, Hark. She's going to be just fine, mate. You know that?"

I paused for a second. Oh. Marisa. Yeah. Her. "Thanks. Thanks."

"Eh, you know. I'm that kinda guy." The big blond oaf inhaled deeply, and I swear to the gods just fell asleep right after that. Just one deep huff and he was out cold.

Marisa. Reason behind all this, right? To…to save her. I started thinking about Granger's tale, what all this meant— what the hell we'd even gotten ourselves into—and suddenly found sleeping on that satchel was next to impossible.

XII

slept for two or three hours and lay in the…well, not quiet. Karla's snores, you know. Aldric and Karla were dead to the world, and I would've been too if the damned satchel hadn't given me a crick in my neck. I rolled my shoulders trying to get comfortable and—

Wait. They were asleep. *Asleep* asleep.

I…I wasn't gonna get another chance like this.

I shifted quietly, slowly, making sure not to wake Aldric. I'm not sure I even could've. His broad chest rose and fell, drool pouring out his mouth. He was out like a narcoleptic baby.

I stood up on the creaking floorboards, cursing the stupid inn for being so crappily constructed. The satchel hardly made any noise as I picked it up, slinging it over my shoulder and cinching it tight. Couldn't have it swinging and knocking something over on my way out. *Oh, hey, kids, I was just going out for a smoke. Be right back!*

I was lifting my father's sword—my sword, now—off the wall when heavy iron slammed against our door, shaking our entire room. Like, the floorboards, the ceiling, the window, everything. *Dear gods this place is architectural blasphemy.*

The clank of armor on wood got louder—my sleep-addled brain realized, oh, hey, that's the sound of the door breaking. One of my sidekicks had the brilliant idea of blowing out the candle before we went to sleep, so I couldn't see jack shit.

"Open up this door right now!" A baritone growl shook the door a second before a fist rattled it. *Gods, just shout a little louder and the thing will probably come off on its own.* The other two had gotten up and out of bed faster than anyone would have ever assumed teenagers capable, and my hand fumbled to draw my sword in the dark.

"Harkness!" Aldric hissed. "Give me your sword. Use Layana's!"

I felt my blood run cold, even with the imminent threat of whatever the hell was happening with the yelling and shouting outside our door. "No. No I can't. I…it has to wait. Until the dragon. I'm sorry."

"We know you're in there, thief!"

Aldric frowned, his head cocked to the side as he looked at the door. "Hey, don't they know there's not a loc—"

"Shut up!" Karla and I both shrieked at once, desperately trying to make our way toward the window in the dark. I was just generally pissed off at the universe for throwing another needless obstacle in our way. What had I done to annoy the gods? I'd been nice to Layana and Aurea and everything. And I am *never* nice to people.

Something heavy-sounding smashed against the door and it visibly bent inward. My eyes were starting to adjust, which was nice, because I'd be able to see fully who was beating my ass to death in a second. I finally grasped my sword and, without thinking, ripped it out of the sheath—I cursed silently, feeling around for it in the dark, but I'd knocked the sheath aside. We were never going to find it in time.

"What are you doing?" the owner shouted—I recognized his voice clearly, and my brain frantically began putting together the pieces.

"Oh shit. Oh shit. Oh shit. Out the window. Get out the window right now you two. Go!" I kept my voice quiet enough to avoid being heard by our friendly visitors, but something in my voice must've kicked their asses into over-drive. Karla scrambled for the window but Aldric stopped her, throwing out a thick arm and blocking her way.

"Too big a drop for you. I'll go and catch you." Karla nodded and Aldric squeezed through the small space, grunt-ing, and held onto the ledge with his fingers. A second later, he dropped down out of sight. There was a thud and a grunt, followed by Aldric's whisper. "All right, Karla!"

"No, Harkness has to go next! He has the Blade!"

"They refuse to open the door. We must break it down!" roared the baritone from outside.

"You cretin, did you try opening it?" the owner shouted, his voice equal parts resignation and anger. "There aren't even loc—"

"Damnit!" I hissed, turning and running for the win-dow. The room was too small to get a good run in, but it was one of the rare acrobatic moments of my life. I man-aged to dive clear through the window, one hand clenching the leather satchel and the other holding the naked sword, my legs straight out to avoid catching on anything. I was totally psyched about pulling that off until I realized what I'd just done.

I heard the door get thrown open, and Karla shouted something I couldn't understand. "Thief!" the voice roared. "You will pay!"

A half second later I smacked into Aldric, who had been expecting the graceful, controlled jump of a much lighter Karla. He immediately yelped under the impact, his back smacking against the cobblestone. *And cushioning me.* Not to say it didn't hurt me—the wind was knocked clear out of me, but Aldric definitely got the worst of it. My elbow had smacked into the street, and my fingers tingled and burned from the impact as they clutched onto the sword. The flint and steel in my satchel jingled as it slammed against the cobblestone.

Time slowed down to a crawl. The stars above glittered, quietly witnessing.

Somehow in the middle of the blood-trembling panic of being attacked like this in the dead of night and having to jump out a window for dear life I found the time to stop and think. About warm beaches and goddesses and chilling words. About debts, and balancing the scales.

Karla yelped and came tumbling out the window, too hurried to make a collected exit. Her foot caught on the ledge and she careened over, arms spiraling wildly into the empty air.

It was dark and the night was all guards roaring above and people throwing open windows trying to make sense of the shrieking and the chaos. No lanterns adorned this part of the street, but my sword reflected the moonlight for a split second before Karla fell straight down onto it.

Karla screamed.

"No!" Aldric threw me off of him—I mean literally, I went rolling for several feet as he scrambled up, kneeling over his Karla and pressing his hands onto the wound, a massive gash on the outer side of her right leg. Even in the witching-hour, I could see the blood stain her clothes darker than the shadows around it, Aldric's hands coming away scarlet and soaked. "No, no, no, I swear this isn't—"

"Aldric," I croaked, struggling to get to my feet. I could hear the guard yelling from inside the tavern—how long until he got outside? Five seconds? Ten? How long until they killed off Karla for whatever it was they thought we'd done? "Aldric pick her up. We—" I was trying to speak but I could only wheeze, my stomach refusing to hold air. "We have to go."

"We can't move her. She'll…"

Karla was, bless her, trying to be stoic. She was biting her tongue hard enough to draw blood, tears welling up fast and heavy in her eyes. "Aldric," she hissed. "Do it. I'll be fine." Aldric nodded, lifting her quickly but gingerly, carrying Karla (who looked so small now, so frail) in his arms, held fast against his chest. I saw Karla numbly try and press a hand to the wound, in an attempt to staunch the bleeding. Blood oozed out her lips as she bit down hard, muffling a scream as Aldric had to shift her weight. I staggered over to my sword—which felt like an abomination to pick up, suddenly I didn't want a sword anymore, suddenly I had seen what it looked like with blood all over it and I wanted to leave it there and never come back to this place. But I couldn't. I couldn't. I gripped the slick, wet handle of the blade and fastened my satchel over my shoulder. It was so light.

We took off into the night, only two sets of footsteps sounding to our usual three, the road before us bathed in lantern light as the bloody-murder screams woke everyone nearby. People stuck their heads out to see what was wrong, only adding to the hysteria with (incorrect) explanations shouted out to their neighbors and families. Fine with me. The more chaos and commotion, the harder for the guards to organize and find us. Behind us, the guard frantically looked, shouting over the waking city for help, for reinforcements, but we'd darted into the first alley we saw.

"It's okay," Aldric whispered, his voice gentle. "It's okay. It's okay. It's okay."

"Aldric," I gulped, my stomach still refusing to unclench, "You have to help me find the temple. She'll be safe in the temple."

Karla let out another muffled whimper, her fingers digging into Aldric's back as she clung to his shoulders, trying to help support her own weight.

This was all my fault.

We tore through the alley in four seconds (roughly a hundred heartbeats), knocking some unlucky bastard to the ground as we did so. I fell with him, shifting my weight so I smacked into his chest and came up in a roll. Before he could recover, I put the already-bloodied blade right under his jaw, pressing against his throat. His eyes bulged trying to run out of his sockets, torn between the sword and the hulking, bloodsoaked Aldric standing next to me. Karla probably looked dead to this guy. No. Karla couldn't look like a dead girl to anyone because she was going to live. She was going to live. She was going to live. We were going to be okay.

"Where the hell's the temple? Remos' Temple. Where is it?" I said, struggling to be as intimidating as possible while also staying relatively quiet.

"Th-that way. About half a mile. Straight up the road! You can't miss it! P-please do—"

I didn't get to hear whether he had a wife or kids or whatever. We were already moving, the earlier fatigue gone.

Somewhere behind us, over my left shoulder, I heard the loud, sharp orders of the guard who'd come knocking for us, and the chink-chink of armored boots smashing against cobblestone. Both of us ran faster, legs and chest burning—and Aldric was always two steps ahead of me, entirely unaffected by the extra weight he was carrying.

"It's okay. I've got you. You're gonna be fine."

"Aldric…"

We kept on as hard as we could. As the guards' torches and lanterns of sleepy townsfolk sprang to light behind us, our shadows grew out ahead of us. Karla let out a pained shriek, and Aldric roared as if he had been torn open and not Karla, pushing himself faster still. I struggled to keep pace, empty chest gasping for summer air.

"Thief! We found the thief! She's hurt!"

What did they think we'd stolen?

We rounded a corner of the road at breakneck speed, refusing to slow down at all, and two guards cut us off, swords and shields at the ready. Damnit. Damnit. Damnit!

Aldric was going way too fast, carrying way too much weight—he could never slow down in time. Aldric met their raised swords with another guttural howl, and showed no signs of changing course. He would've skewered himself on their swords before slowing down.

I screamed as loud as my throat could bear and hurled my sword right at them. Of course, it didn't work—swords aren't meant for throwing. But to the guards, staring at blood-covered renegades (of whatever crimes, I didn't know) fleeing from half the Drowduss' guard, they didn't stop to think about it. They just acted. The one on the right dove to the side, even as the sword fell five or six feet short of him, and the one on the left took a more cautious half-step to the side.

He, however, made the mistake of focusing on the weapon, and not the very desperate man sprinting right at him. Aldric nailed him—in the dark, running full speed—with a haymaker, his fist making a horrible splitting noise against the metal helmet as it impacted. The guard went down, where his helmet dented against the cobblestone with a second crunch. I turned to pick up my sword, but there was no chance—the diving guard had already begun to recover, and the mob behind us was rounding the corner, elated with the thought of closing in on their prey. I whipped back around, abandoning our only means of defense (covered in Karla's blood) and held the satchel with both hands, tucked tight against my chest as I ran as hard as I possibly could.

Screams and shouts echoed on all sides of us. Guards roaring commands to cut us off, normal citizens trying to figure out what the source of confusion and chaos was, children either yelling in terror or naively cheering it all on. The dark only amplified everything, even with the guards bringing out torches, and was probably all that kept us alive. Trying to coordinate a city guard in the dead of night, with the occasional confused shopkeep walking out into the road to find what was going on, was much harder than just outrunning them. Whoever the real thief was, we were giving them one hell of a smokescreen.

Before us, growing larger with every step, was the temple. I might have found it beautiful if I wasn't about to die. Wide pillars flowed into the domed roof, smooth and gorgeous marble that caught the moonlight gently (as I'm sure it reflected the sunlight harshly), braziers roaring furiously on either side of the gargantuan staircase. The building was the single largest one I'd ever seen, the temple's entrance shadowed beneath a tremendous archway, giant reliefs of mythic figures I didn't remember the names of lining the temple walls. The stairs were individually small, but there were a thousand of them. I could hear our hunters drawing in closer, and I knew they would overtake us on the stairs. No. This wasn't fair. This wasn't right. It wasn't supposed to be like this. None of it. I didn't want to be here. Aldric and Karla weren't supposed to be here. They were supposed to be gone.

"You're going to be okay!" Aldric said, his voice breaking from the pain or the lie, I don't know which. "I promise, Karly, I promise—"

Twenty yards. Fifteen. I felt a hand brush the back of my tunic. That got a hollow scream from me, coaxing my legs to burn harder than they already were. My breath came heavier and harder. Fire was beginning to twist up and down my calves and pour into my chest and throat. I couldn't imagine what Aldric felt, but he didn't show it. There was just a manic look on his uneven features. His face was almost glowing in the light of the temple's flames. His blue eyes were wide and confused.

Karla let out a full, uninhibited scream as Aldric hit the steps, not slowing, her body jostled up in his arms, the gash torn open a little further. I was hoping we could get inside and then…then…then I don't know. No. No, I realized this was it. We'd been run into a trap, game driven into a dead end. They'd take us to prison, surely…surely they'd let Karla die. And that was assuming they didn't gut us on the temple steps for all of Plagiar to see. Karla shrieked louder with each step throwing her back and forth.

This couldn't be it. This couldn't be where we died. That's not how these things end, is it? It couldn't be. Why was this happening?

My foot couldn't bring itself up high enough—my legs had reached their breaking point. Halfway up the stairs my left foot slipped, toes catching one of the ledges. I tripped, hitting the marble staircase with all my momentum. My ribs all threatened to shatter with the pain. I just lay there, trying to ignore the broken feeling in my chest, the deadness in my legs and heart. I barely managed to roll over, staring up at the stars. Plagiaran justice wasn't fond of due process. *At least it'll be fast.* I heard the thundering of Aldric's steps—he hadn't slowed down.

A guard came stumbling to a halt on the steps next to me, chest rising and falling beneath his armor, his shield abandoned somewhere on the road behind us. He still had that wickedly sharp sword in his hand, holding it a few hairs from my jugular…carotid…heh, I still didn't know what it was called. Guess I'd die not knowing.

I stared up at the guard, too tired to be afraid. I just stared at his face, memorizing every little detail. He hadn't shaved this morning. An old dueling scar over his right cheek. Messy black hair, slick with sweat. A few more bolted up the steps past me, surrounding me, as if I somehow still posed a threat. As if I'd somehow find a way out of this one. The guard raised his sword. I noticed the spot of rust on the side of the sword, the sounds of the heavy breathing all around me. I was keenly aware of every stitch in my chest and cramp in my thighs. The fine edge of the staircase was less than pleasant on my neck and back. The satchel was by my right side. I dug my fingers into it. Well, they were in a hell of a surprise when they opened it up, that was for sure.

"Put the sword down." The voice was calm but stern—an order that demanded obedience. The guard hesitated, neither lowering his blade nor driving it down into my throat.

Which I guess, all things considered, was a victory. "These are not the ones you seek."

The guard looked up at him, eyes narrowed. A snarl began to stretch his lips out, baring his yellowed teeth. The voice was coming from somewhere behind me, somewhere I couldn't see without turning and moving—which I didn't think would go over so well with the guards.

"You gave us the description. A young girl, newly arrived, dressed like a savage! The others were conspiring with her, planning their getaway in an inn at the edge of town."

"And this," the priest spoke, his voice rising both in volume and intensity, "Is neither a young girl nor a thief. She is guilty of no crimes, and neither are the other two. We have already found the one we seek—" he continued, despite the beginnings of an angry protest from the guard, "And as we have already established, those who interfere with the temple are under our jurisdiction. If we deem it necessary, we will turn the thief over to you." There was a pause, and the next line came out with the sound of silk and the force of steel. "And only then." There was a clop-clop as the priest came down a step or two, presumably using a staff or cane or something. "Can you get up?" he asked me, more quietly, and I was finally able to see him. Yellow robes, tied at the waist with a golden rope—not literally gold, I mean, gold-colored—wrapped in some intricate knot. Nothing else. His staff was simple oak, no embellishments or trophies. Silver hair engulfed almost all of his face, with a long white mane reaching down his shoulders and a scraggly beard coming halfway to his belt. The rest was all wrinkles and wisdom. He offered me a hand, soured with liver spots, but I managed to push myself up on my own. My body felt like it died a couple days back, but I still had a shred of pride left, at least.

My head shuddered with the blood surging through it, and I couldn't shake the distant feeling across my skin, a sort of numbness to my mouth and fingers.

"Yeah," I said. "Uh, I mean, yes, sir," I added quickly. There was another moment of uneasy tension between the guard and the priest, until the former slowly sheathed his blade, refusing to look away from the holy man. "Very well," he said stiffly. "Please alert us if you need any assistance, your holiness."

"Indeed, we will. A pleasant night to you all."

I wasted no time in scrambling up and putting the priest between myself and those assholes. My chest was still throbbing, my breaths coming too slowly for my legs to manage bending all the way, or for my eyes to see clearly. The golden-robed priest held the intensity for a few seconds longer and then turned and began to move up the stairs, slowly and methodically. I followed him, my gaze lingering on the soldiers (who watched us go, refusing to budge) for a bit. As he turned away, I saw the priest's visage begin to falter—some of the fire went out of his eyes, he stooped over a bit more. He looked much, much older by hunching over just a bit. His joints creaked and popped as we climbed up the rest of the steps.

"Are you all right?" he asked in a grandfatherly tone.

"Yes, sir. Thank you."

"It is nothing. I will not have children killed on the temple steps if I can help it."

We were following a trail of blood.

"Um, do you know…my friend, the wounded girl…"

"Ah," he said, nodding, which had the curious effect of moving the mass of silver hair around him all at once. "Normally, we would not allow a woman within the temple, but here we have made an understandable exception. The others are tending to her at the moment. I cannot say if she will live or die, truly." He stopped talking and sighed, fingers fumbling on the cane for a moment. "Regardless, you were wise in bringing her here. We shall do what we can."

Well, there was some good news. Not much, but a slight chance of Karla's survival was a huge step up from what it had been two minutes ago. I focused on taking a few more deep breaths before I had the air to spit out another sentence. "Sir, um…we didn't come here for her…I mean, not entirely. There…." I stopped, gasping.

"The dragon?"

"Yessir. The dragon."

The old man grunted, expression hard to discern on his face. "I assumed as much. When I heard the Reckoning happened not thirty miles from here, I had a suspicion we would be entertaining visitors. I am merely grateful we are able to perform our duties, what with our recent crisis with the guards."

"Duties?" My lungs could handle one-word sentences much more easily. I clutched my ribs. I needed to sit back down. Ugh.

"Yes. A…lesser known facet of our priesthood." We were perhaps three-fourths of the way up the temple now, marble faintly glowing in the brazier-light, screams and shouts of a wide-awake city fading slowly behind us. "Most of the time, we have our regular tasks. Sacrifices. Blessings. Prayer. Reflection. The Reckoning, however, is one of our responsibilities as well."

So…so there…there might be help after all? I don't think any of these old guys could really help us in terms of fighting the damn thing, but at least they could point us in the right direction or something. I mean, keeping Karla alive would be help enough, but I guess I was still counting on some badass to come in and save us at the last minute. *None of this was supposed to happen. None of it.*

"We—not merely the children of Remos—all priests, for all the gods and goddesses, are tasked with the maintenance of the Old Gates." He glanced at me and saw the limits of my theological knowledge clear across my face, and hastily added "Passageways. Tunnels. Gates. Doors between somewhere and nowhere. Each of the temples—of course, aside from Layana's—is primarily a temple. But it's something of a watch tower as well. And once every ten years…a gateway. It is not our duty to pass through. Merely to keep watch."

We had reached the flat pavilion at the top of the stairs, and the noise of the priest's staff hitting the ground echoed out through the darkened archway before us. We slipped between two of the pillars, beneath the contorted stone faces of old heroes, and I slowed my pace a little more—the brazier-light was distant. I couldn't see anything, but the old man moved comfortably through the ancient hall around him. The marble below us began to shift into paintings, colors and images I couldn't discern in the darkness. Even with everything going on, I couldn't resist twisting around, staring out over the miles of candle-ridden buildings behind us, watching the guards swarming and arguing at the foot of the steps.

"We are not the ones to slay the dragon. That is not our purpose. We are not, perhaps, even meant to aid those who try. We merely keep watch over the Old Gates." His voice changed suddenly, as if some rather nasty possibility had crossed his mind. "Who told you to come here?"

"What do you mean?" I asked, hesitant of where this was going.

"You are from the village that was Reckoned, are you not?"

"Well, yes, sir."

"Who sent you here?" he repeated, as if I should've understood the question to begin with.

"An old storyteller in our village…and, um, Lady Aurea. Sorta Lady Layana too."

It was mostly true.

"They pointed you here, to this place…" he murmured, thinking it through. "Ah. Yes. You could not have reached any of the other Gates by sunset tomorrow. You, unfortunately, do not have the luxury of choice."

"I don't understand, sir." We had passed through the archway and into the atrium of the temple, the roof of which was entirely glass. Not normal glass—it almost seemed… magnified. The stars above looked larger and closer, bathing the entire room in a faint silvery light. I could easily pick out constellations, shooting stars far in the distance. In the center of the room, a fountain quietly bubbled and whispered. The place was calm, quiet. Even the bloodied trail that Aldric and Karla had left seemed gentler, and the few priests still moving about at this hour were doing so serenely, exchanging solemn nods as they went about their duties. Around the atrium I saw a few small clusters of plants—they were tough to make out in the dark, but I thought a few were wise man's willows.

"Were you, say, closer to another temple—another that guarded one of the Old Gates—you could choose which of the pathways to the dragon to take. Unfortunately, you have but one. Unless the goddesses bid you otherwise?"

"No, sir," I said quickly. I did *not* want to be mistaken for speaking on behalf of the gods. "The guardian of Layana's shrine said…said to come here."

He stopped entirely, confusion etched across his wizened features. He turned and looked at me, his ancient blue eyes studying mine for a moment. His gaze went down to my satchel, and a look of knowing spread across his face. He returned his eyes to mine, not blinking, not wavering.

I looked away.

"Are you sure you wish to walk this path, child?"

"I…" My voice broke. "What choice do I have?" My hands were still shaking from the running, from the chase, but they felt cold, thinking of the eyes of everyone in Sorro on me, of the pain of dragonfire, of hollowthroats, of everything. I could almost hear an echo of laughter.

He sighed, and something crawled down my spine, pulling my stomach down to my feet and twisting it into knots. "Go and speak with your companions. I doubt the girl will be well enough to travel for many weeks, but the boy may yet wish to come with you. If he does…" The priest paused, staring at me.

"What?"

The priest started to speak and caught the words, biting his tongue for a moment. He shook his head, turning and walking away.

Whatever that even meant.

"When you are ready, through those doors lies the inner sanctum." He pointed to the hallway directly opposite the entrance, where the starlight didn't seem to reach—a pitch black tunnel burrowing into nowhere. There were six tunnels leading away from the fountain in the center, including the archway we'd just come through. There was a simple symmetry to the temple. Precise, but intuitive. I couldn't imagine how long it took to build this place, which had more architectural thought put into it than my entire village. Everything was smooth and pristine.

"Thanks," I whispered, as the high priest hobbled away. I stood there for a little while, watching the fountain bubble in the starlight. I suppose they paid such close attention to the stars so they could mark the passage of time—Remos being lord of the seasons and all. I thought the temple wasn't that bad. It was quiet. There was nothing going on. No danger. No death. No urgency.

If your friends died here, they went…quietly. After many years of peace and quiet.

I turned and left the gurgling fountain behind me, walking into the room where Aldric and Karla were. Some equally ancient priest was down on his hands and knees wiping the blood off the floor with a rag, looking not at all bothered by what he had to do. The room was an infirmary of some sort—there were eight or nine cots, all made up and waiting to be used. A lantern hung over the cot with Karla, but the rest of the room made do with starlight from the glass above. She was laid out, naked and pale, on the bed. A small blanket was carefully placed to afford her some degree of privacy, but even with it masking most of her body she looked…fragile. Was she really that thin? What looked like all of her right leg was wrapped in bandages, white cloth that was already soaked through. The priest was busy smashing some kind of plant with a mortar and pestle, and another one walked past me carrying more fresh bandages and a clay jug of water. Aldric was next to her, kneeling by the bedside, gripping her hand tightly with both of his. I don't think either of them even saw me there.

I didn't belong there.

"Aldric," she whispered, straining hard to speak even that softly. Her voice sounded rough and forced, not sing-songy and melodic.

"It's okay. It's okay. I've got you."

"Promise you'll make it back."

Aldric nodded, blinking a lot, swallowing heavily. "I will. I promise, Karla."

"I don't want you to go."

"I don't want to either. But y-you've gotta have somebody to sing about, don't ya?"

Karla smiled—I think she was too scared to really laugh. She leaned back into the pillow, eyes closing. For a moment I thought…but no, she was breathing—faintly, but breathing. Aldric took one of his huge hands and gently swept the hair from her face, kissing her on the forehead before letting her hand slide from his. He grabbed another blanket and laid it over her, tucking it in around her. Just barely, you could hear him sing that nightingale song—Karla's favorite lullaby as he swaddled her in the cloth. I slipped out of the room, walking quietly over to the fountain. I stared at the marble, traced my finger along the lines in the stone, and tried to ignore the sound of Aldric sobbing and praying over the rushing water.

XIII

Aldric came and stood next to me by the fountain. What remained of his clothes were ripped, more dirt and blood than fabric. His face was blotchy and puffed, bloodshot eyes forced into permanent squinting. He was nursing the hand he'd punched the guard with, and I rather pointedly stared at the water as he sniffed and choked for a minute or two.

"You ready?" he asked, hoarsely. There was no more optimism in his voice, no more excitement for what lay adventures lay in wait before us.

"Yeah. You?"

"I guess."

I turned and gave him a quick half-hug, patting him on the back for a sec. "Karla'll be okay. They'll take good care of her."

Aldric's painfully tight hug conveyed his thanks well enough. We broke off and made our way around the atrium, noting that all of the priests had retired for the night now. It was late. I don't know exactly what time. Sunrise wasn't more than a few hours away. We reached the corridor and began walking down it, quiet in the absolute dark. Aldric brushed up against me nervously a few times, to which I said nothing. After ten or so seconds of walking we came to a curtain in front of us, which I slowly pushed open.

Another starlit room. This one…this one looked older than time. We stepped inside (Aldric somewhat hurriedly) and looked around, taking in the sight. It wasn't terribly wide—perhaps fifteen feet—but it stretched tall, an arching ceiling reaching up to the heavens. The walls were covered with murals, some stories of the gods that I was familiar with and others I was clueless about (Karla, I bet, would have a field day in here once she could walk this far. Assuming she…*no, no, don't think like that*). There was one corner that was entirely blacked out, but all the faces and people and beasts around it were recoiling in fear.

"The dragon," said the priest. "We were unable to depict it, given that no one has…" he paused, but the damage was done. Ouch. *Well, that was reaffirming.*

The center of the room had a small shrine, an ivory table with gorgeously crafted legs. Each leg was a different sculpture, small but meticulously designed: howling wolf, slumbering bear, singing songbird, and some strange insect I couldn't quite make out. Resting on the table was a chest, all gorgeously stained wood with gold and silver inlay. It was lying unceremoniously open, with nothing inside. Hm. The thief had good taste, at least.

We stood there, taking in the sights, and barely noticing the high priest. He stood with his back to us, looking at the wall before him. There was a small area in which no murals covered the stone, and as he turned and stepped to the side, we realized why. It was a door—the Old Gate. It was hard to see, but I could faintly make out the lines in the marble wall, etched into the stone, and the keyhole in the dead center was unmistakable.

"Are you ready?" the high priest asked, looking between the two of us.

"We have to be," I said quietly. Aldric gave me a strange look. "I mean, that's what they said…at the shrine. Remos' gate only opens at night, doesn't it?"

"Correct," the priest said, with a faint note of pride in his voice. Heh. He'd love getting to talk to Karla, then. Her knowledge of the mythical was a touch better than either of ours. I realized we were going to face whatever was on the other side of that door without any of Karla's knowledge. That was not a comforting thought. "And given your deadline of sunset tomorrow, waiting another night is not an option. You still have a few hours of darkness left, however, if you need sleep or food."

"No," Aldric said, barely above a whisper. "I don't think I could fall asleep. Or eat." He blinked, perhaps realizing it came off a little harsh. "Thank you though," he added.

"Very well. And you?" He turned his head to me.

"I…I suppose so. Aldric, look, if you want to stay here with Karla…."

Aldric shook his head. "No, I…." He closed his eyes, taking a deep breath. "If she doesn't—if…if she…then I want to help you. I don't want this to…to be in vain."

Oh, Aldric. I didn't want any of this to happen.

"Aldric, please, I can't…I can't be the reason—"

"Shut up, Harkness," Aldric said. "I'm going."

"I understand." I took a breath. "I guess we're ready then."

"You came close to being stopped. The commotion with the guards was over a burglary that occurred here earlier." He gestured towards the chest. "Someone stole the key to the Old Gate."

"Wait," Aldric said, "can we still get through?"

The old man snorted, taking his free hand and pulling out a small key on a string around his neck. "Boy, we're assigned to guard a portal by the gods themselves, and you think we only have one key? We all have an extra copy, just in case. The thief, unfortunately, will be able to get through here as well. I don't know why they'd desire such a thing, but it's possible you may cross paths."

"But you told the guards you already caught the thief," I said.

"Well, sometimes…." the priest paused, for the first time seeming at a loss for words. "There's an intersection of moral responsibilities…." He fumbled for a moment, cheeks reddening a bit. "It's a… Sometimes you have to lie. You shouldn't," he added quickly, "but you do."

I liked this priest.

"Had the guards come in here, they would've interfered with things. Remos is steady. Solstices, equinoxes, he doesn't vary. He disapproves of interference." He beckoned for us to come over and we parted around the empty chest, moving toward the door.

"What should we expect?" I asked. If either of them noticed how much higher my voice was they didn't comment on it.

"Remos," the priest said, "is the god of seasons. You will pass through each before coming to your final challenge. I would warn you to stay on your guard. The Old Gates and the trials beyond were not meant for the faint of heart." The priest stepped over, putting the key into the lock. As he did so, the small, unmarked portion of the wall began to glow, with lines radiating out from the lock. One gold, one orange, one silver, one green. Summer, fall, winter, spring. The pulsating light was beautiful to look at, but it didn't bode well. This was just a glimpse of the kind of power Remos had, and the sorts of things we might see on the other side of that door. I thought about what sort of tests Aurea might've schemed up.

I prayed Remos was more merciful.

After a moment the entire door was covered in shimmering light, flickering and dancing, and the priest turned the key.

The starlight from above intensified at the same time the gateway did, with the heavens above us and the hell before us igniting with light and force. A warm gust of wind ripped through the portal and with one final ripple the door simply vanished, and the stars' intensity lessened. There was empty sky through the doorway, the floor ending right into a huge field of grasses and wildflowers. In the distance, the sun straddled the horizon, bathing the sky in oranges and purples, and the faint glow of fireflies danced above the trail. I looked up at the night sky above us, then at the sun hanging over the horizon ahead. I felt small, again, the same way I had before that mountain. *This is a place the gods have wrought, and humans were not meant to go.*

"Summer," Remos said plainly. "It always begins with the current season. Gods be with you, children. We will take care of your friend until your return."

Aldric and I both muttered a quick thanks, trying to gather up what nerve we had left, and then we stepped through. Behind us, there was the sound of door closing—hinges creaking and all—and the hole in reality simply blinked shut, replacing the sight of the sanctum and the priest with a seemingly endless field. Two wildflowers, vibrant and colorful, sat quietly by the edge of the path, the sole interruption for the field around them. We were standing at the very beginning of the road, and it did not look that there would ever be an end.

The other side was...surreal. I was at that point of the dream where you realize something's not right, but you haven't woken up entirely yet. There was some fundamental little difference, one that was too slight for my eyes or ears to notice, but one I could feel in my gut. This wasn't...reality. A very well-done imitation, sure, but this wasn't Plagiar. It was Somewhere Else. I looked over at Aldric and saw the same unease on his face, and my stomach unclenched a bit knowing—hey, at least I had somebody else going crazy with me.

The grass, some too-brilliant shade of green, swayed in the sunset breeze. This was the place Layana had shown me in my dream. *Or maybe it was a vision? I think it's a vision if it actually happens later. Screw it, there are more pressing issues.*

Well, if this was a dream, or a vision or whatever, then that meant. I scanned the horizon, but I couldn't see that... other place. The dragon's lair. Nowhere to be found. Well, that was good news for the short-term, at least. Another surge of air sent a few of the fireflies before us drifting to the side. Aldric and I stood still for perhaps a full minute, making sure nothing was about to jump out and rip us apart. The most unnerving thing was the sun—it was frozen in place, entirely motionless. Had we jumped ahead twelve hours? Was the dragon about to finish off its two captives, or...no, no that couldn't be right. I had no way of proving it, but I sensed we would get to the dragon in time. We'd made it to the Old Gate with a few hours to spare, and we had a full day's time to make it to the end.

I tried not to think about what "the end" entailed.

I glanced over at Aldric, who was nursing his hand. His knuckles were all split open, courtesy of that guard's helmet. He grimaced but caught my eyes and gave me a sharp nod—*I'm good.* I nodded back and we slowly started to walk along the dirt path.

I was hoping whatever this place had ready for us was something we could handle—my sword was gone, one of Aldric's hands bruised and bloodied. Somewhere in the streets of Drowduss, Aldric had lost his wineskin, which meant we only had the one between us. If this trek was an all-day ordeal, things might get bad. Heck, if anything came close to us, our best chance was running away.

All that being said…it was hard to stay alert in a place this pretty. Aldric slowly loosened up, the occasional firefly buzzing by and landing on one of our shoulders or arms, flickering awhile, then drifting off. Ahead of us, the path continued on as far as the eye could see, but everywhere else there was nothing but endless steppe, and a bunch of annoying fireflies blinking through the air. They circled around us like the smaller, luminescent cousins of vultures. The good news was that the grass only came up to our knees, so it wasn't like something could hide in it that well. Hey, more good news— we really couldn't get lost, either. It was a pretty straight shot, just one dirt road going on for…infinity. Even the two of us weren't dumb enough to go trailblazing. Something about that never-ending field was terrifying—I imagined walking off, getting lost…no landmarks at all, not even stars to try and find your way back.

We continued walking for about five minutes, feeling like we hadn't moved at all. There was no discernible difference in the landscape around us, no change in the sun's elevation, no nothing. Everything was exactly the same. Was this the trial of summer? I mean, summer had the longest days, so maybe we just had to keep walking for some obscene amount of time, and then we'd be in the clear? Or maybe the heat would slowly crank up? What did all the old tales say about Remos?

"You think maybe it's a trick?" I asked, keeping my voice down and checking over our shoulders.

Aldric chewed on his lip, head on a constant swivel. He wiped his brow, smearing a bit of blood across his forehead. "Maybe. Dunno. Remos isn't that much of a trickster, is he?"

I shook my head. "I never paid that much attention to those stupid stories growing up. If only we had Kar—"

Aldric winced, recoiling as if I'd punched him.

"Sorry."

"S'okay. Let's just…walk. If there's some other angle to this we'll, uh, figure it out."

I watched Aldric walk for a while. Karla might die. No. She was probably going to die. I left the sheath in the hotel room. I brought her along this quest. I didn't make them leave when they should've. I stared back from where we'd come, but even if the way back was still open, it was too far in the distance to see, the beginning of the path out of reach.

I don't know exactly what step we were on when things became…wrong.

Instantly, the sun plunged below the horizon, the air dropping thirty degrees in half a second. The orange sky turned dark, all the blues and pinks of sunset ripped off the horizon, replaced with midnight black. Without any clouds or lights to compete with, the sky was flooded with stars, all cramming into the heavens to get a good glimpse of what we were up to. Aldric and I went still, then quietly backpedaled a bit to see if it would reverse itself—whatever…whatever *this* was, it did not seem good. Things had been quiet and mellow in the sun. I did not want whatever the dark had to offer.

The fireflies began to burn feverishly, clinging tight to us. They illuminated the path, perhaps a hundred of them settling on our clothes, swirling in the air. We shifted a bit, scanning the plains around us. The wind had picked up, sure, but it sounded like *rustling*, movement just at the edge of earshot, something scraping low against the ground, hidden in the grass that now seemed much higher.

I flicked a few lightning bugs off me and they flew off for only a moment before turning around, coming and latching back on. Weird. I did it again, watching them cling back to my forearm. I looked back out over the lightless fields and—

Oh.

"Aldric."

"What?" he asked, breathing hard. Darkness, right. Even with the fireflies and the stars, there was a lot of it.

"We're…giving off the only light for miles."

Aldric realized what I was saying about halfway through my sentence. We took off at a dead sprint, the fireflies breaking off in the rush but trailing us with silent determination. There was definitely rustling in the grass now, but there was something along with it—hissing, rattling, loud and coming from all sides.

That was a lot of snakes.

I began slapping at the fireflies, trying to knock them out of the air, knock them away from me, get rid of the halo that was drawing a hundred thousand venomous bastards toward us to—

"Duck!" Aldric screamed, hunching over and trying his best to keep his momentum. I barely managed to dive down as a lynx leapt clear over where Aldric had been, claws ready to filet my throat. It sailed over me by half a foot (there was a whistle in the air where its claws tore through the empty space) and fell into the grass, snarling furiously as it turned back around for another pass. More cries like it rose up, all within a hundred feet or so, and my legs had pushed me back upright and moving before my brain had even begun to grasp what was going on. I must've knocked half the fireflies off, but more were coming, rising out of the grass and igniting from above and falling down.

Even between the screaming lynxes and the hissing snakes I spared a half second to look up at the sky. The stars were getting brighter, and closer.

Stars didn't move closer. So…those couldn't be stars, they…were they…

That is a lot of fireflies.

The bugs began to cling onto our clothes and skin, undeterred by the now violent summer gusts that threatened to uproot the steppe around us, pushing the wild grasses flat to the ground. It must've carried our scent for miles, but the upside of that was by the time anything smelled us, we'd be long-since dead. There was a snapping of teeth far too close to my ankles, and Aldric roared as a coyote—too small to be full grown—lunged out of the darkness. He turned and drove his arms against it with all his force, catching the thing in its gut and knocking it down to the ground. He snarled, clutching his wounded hand as we ran on further. My legs were too tired from Drowduss to keep this up much longer. What was the twist? What was the catch? What was Remos trying to prove?

Before us, thousands upon thousands of the glowing insects rose up out of the grasses and began to swarm, a single luminous cloud that lingered in the air, blocking our way. Behind us, the noise hadn't let up, and there was the thundering of paws on dirt, the rustling of snakes through grass. Something hot splashed against my shirt sleeve. Oh gods, they were spitting now, I didn't even know snakes could do that. The halo of fireflies clinging to us began to burn brighter and brighter, as if signaling the ones ahead of us. In the darkness on either side, I could see hundreds of red eyes glinting back, thousands more behind them stretching back into the endless night. I clung to the satchel for dear frigging life and tried to focus on the dirt path, hoping, praying something would come up.

"Harkness!" Aldric screamed, still running full-speed toward the cloud, maybe thirty feet from us. "What do we do?"

"Just keep running!" I closed my eyes and dove into the cloud of fireflies. I lost sight of Aldric almost instantly, a wall of buzzing, swarming light cutting us off from each other. I kept running forward, slapping and shoving, but there were *millions* of the damned things, swirling and glowing, crawling over our skin, and suddenly the coyotes and snakes were loud. They were right there. They were *right there*—

The wind roared, cold and strong. I felt the fireflies tear off my skin and clothes, ripped away by the brisk air. The howls echoed for a moment or two longer before fading out, and I slowly, *slowly* peeked my eyes open. Aldric and I stood not a foot from each other, gasping and sweating. We didn't waste any time putting ourselves back to back, but the threat was gone, the fireflies all vanished. So had everything else.

There was no trace of the beasts behind us. No trace of anything in our wake—just a narrow path leading back into the steppe. There was a definite divide, a plane stretching three or four inches from where we'd been. Back behind us, it was lit up like sunset, and all the animals had suddenly returned to their hiding places. Deep, deep breaths. I rolled up my sleeve and made sure I didn't have any open wounds on that spot on my shoulder. Thankfully, none.

Well, maybe that would've been more merciful. There were still three seasons left.

Aldric and I stayed pressed against each other for a little while, simple comfort in knowing that nothing could sneak up and tear me to shreds from behind, but nothing came. All quiet. Slowly, we turned to look at where the path led next. How stupid I was for dropping that sword a while back? Not that it would've helped us against the sheer numbers we had faced, but it would've at least made me feel a little better.

"Are you sure you can't use your sword?" Aldric asked.

"I dropped it on the run from the guards," I said, looking at what was waiting for us down the path. Aldric's head whipped around, his eyes wide and full of fear. "Oh. *Oh*. Not the Blade, my father's sword. I…." I patted the satchel. "I… uh…I can't use it. Not now. I'm sorry."

Aldric grimaced. "Well, let's…keep going, then."

Our thin clothes did very little to stop the autumn breeze. It had picked up, now, and the wind buffeted us every few seconds. We walked on ahead, abandoning an ocean of grass for the thickest forest I had ever seen. On both sides, broad, gnarled oaks reached up to the heavens, branches leaning out over the road and wrestling with each other for a spot in the sun. There were spots of the sky peeking in between the canopies, but they were doing their best to replace the blue with changing oranges and reds. The sun was higher up in the sky, if the shadows were any indicator, I figured somewhere in the late afternoon. The leaves were beginning to die, I think, hanging just barely onto the tips of the branches, getting tugged and torn in the bursts of air. This place was gorgeous.

It was the most nerve-wracking thing I'd ever experienced, but gorgeous.

"Aldric, you ever wonder if maybe we shoulda just gotten our asses kicked by that blacksmith and just called it quits?"

"Yeah." He chuckled. "It crossed my mind once or twice."

"Heh, I mean it though."

We walked slowly, waiting for the sun to drop again, waiting for…anything, really. We continued along the path, which was still perfectly straight, leading undeniably onward. At least now we knew the general idea—something was going to change, and then something would probably try to kill us. The road led straight, and the road led to the next season. Winter, I guess? Regardless, we had only right now to worry about. There weren't any animals thus far, nothing moving in between the trees, nobody scampering across the gnarled roots. The roots stopped just short of the road, curling back on themselves or going straight down.

We were moving a lot slower. It was just cool enough to be chilly, but not outright cold. Worse, there weren't any signs about when things were going to get awful again. It'd just happened out of nowhere last time. Aldric and I were glancing around, looking for marks on trees or a spot in the dirt, but…nothing. I checked behind us every now and then too, even though I was pretty sure we were clear on that front. But, hey, a week ago, I'd been pretty sure a dragon would never destroy my hometown. *Best laid plans, huh?*

Aldric threw an arm out and caught me across the collar. Normally, I would've said something snarky, but instead I just backed up a few feet, hunching down. He pointed ahead, and my eyes followed it to a small brown clump about thirty feet away. I grabbed the wineskin, squeezing some water in my mouth. Didn't fix anything. My throat was still dry. We inched ahead, focused on that…whatever it was. Nothing on either side but the trees, swaying in the wind and showing off their leaves for the world to see. The brown thing stayed motionless. Aldric and I crouch-walked as quietly as we could, stopping when we were about ten feet away. It was… moving, up and down, brown fur and gentle snores.

I locked eyes with Aldric, who nodded.

It was a bear cub.

Which meant a very angry mother was very close.

Never thought I would miss snakes.

We stayed absolutely still, checking as far around us as we could see for the mother. Bears are big, right? They couldn't be that hard to find. For a solid two minutes we looked, but nothing. No mother bears. I glanced at Aldric and saw him looking at the thing with a little pity, hesitation splashed all over his features. *Aldric, I swear to every god I can name if you pick that thing up I will let its mother eat you.*

Gods above, there were no other options. We could've gone in the woods, but something about it felt wrong. Fundamentally wrong. There was a path, and we were to follow it. Getting turned into a bear's mid-hibernation snack would've been better than facing something else out there. We tiptoed closer, getting to be about five or six feet from the cub, but it stayed asleep. Snoring, chest rising…and falling. Still no mom. Aldric's face twitched, hesitation and compassion overtaking the fear and stress for a second. He started to lean down, wounded hand opening up. Without having to look at me, he felt my glare, and stopped dead. He looked sheepish for a second and drew his hand back. The cub yelped in its sleep, tensing as if it were in pain.

This…this couldn't be right. Something was up. About half an inch from each other, we sidled past the bear. Little thing snored, curled up small and tight as he could get.

The minute we cleared the other side of the cub, it happened. The sharp breeze came back through.

The leaves began to fall. Not all at once, but the wind was coming through harder, clawing at the trees as it surged down the path. Every few seconds it would send a shiver down our spines and rip a few more leaves off the trees. They'd fall down gently, spiraling to the ground. We kept inching forward slowly, and we began to see more grizzlies. On either side of the road, the beasts were asleep. Mothers and massive old males and five or six cubs all dogpiled on each other. All hibernating. Because this was autumn? So what was the challenge? What was our trial? Nothing moved but two very lost travelers, the gentle rise and fall of sleeping beasts, and the leaves floating down to the forest floor.

Without thinking, I put my foot down, and nearly pissed myself at the *crunch* of the leaf breaking beneath my foot. Aldric froze, leg halted mid-step. Slowly, *slowly*, we turned our head to the side, seeing a freaking fur-covered mountain sleeping with its mouth open, wickedly sharp fangs bared out of old habits.

It shuddered.

It stopped snoring, one eye opening, half-lidded. A heartbeat passed. Then two—then I think my heart honestly might've just stopped beating. We stayed there, not breathing, not moving, listening to the breeze knock even more leaves down onto the path before us, chill us to the bone beneath our ragged clothes. The bear's eyelid trembled, half a glassy pupil staring blindly at us.

Its eye closed, and a few moments later, it resumed its coma. Close. Too close.

I now realized what the predicament was. The longer we waited, the more leaves were going to get in our way. Eventually, we'd have no choice but to make noise—and I had a feeling next time, we wouldn't get so lucky. Aldric had pieced it together as well, and in absolute silence we moved as fast as we could, tiptoeing around leaves and darting around the falling ones as the wind howled down the path every few seconds. What was the catch? What was the secret? Was there some other way? The dirt path was quickly filling up, and we began to move more and more quickly, struggling to stay quiet. After perhaps thirty seconds, there were next to no empty spots on the road left, and we were forced to try and brush some of the leaves out of the way with our feet before stepping forward, which slowed us down considerably.

More and more leaves fell.

Oh gods. We weren't going to make it. We weren't going to. On either side, the rumbling snores and heavy breathing of the biggest animals I'd ever seen filled the pauses between gusts of wind, a steady reminder of what was going to happen if we crunched any of those leaves.

They just kept falling. Orange and brown and red, the breeze knocking them right in our way. Slowly, the sky got more and more open, the glare of the late afternoon sun piercing through. All the branches were stripped bare. We stopped, looking around. Nothing. No other way. We'd taken too long—where there weren't grizzlies, there were leaves.

Aldric caught my eye, and I saw the big guy, leaves sticking out of his hair and caught on his shirt, shaking with fear. He gave me a reassuring smile, trembling as he did it.

I didn't know how much further we had to go. I…I had a plan, but it wasn't going to get us much further than a couple of yards, tops. I met eyes with Aldric and put my finger on my lips, then nudged my head toward the road ahead of us. *Get ready.* He turned his head quizzically, but nodded. As slowly as I could, I shifted my satchel around, opening it up. Aldric's eyes widened, but he was going to be disappointed—I pulled out one of my blankets and tossed it to him. Thank the gods he caught it, now looking even more confused. I pointed at one of the bears, mimed biting at something, and then throwing it. He understood my charades and readied the blanket, a bit of blood oozing from his knuckles onto the cloth.

Then I drew out the little kit of flint and steel, kneeling down. I waited for the wind to falter and die out before I struck it, the faint noise drowned by the snoring apex predators around us. In a way, it was almost soothing. *Still not as bad as Karla.*

A few sparks but nothing lasting.

A few more seconds. Another gust, another strike. The whistling breeze and the sharp *clink!* of flint on steel.

It was getting colder, the air chilling the sweat that had run down my arms and neck. I struggled to keep my hands still, to time the clinking of steel to the noise of the wind. It was working against us, throwing leaves at our eyes and lips, becoming erratic. On the third try, the sparks caught, and the dried husk of a leaf below me flickered with a tiny flame, which quickly began to gnaw its way through. I nudged the burning leaf a little closer to some of the others and then pulled out the second blanket I had, pressing the corner of the wool blanket to the embers. It took for-freaking-ever, the flames licking the edge of the wool before it finally started to flare up. I twisted, grabbing the ends of the blanket furthest from the slowly growing flames. I glanced at Aldric and mouthed. *Three. Two. One.*

We turned and ran, me holding the blanket behind me, keenly aware of my hands feeling hotter every second. The minute we started to move, the wind died entirely, offering no white noise to cover the crunching of our feet on the leaves.

Running through the ankle-deep leaves was clumsy and strange, making us pick up our legs too high and move far, far slower than I would've preferred. I could've dealt with slow, but not loud. The bears sluggishly lifted their heads, mothers looking blearily for their children, fathers sniffing the air and pulling back their lips, low, steady snarls echoing out. The blanket erupted into flames behind us, catching their attention for a moment. As we moved, the fire was supposed to catch onto the leaves, keeping the bears from following us.

It wasn't working at all. This was worse than faking crazy for the muggers, damnit. Were bears not afraid of fire? Even the blanket looked like it was sputtering out. A few places glowed, embers slowly starting to catch, but it would take too long. My feet caught on a fallen branch as I ran backward, my boot tugging the blanket down and out of my hands.

"I messed up," I said, my throat having trouble putting the words out. I didn't care about speaking loud, now. They heard us. They knew. "I messed up, Aldric."

He glanced over his shoulder and saw the failed blanket, the slow lumbering of drowsy beasts coming to the edge of the woods—one, awake faster than the others, came and snarled to the left of Aldric. I screamed, jumping to the far side of the path, trying to get myself a few more feet of space. Aldric grunted, turning and throwing his blanket without slowing down—I don't know if he managed to get it over the bear's face and confuse it, or if something flying past it distracted it, but it kept Aldric from getting ripped in half for a few more seconds.

Behind us, we could hear heavy thump-thump steps as the beasts began to truly wake and realize that there were trespassers in their woods. The wind burst through, throwing our scent down the path and killing whatever fires we'd managed to start. The grizzlies answered back, heavy roars—deeper and louder than anything I'd heard before—filling the forest, building off each other and rousing whichever ones were still hibernating.

Dear gods, there were so many. Even if that fire trick had worked, there was still all the trees before us to consider, and they were all awake, all coming for us. And if this forest was as wide and massive as those plains were....

"We're gonna die here," I whispered, not wanting Aldric to hear, not sure why I wanted to giggle and cry and sit down all at once.

A small one—no, that's not right—a *young* one—burst out of the trees ahead of us, turning and snarling, planting itself down as it tried to size up the two of us.

"Split!" I shouted. Behind us, the thundering of claws on the road (the lynxes had been nothing compared to this) met the guttural roars from further back.

Aldric moved as I did and the beast tried to turn two ways at once, stumbling forward. It would've worked if there hadn't been another one. The second lumbered from behind a tree and slammed against my thighs. It was like being hit by a house. I fell straight down, crashing into the dirt and practically bouncing away. I scrambled back, kicking out furiously, trying to get my feet under me to get back up. The grizzly turned and roared, jumping in faster than it should've been able to—gods, it was that huge and still moved so damned quick. I threw my foot back with everything I had, aiming for the center of its chest as I swung the satchel up to knock it off-course. I didn't know which one worked, but the satchel took the worst of it: my ankle felt like I'd kicked a fur-lined brick wall, but the cub rolled off, strips of leather from my satchel lodged between its claws. I jerked the satchel back and turned as Aldric pulled me up to my feet, but I'd cost us too much time. The children had gotten up and were stirring faster, but their elders were upon us now—they poured out of the sides of the trees, muscling their young out the way as they came in closer to—

The wind came in one triumphant final scream, loud enough to drown out the rumbling growls all around us. It brought us to a stop, threatening to slide us backward toward the beasts. The gale was so strong we couldn't run forward any longer. Aldric and I quickly sank to our knees. We had to fight to keep from being blown back across the leaves, which were being thrown everywhere around us, every tree stripped bare.

I made the mistake of looking behind me. Its teeth were lunging out for my back, eyes dark and furious. I dug my feet in harder to keep from being pushed back any more, my screams lost in the windstorm. The hurricane brought a wall of dead leaves between us, and I noticed the air was growing colder and colder, the debris whipping around faster and faster. The leaves cut off everything just as the fireflies had, masking the bears behind fading reds and yellows. A few times I saw claws pierce the whirlwind for a second, and faintly heard grizzlies roaring, the far-off sound of a woman's shout above the sound of the wind.

Then it all went quiet. The branches and leaves fell to the earth as the wind petered out. I pushed myself off Aldric—I hadn't even realized I'd wound up pressed with my back against his again.

The autumn path lingered behind us, a small, sleeping brown cub just barely visible far back, with something moving even further behind it. We were at the beginning of another road, sealed off on all sides by one mother of a snowdrift. Drooping icicles hung from the edges, and everything had the hard look of frozen-over snow, the kind you get in deep winter. The sun had entirely vanished now, the sky dark save for the distant stars.

"Harkness," Aldric said, breath misting and teeth chattering, "I can't tell if that thing with the blanket was brilliant or really stupid. I'm l-leaning toward stupid."

"Hey, we made it, didn't we?" I muttered, rubbing my arms as much as I could, hoping the friction would start a fire. There had to have been some…some secret, some trick. I just couldn't think of it. Damnit. Karla would've known how to deal with riddles and puzzles.

My nose was already going numb, and frozen air was working steadily on my ears, crawling down from the tips and chewing off a bit at a time. I prayed there were no animals here—we'd be doing well just to fend off frostbite. Above us, the stars were aloof, grey clouds interrupting our view periodically. It felt quiet, but it wasn't peaceful. The cold and the skies were just waiting with held breath. A highwayman's silence. On both sides the snowdrift reached up above my head (the top of Aldric's head was level with it), the wind somehow getting sucked down into the trench we stood in. Flurries danced down from the heavens and fell seamlessly into the endless white.

Something occurred to me. If we had to push our way through the snow like we did the leaves, we were dead. Even if we made it through we'd die an hour or two later. Why couldn't we have ended on summer instead of starting there? That might have kept us alive at least. I curled up, trying to clench my chattering teeth shut and my toes wiggling.

On either side of the massive snowbank, at some impossible distance that humans hadn't named yet, were mountains, but it almost seemed like mountain peaks. We were atop them, running in a valley between the highest points. The air seemed…empty? Thinner. I was having to breathe more, I thought, but I may have just been imagining it. Aldric wheezed softly next to me, eyeing the snowbank.

"You think…" he held up his wounded hand. I chewed on my lip and split it, cursing. Blood was running out faster, now, and it was already starting to turn a nasty shade of purple.

"No, I…I wouldn't even reach off the path, honestly."

Aldric paused, staring at the snow mound, and then reaching back from it. "Y-yeah. Good point."

For a brief moment, the same part of me that was so thrilled to have my own sword marveled at the fact I was physically higher than anyone in our village back home had ever been. We…we had done it. We were on an adventure. We'd gotten to the edge of the world, then gone even further. Gods, if they could see us now. Torn to shreds and limping half-naked in the cold. I hoped they left those details out of the stories.

Before us, the highest mountaintop cut a cloud evenly, sending its halves drifting around either side (well, I guess this path would end eventually, then—I hoped to every single one of the gods that this one was shorter than the rest, because we could not make it to that horizon). We were not powerful enough to contend with winter. There was hoarfrost that had not been thawed for thousands of years, an unshakable feeling that the sun had never shone here. I reached in my pack for the flint and steel and cursed again. Dropped it back in autumn. And even if I had it, there was nothing to light...we'd even thrown away our blankets.

"I swear," I said. "Couldn't that damn priest have given us some cloaks? I wouldn't have thrown away the blankets if I'd known we had to deal with this."

"Hark, I d-don't think you're supposed to say 'damn' and 'priest' in the same sentence."

"What, you think that's g-gonna make it *worse?*"

Aldric shook his head. "We'll be fine. C'mon, let's keep moving, I can't stand still much longer."

Frantically hunched inward, trying to preserve what body heat we had, Aldric and I took off at a jog, figuring we'd die of exposure if we tried to be cautious and assess our surroundings. Definitely die if we moved slowly, or risk getting hurt if we charged headlong into whatever was waiting in the dark. *Wonderful choices we've got here.* Gods. This wasn't supposed to happen. It wasn't supposed to be like this. At least if that dragon showed up now and burned us alive we wouldn't be so freaking cold.

"Hark," Aldric said, speaking soft. I could hear him easy over the quiet snow. "You...you think Karla's gonna make it?"

I'm a little more worried about us at the moment. "Yeah," I said back. "She's gonna be just fine."

"Thanks." He took a few breaths, which made me a little envious. Every deep breath made my ribs hurt like all hell. If I didn't think it would've killed me with hypothermia, I would've lain down in that snow just to take the edge off.

"You…she, um, did….do you ever think…after we're…." He stopped, trying to put together the words.

I clapped him on the back. "You don't have to say it man. I think so."

He gave me a tight little smile and a word of thanks, and then we ran a way in silence.

The stars were hardly enough to see by, but there was this weird were-light because of the snow. There wasn't much light to begin with, but all of it got reflected back. It made for an eerie reversal, with the snow glowing faintly as the skies were dark. Snow was falling all over even though the clouds above were sparse, wispy, and grey. But more than that, this…strange…I don't know what it was in the sky, lingering over that cloud-breaking mountaintop directly in front of us. It was…a kind of flickering light, swaying and swirling, all greens and blues, glowing and pulsating. There was a whisper, some kind of *whooshing* noise that danced across the ice—and I swear it was coming from that light show. I kept my eyes locked on it, thinking lights had to be fire, and fire had to be warm. If nothing else, I could die looking at something pretty.

Aldric and I hustled on forward, brushing up against each other. Maybe in the streets of Sorro we would've been self-conscious but not here.

"Hey Aldric," I huffed, trying to ignore the way my shoes had been soaked through, and then seemingly froze back again. "Did I ever tell you about that girl I knew? The one who lived in the mountains?"

"What about her?"

"She," I said, fighting to keep a straight face, "asked me out on a date once."

"Y-yeah?"

"Yeah…but I said snow way."

There are many different kinds of laughs, but my favorite is the reluctant, I'm-annoyed-you-wasted-my-time-with-this laugh, which came out of Aldric hard enough to make him fall over. I wheezed for a second and helped him up.

Maybe ten seconds later the light show above us exploded across the horizon, painting over the constellations with that weird, shimmering light. Greens and blues and yellows painted the night as the stars burned harder, shining furiously down at us. A blizzard stormed from nowhere, sliced across the face of the snow field making it somehow colder than it had been before. Where there had been flurries of snow before, now it seemed like entire snowballs were dropping out of the sky, making us blind beyond a few feet. I turned to make sure Aldric was still with me and saw tiny snowflakes stuck throughout his hair. Between that and the leaves, it just wasn't a good hair day for him. He tried to knock them off with his fingers, but they didn't seem to be bending so well, and the storm simply drenched him again a few minutes later. My head was below the trench's wall enough that I got spared a little, but I knew I was looking the same. There was a strange noise to the snow, a kind of echoing cry.

"I don't get it," I shouted. We got the occasional snowfall in Sorro, but nothing like this—never this cold, never this much. "The way the snow howls. It sounds like—"

My voice died in my throat. *Oh gods.* Aldric went completely pale as he realized what I hadn't said, and I saw him start running faster, pushing me to keep up.

"D-dogs," Aldric whispered. "It sounds like a lot of dogs." He turned to look at me, the both of us somehow holding eye contact as we sprinted faster. We couldn't outrun this, not like we had the grizzlies, not like we had the things in the summer dark. These were faster, and we were both exhausted. *Damnit. What was the catch? Why couldn't I figure it out?* The snow banks on both sides and the blizzard had us in a blind tunnel, unable to see how close they were getting. Any second, they could just pounce down and….

The howls got louder, closer. It wasn't one or two coyotes whining at the moon. This was a war party, a bloodlusted scream that told the others there was warm, fresh prey, and it was close.

I forgot about the cold for a second, forgot about the sores that my satchel had rubbed against my shoulder, the blisters on my feet. This felt harsher than the last two places, this felt…this felt…

I saw a glint of light ahead of us in the snow and dropped down, sliding to a stop. "Aldric!" I said, barely warning him in time. He couldn't slow as quickly, but he managed to avoid smacking into whatever it was with as much force. I scrambled up peering through the blizzard to see what it was.

A dead end.

I giggled.

The giggles burst into full, dead man's laughter. *This was a dead end.* I ran my hands against the glacier, desperately feeling for a handhold or a rough spot that would offer traction but it was slick, burning my stiff hands as I traced the ice.

I crouched down and sprang up, throwing my hands up high as they'd reach. Nothing, I didn't feel a ledge or… or anything. Aldric screamed, pounding his wounded hand against the glacier, maybe trying to break off a piece or… or something. He looked around with wide eyes, staggering back for a better view. It was pointless. They were getting closer, the pack—no. No, it wasn't right to call them a *pack* of wolves, this was a *legion*, a…a…I don't know the words. They were predator and we were prey.

I pushed up as hard as I could again and caught a glimpse of something. "I can see it up there!" I said. "I can see the ledge when I get up but I can't reach it!"

We scrambled onto the wall, trying to get a grip, but the wall was slippery, the ice almost actively squirming out from under our stiff fingers. There was absolutely nothing to latch onto. My hands—too numb to properly close around the just-barely-there juts of ice, slapped uselessly against the pitiful excuses for handholds. When I managed to get my foot on something, shifting my weight even a little sent my ass falling back onto the hard-packed snow beneath me.

I panicked. I *broke*.

My lips split further as I shouted, Aldric's brutal shrieks joining in as we feverishly tried to scale the ice wall. Our hunters roared back in reply, feeding off the terror in our voices. We couldn't get up. I turned and tried to climb up the snow drift, but it was equally impossible, crumbling against me, making me sink deeper and—

There were more howls and they were closer.

Aldric was pale, staring at the snow behind us. How well did sound carry here? Were they a hundred feet or a hundred yards away? Was it the cold and the fear, or were there glimpses of grey and black in the blizzard, flashes of yellow eyes?

"Aldric," I turned to him, my voice near breaking. This was the end. Oh gods. "Please tell me you have a plan or… or…or something."

Aldric shook his head, tears welling up in his eyes. "No I-I-I don't have anything—" he stared at my satchel. "The Blade. Dear gods please, Harkness. The Blade."

I…I couldn't look at him. I couldn't let him see. I didn't want him to know.

"No," I whispered. "It's not…I…."

The howls were closer. There were things moving in the snow. There were a lot of them.

I managed to look back up at Aldric. He stared me in the eyes (my gut rolled and twisted and threatened to carve its way out through my chest), snow-caked, messy blonde hair all askew, his bloodied, filthy face somehow calm. A sad and horrible smile stretched across his features. "You can do it. I know you can, Hark."

"Aldric…"

Aldric stepped over and knelt, grabbing me around the legs and standing back up. He grunted, readied himself for only a moment, and threw me up with all the force he could muster. He screamed as his wounded hand bore my weight, if only for a moment. I swung the satchel up, and just as I started to fall I felt the leather snag around a thick horn of ice that stabbed out from the wall. I struggled for a minute, squirming and wriggling, the leather threatening to tear under my weight, but Aldric pushed my heels up, helping swing my legs up onto the edge. I rolled up onto the top and felt the ice brace against me. It would hold. I squirmed over to the edge and hung the satchel down by the handle. "Grab on!"

Aldric—just barely visible through the blizzard—looked to me, started to reach up with his good hand. "No," he said softly. "It's too far, I think."

"Shut up!" I screamed. "It's not! Grab it, Aldric! You don't get it! You don't fucking get it! You have to! This wasn't supposed to—"

"Hark," he said, cutting me off. I could see him shaking, part from the cold, part from the howls. He stared up at me, tears running down his face, off his cheeks. They froze before they hit the ground. "You'll tell Karla—"

"No, you don't—"

"Please just lie. Tell her it was painless, okay?"

Somewhere between my hollow stomach and broken throat the words got lost, swept away in the screaming air. They wouldn't come out.

"You can stop the dragon. You c-can. I know it." Aldric looked away, his chest heaving as he pressed back into the wall, a flood of his worst fears converging on him. I could see them, more wolves than I could ever count storming down the tunnel we'd come from, dark grey and black and silver fur pressed in tight against one other, all surging closer. "G-go," Aldric said, his voice shaking and breaking. "I d-don't…want you to see."

I pulled back from the edge, curling up and closing my eyes, pretending it would shut out the blizzard and the dragon and this whole stupid quest.

There were maybe two or three seconds.

Then Aldric started to scream.

I started to crawl, my legs refusing to unbend all the way and stand me back up. I didn't bother opening my eyes. It wasn't like I could see anything through the blizzard anyway. But the snow would only blind me. It wouldn't cut out the sounds of…of…screams giving way to…to *ripping* and….

I stopped, my body shaking with the decision to just turn back around and fall down into them, end it all, rather than go on to what was waiting on the other side. It would've been faster. So much faster. But instead my body refused. *You coward.* I don't know for how long. A rumbling shook the earth, loud enough to break the mountains and sky and mercifully loud enough to drown out the awful sounds of Aldric being torn apart.

The walls of snow came down, the glacier below split open, and I tumbled down into a newly formed tomb. That was okay. The snowdrift collapsing upon me threw me from side to side, tearing the satchel from my hands. I let the avalanche take it wherever it would. Maybe back to Aldric. Maybe all the way back to Karla.

It was all quiet for a few seconds, and I thought maybe I'd gotten lucky and—

No. Something warm tickled at my sides, and slowly the spring air blossomed through, melting the snow and the screams and all of winter behind me.

XIV

I guess I've put off talking about what happened at the Shrine for as long as I can.

Jungles suck.

I was five seconds in when I realized how much they blow. Unlike the beach, which was warm and sandy and nice, the jungle was way too warm, the ground was uneven, and everything was full of mosquitoes. Slapping away the little pricks without impaling myself on my father's sword was a lovely little challenge, interrupted only by hacking branches and vines and other equally irritating jungle stuff. I'm pretty sure using your sword for that ruins it, but I didn't really care. It had to last me like, two more days, and then I'd have enough money and fame to buy whatever sword I wanted. Or, hey, I'd have a very lovely Blade to last me the rest of my life. I assumed Layana would let me keep it as a keepsake. Maybe some dragon boots too, who knew. If the goddesses were really throwing this much weight behind me, I was feeling pretty good about this whole deal. *Maybe sticking to the quest wasn't such a bad idea after all, eh?*

It was going to be pretty smooth sailing from here on out. I mean, figuring out where the temple with Layana's Blade was the hard part. One quick hike through the jungle, one quick drawing of the Blade from the stone or whatever, and I'd be on my way to kicking a dragon's ass. It was hard not to be amped up, you know? It'd been all of ten minutes since Aurea almost turned me into a scorch mark on the sand and I was already over it. She was just bluffing. Deep down, she liked me. I could tell.

"Gah!" I smacked another bloodsucking *thing* off my arm. Plagiar (and by extension, me) is not exactly up to date with germ theory and disease transmission, but I was pretty damned sure I was catching something from all these little bastards. I'm not sure if it would've felt better to wear absolutely nothing (because of the heat—calm yourselves, ladies) or to get long sleeves to keep these bugs off. Either way, lose-lose.

As I said: jungles suck.

A hellish mix of humidity and sweat drenched through my clothes—walking uphill felt more like swimming. Trees—small and thin, were enjoying getting in my way, curling up their roots to trip me and drooping leafy branches right at eye level. There were vines draped all over the place, and if I stopped and paid attention, I could pick out thousands of spiders and lizards and similarly freaky things crawling around me.

So I made sure not to pay attention.

The whole place felt alive, overdosed on movement and energy. Birds were crying out harsh warnings instead of chirping songs, and it didn't at all feel like the still, empty woods back home. Back there everything was trying to blend in, you know, but here the birds were colorful, the frogs were bright red…weird stuff. Everything was in motion. Predators and prey carrying on a never-ending game of high-stakes hide-and-seek. It was unnerving, but at the same time, I could see how a Goddess of Love could make her home here. There was…energy. Everywhere. Everything was vibrant and explosive and throwing everything it had into everything it did.

Navigating through the jungle wasn't exactly something I was qualified for. I was hoping for a clear-cut path, but I had no such luck. I was just going straight as best I could and hoping I'd pass somewhere near the center of the island, which I figured was where the temple would be. I mean who the hell puts it on, like, the far side of the island or something, you know? These sorts of things are always in the center. I realized that finding this stupid Shrine might take me a long time if it was hidden by some weird goddess magic or whatever. Although, honestly, at this point, it wouldn't have thrown me off-guard.

I pressed on, cursing pretty much every time I breathed. I mean, I generally try to keep my language under contr— oh gods, that's a lie, but I mean I really got out of control going through that jungle. I think anyone would've, though: you've got to be a certain type of crazy to *like* clouds of mosquitoes, to *like* enough venomous assholes to give Plagiaran witch doctors job security for life. I passed under a fallen tree, which had a rather large, green lizard looking thing lazily sprawled on it, soaking in some sunlight. He opened one eye and gave me a "stop disturbing my beauty sleep" stare. Even the animals were dicks here.

"Yeah, real cocky now," I muttered, moving around him. "But when I slice up your older, fire-breathing cousin in a few hours we'll see how tough you are."

After one final bout of getting smacked in the face with a branch, which honestly just seemed like Mother Nature was taunting me, I burst into a clearing, the jungle ending as sharply as it had begun. The clearing was a perfect circle, maybe fifty yards wide, although I was too busy spitting and trying to slap a spiderweb off my face to appreciate the divine order of the place.

Ahead of me, was, unmistakably, the Shrine. There was a wide, open pavilion, an architectural marvel held up only by four statues, one at each corner. Just as obviously as this was The Shrine, it was pretty clear whose Shrine it was—the statues were ornately carved figures of unattainable beauty. *No ass like divine ass.* I don't really know anything about sculpting, but you don't need to be an expert to tell when something's been done well—and, hey, I could tell this was done well. *Under "adventurer" and "intern at a tanning firm," you can add "art critic" to my list of marketable skills.*

I did my best impression of a snail as I inched toward the pavilion. As a rule of thumb, when you're dealing with the supernatural, running headfirst into a building older than you are tends to end horribly.

The soft-as-kitten-fur grass beneath my shoes gave way, the air crisp and lacking any of the jungle's humidity. The clearing had just the right amount of light, not too harsh. Had there been a hammock, I might've taken a nap. There were roses sprouting up out of the grass, too haphazard and unrestrained to be anything but wildflowers, nature's way of showing unrestrained love. *I would've gone with deadly nightshade, personally. Or maybe wise man's willow is a more accurate depiction of what love is like.*

I gingerly tapped the pavilion floor—made of some blue stone I didn't recognize—with the tip of my boot. I jumped back, holding my sword up to stab whatever leapt at me. Nope. Nothing. I tried it again, and then a third time.

Huh. All clear. Maybe I was just being paranoid. I moved onto the pavilion all the way and looked around, making sure to check the arch above me, checking behind my shoulder every few seconds. The statues looked down at me impassively, and you kinda got the feeling when you turned away they came to life, giggling and gossiping behind your back. It was probably an intentional feature, what with this being the Shrine of the Love Goddess. As I walked further onto the pavilion something *crunched* beneath my boot and I scrambled back, sword raised and ready to rip someone apart. Huh. A small, shattered glass vial—exactly like the one I had—was on the floor. None of it had pierced my shoe. Maybe somebody liked coming out here and getting wasted or something. It would be a pretty fitting make-out spot, I suppose. I brushed the shards away with my foot and glanced around again.

"Um, anyone there?"

Silence. The trees swayed lazily. Somewhere, a bird cried out.

Maybe I had to do it all official and shit. "Um, hail, Lady Layana! I am Harkness, come to retrieve your—I mean, uh, thy Blade! Come forth...guardian." That sounded way better in my head.

No response.

Okay, it was not my best moment, but at that point, I was sick of all this crap. *I hauled ass through a jungle to get stood up?*

"Hey! Anybody out there?"

So, of course, when a voice came from a foot or two behind me, I almost pissed myself. At the rate these pants-pissingly-terrifying things were happening, I was bringing diapers on the next adventure. *And alcohol. Things have been too sober lately.*

"Yes. But I do not think you will gain much from speaking with me."

I recognized that voice.

No. No. *No.*

Very cautiously, not wanting my eyes to prove what my ears were telling me, I turned around.

Just as I'd seen her last. The wavy ginger hair, somehow glossy and gorgeous despite the lack of conditioner and running water in Plagiar. Mouthwatering curves, made all the more alluring by an unhealthily tight corset. Black silk stockings riding delicious white flesh. Dark eyelashes fluttered, and the sweetest grin for a hundred miles glinted at me. Her lips were plump and some wild, painted-on shade of red, one that was so obviously unreal but just as obviously good. She stood with just the slightest curve to her spine, one that took your eyes by the hand and led them right where they'd been wanting to go.

"Hey, Eva," I whispered, the sword lowering in my hand.

I am not the smartest man in Plagiar, but I had pieced together what the Shrine's guardian was. How it worked. "You…you're a long way from Hammerk."

Eva giggled, echoing somehow in the open air of the Shrine. It bounced back, ringing like all the laughter from the streets of Hammerk. Just like it. "Oh, aren't we?" she moved in a step closer, her smell intoxicating. All of my senses wanted the exact same terrible thing, and they were very quickly gaining ground against the part of me that knew better. I closed my eyes and took a step back, but heard her—

felt her, gods, I could almost *taste* her—sidling closer regardless. "Why are you here, Harky?"

"Piss off. This isn't real."

"What were you expecting?" she whispered, her lips a half-inch from my ear. A part of me wanted to drop the sword and grab her and put on one hell of a show for the mosquitoes. The other part of me just wanted to turn and run through the jungle until I hit the ocean, and then keep going until I reached the far shores. I guess they compromised—I stood there paralyzed except for my racing heartbeat and trembling knees. "What did you think would be here?"

"Well, um…the Blade, for starters."

Eva giggled again, and I opened my eyes to glare at her. I'd told her how much I hated that—it felt so fake. Like she was mocking me. But this couldn't really be her. She shook her head, whatever magical glamour that gave her doppelgänger life somehow made her hair fall perfectly into place, her mischievous grin almost literally lighting up her features.

For a few seconds my vision gave way, the pavilion blurring into that hotel room over the cheapest tavern in Hammerk, a window open to the grimy street where brawls raged and drunkards drowned in their own vomit. Everything—the smell of her perfume, the reek of cheap liquor, the creaking of the piece of shit floorboards beneath the bed, the screams from the rooms around us, it was all so real. I closed my eyes hard, and opened them to see the Shrine again, the smells and sound barely at the edge of perception, hallucinations only just kept at bay.

"And you thought," Eva purred, "you could take it?"

"I didn't have any other choice. I—"

Eva clicked her tongue at me. "Oh, Harkness. No other choices?" she said, throatily, a tone she'd rehearsed in a mirror a thousand times. It paid off. I forced my starving eyes shut again. "Life is *horrible* like that. Never giving you a fair choice. Putting someone as brilliant as you in that cesspit of a hometown—"

"C-coming from Hammerk's resident whore, I'm kinda—"

She pressed a finger to my lips. Something electric seared down my chest and settled between my legs. "Hush, now. I'm the resident whore Marisa can't know about."

"You're not real. You're just some—" My brain didn't want to produce words, it was preoccupied, and that was the trap, that was what this was. "This is all a trick. An illusion. You're not real."

Not-Eva traced a nail down my chest, pressing it into my flesh for a moment. I felt a sharp pain and looked down. A trickle of blood bubbled out. "I'm plenty real, Hark. Real enough to love you."

I knew the right answer, but even as I said it, it didn't sound convincing at all. Gods the woman looked gorgeous. No, she didn't look gorgeous. She *was* gorgeous. Sex radiated from her every movement, every breath a throaty sigh, every blink of her lashes some half-lidded, feverish temptation. Some quiet logical part of me that was struggling to be heard over everything else, knew this was all a test, all a trick. But there was a place for quiet and logic and it did not exist in Not-Eva's curves and Not-Eva's kiss. "You…you don't love me. I don't love you. That's…that's not love."

She gave me a faux pouting look. "Well, if you don't love me, you certainly don't love your little fiancée. Do you?"

There was silence in the pavilion between us. The birds screeched. The statues watched, almost grinning, almost laughing.

I didn't want….

Somebody else's voice, slow and somber, came out my lips. "No. No…I don't."

"How often did you even think of her on your little quest? Was she the last thing to leave your mind at night, the first to dance through your thoughts in the morning? Or was it you? Was it what you would gain, what glory you could win? The gold you'd have? The stories you'd tell?"

I…I said nothing.

"Then," she continued, wrapping her arms around my neck and pulling her head in close, staring into my eyes—I tried to make them close but couldn't, just *couldn't*. "How did you ever think Layana would let you pick up her Blade? Did you think true love for yourself would suffice?"

I had a moment of lucidity, which probably saved my life. Eschewing that whole "don't hit girls" thing, I brought my knee up with as much force as I could muster into Eva's groin. It was both a cheap shot and totally effective. She grunted, pain shattering the *femme fatale* act for a moment or two as I stepped back, raising my father's sword.

"I may not love her but I'm not dying here, damnit! You're not Eva."

"I'm"—Not-Eva giggled—"whoever you want me to be." Her skin rippled, which was both nauseating and mesmerizing, hair shimmering and warping into a worn red, spine shrinking and hips thinning until she was Karla. A fuller, sexier Karla than I'd ever known, staring at me in silk lingerie Karla could never have afforded. "Does the thought," the thing spoke, mimicking Karla perfectly, from her voice to the way she walked, "of breaking Aldric's heart get you going? Because it certainly does *wonders* for me." She was getting close again and I stepped back, about five or six feet from the edge of the pavilion, trembling sword raised high.

"You're—no. Stop! Where's Layana's Blade? Where is it?"

She whistled Karla's lullaby, her whole form rippling as she stalked closer, morphing from Karla to Elaine in a split second. "You're the only one who understands what it's like," she said, head cocked to one side, her pink scarf hanging down between her tits. One hand reached up and began to unhook her corset as the other reached out toward me. "Losing someone you love.... I'm so alone, Harkness.... I know you are too."

"No. Back off, bitch! I'm not interested!"

She did a twirl, facing me as Elaine and then as Aurea the next second, dark eyes alive and hungry. "Oh, but you are, mortal. You *want* this. I can tell."

She was right. That was the worst part. The only thing that kept me from doing it was the fact that I didn't want to die. Nothing...nothing else. Not Marisa, not right and wrong, not the quest, not anything. I just didn't want to die.

I didn't have the willpower to keep this up for much longer. I stepped forward, bringing the sword up to her (dear gods I wanted to put a hickey on that) neck, the tip of the blade a half inch from her jugular or carotid or whatever the hell it was, I didn't care. I just knew she'd bleed like an anemic pig if I cut it. "Back off!" I shrieked. "Where's Layana's Blade? Just give me the freaking thing and let me go! I passed your test. I'm not doing it!"

She eyed the glinting steel and raised an eyebrow at me. "If you're into this sort of thing, Harkness"—she blinked back into Not-Eva—"you should've told me *ages* ago. We could've had so much more fun."

I pressed it even closer, resting the edge of the blade against her skin. "I'll do it. I will." I would've gone for the vial Aurea had given me and gotten out of that place, but I knew I had to at least try to get the Blade. If this bitch made a move—because I had a feeling she was a lot deadlier than the coy slut act let on—I was going to run like hell and try and pull the vial out of my bag before she could pull my intestines out of me.

Eva sighed, the sexiness fading fast. Well, that's not entirely true. She was still real easy on the eyes, but...whatever magical aspect of it that had amplified her, taken all the things about her and Karla and Elaine and Aurea (*but not Marisa...Marisa hadn't made an appearance, had she...*) that were gorgeous and built on them, it vanished. She had bags under her eyes, (one of them was even blackened and bruised, and it looked real fresh) a few lazy strands of hair falling onto her face. "You, Harkness, are out of luck. You passed the trial, I suppose." She brought her hand up to her face, checking her nails lazily. She clawed them against each other, perhaps wiping off my blood. "But you're not getting the Blade."

I started to stutter some badass threat. It died in my throat as soon as she raised an eyebrow at me. Something in her features, deeper than that succubus glamor, was something that could kill me easily if she stopped playing around. I don't think the sword could've hurt her, but I kept it raised, if only to keep my willpower together. "What do you mean?" I asked, desperation and anger bleeding out in every word.

"You're too late. Somebody beat you to the punch, honey." She rubbed at her blackened eye. "Literally."

I blinked. The sword probably dropped a foot or so.

The...somebody else...I...*what?*

"What the fuck?"

"Yeah. And the one who got it? Didn't take half as long as you did to get the best of me, either. I've been breaking every would-be dragonkiller for a thousand years. Now I lose twice in one day." She made a gesture with her hand, conjuring a bottle of wine and a glass from thin air. She wasted no time in pouring herself a glass of something delicious, spilling it all over her lips, the dark liquid running down her front and soaking through her clothes as she drank. *Damn her.* "It merits a drink, I think. Thirsty?" she asked, extending the bottle to me.

"No, I don't...the Blade's just...gone?"

"I'm afraid so." She grinned, her smile dripping with sweet poison. Gods, she was enjoying this.

"Who? Who took it?" If I wanted to have a snowball's chance in hell of stopping the dragon that was going to kill people in a day's time—of not getting made the laughingstock of my entire village and not getting stuck in that stupid town and living that life—

Not-Eva winked at me, taking a deep sip from her glass. "Mmm, I *could* tell you...but I'd rather watch you beg."

Eyes clamped tight. Blood was thundering in my skull.

"No. I don't want you," I lied. "Okay? Just...no. Please. I need some help here, and I swear that's not an innuendo or...or anything. There are a lot of people really counting on me, and—"

"Counting on you," Not-Eva said, and there was no sultriness to her voice now. It was cold, tense as a rattlesnake. She drank from the bottle, clutching it tight in one hand, tight enough to send a spiderweb of cracks etching out across the glass. "You arrogant little bastard. You'd let the dragon burn her alive if you'd walk away from it a hero, wouldn't you? If you'd go back home to laurels and gold and—"

"No, I...that's not...."

"You," she said, draining the bottle, smashing it against the floor beneath her. The sound was sharp and suddenly the

Shrine was dark. It was *angry*, the sweet puppy love given way to vengeful mothers guarding their young and jealous exes with butcher knives and all of it was in Not-Eva's snarl. "You are not worthy to slit your throat on Layana's Blade." She flicked away my sword with her finger, the force of it knocking me to the ground. I hit the pavilion hard, thankfully avoiding the shattered glass. The statues, now, were glaring at me, the entire jungle listening in…a hundred thousand animals all bearing witness to…to this. I tried to scramble back but Not-Eva hooked a foot behind mine.

"Do you know something, Harkness?" she asked, very quietly. "The gods all take a form when they show themselves to your kind. Tell me. What's Layana's?"

"She's…she's the voice, the beautiful voice."

Not-Eva knelt, her eyes mere inches from mine. "No," she said. "Mortals see whoever they truly love in this world." She reached one hand around me, fingers slipping into my satchel and pulling out the small glass vial. She ripped off the top, cork and glass alike, and then downed the whole thing, licking her lips as she threw it back at me. I barely caught it before Not-Eva lifted her hands to my face, nails digging into my flesh as she pulled me in and kissed me, holding it for a moment, two. It felt like I was kissing a blacksmith's anvil, fire searing across my lips and wrenching my teeth out of socket and splitting my jaw.

She broke away and slapped me, sending me skidding a few feet back across the pavilion. I tumbled off the stone and onto the grass, too dazed to try to get up and run. *Dear gods, what if she'd punched me?* The entire world began to roll over and over, and I wasn't entirely sure if it was the potion or just her backhand. I let out some wordless moan, blurry, double-visioned fingers groping for my sword as the world started to go dark.

"Remos' temple, tonight. There, the gods will do to you what I didn't." I blinked rapidly, fighting to stay conscious, but everything was blurring and shadows were creeping over my eyes, into my thoughts. "Good luck," Not-Eva said sweetly, "*hero*."

XV

Spring was something from a fairy tale. Maybe literally.

Summer had been a sea of grass stretching on to forever, but spring was subtler. There were small trees, saplings, every skinny branch full of bird nests. The edges of the path were marked by a dozen different kinds of wildflowers making a rainbow of petals and leaves. There were more colors than I'd ever seen—plants from the jungle thriving right next to the kind that grew back home. Fat bumblebees meandered from one flower to another, buzzing and rifling between the petals. Songbirds gathered in droves on the trees, chirping and serenading each other with wordless love songs. Butterflies settled on my shoulders every few minutes, and I was too tired to brush them off. I didn't give a damn if they were the guardians of this place, or if they were really poisonous and trying to kill me.

I didn't want this paradise. Every step was wrong, some sin I'd never get the chance to atone for. Before, it had been... purposeful. Destiny. Going down the path was right. But there was a nagging feeling in the back of my head, a little whisper, that we'd cheated the cosmos, that it should've been

Harkness who died back in winter, and Aldric who pushed on ahead, that somehow, we mixed it up.

Gods. I let him die. I…I could've….

Spring was very blurry all of a sudden, and I just sat down. I didn't care what came. What it did to me.

I waited for spring to come along and do its job. Nothing came. It wouldn't even do that mercy for me, wouldn't send autumn's bears or summer's snakes. The birds just chirped along, mocking me amongst themselves. They sounded like Hammerk girls laughing.

I dunno how much time passed. Maybe it was past sunset already. Maybe I was still in time. Who knew? Who gave a shit? I couldn't do it anyway.

I must've started walking again sometime. There was a strange emptiness on my back where my satchel should've been, needling at me as if I'd lost an arm or a leg. No sword. No satchel. Definitely…definitely no Blade.

I at least had to try. I was probably going to die up there, assuming I even made it through spring, but I owed it to Aldric, to at least try to make it back to Karla.

A little nightingale fluttered and plopped itself down right in front of me. It looked right at me and chirped. I kicked at it and sent it flying away.

The fields around me fell silent. One bird chirped. Then another.

The nightingale I'd kicked at swooped back and pecked at my arm, hard enough to draw blood. I slapped the thing off of me, sending it spiraling off into the grass, but another was coming a second later. The saplings and blooming bushes began to rustle with redbirds and robins and wrens all coming out of their nests, staring down at me with open hostility.

I'd found spring's guardians.

I closed my eyes because I had a very good idea of where those things would be pecking next if I left them open. I knelt down, bringing my tunic's collar up above my face. No way to outrun these things—they had wings and I had very sore feet. I couldn't fight them, either, not when there were damned near a million of them. I'd either have to blind myself covering my eyes, or risk having them gouged out. Gods, I just kept getting shitty choice after shitty choice. What…what else was there?

There was a moment of silence and I felt two more sharp stabs, a beak piercing my shin and back, and another on my leg. I dropped and rolled, shaking them off but accomplishing little else. The birds began to sing again, all eerily on the same note, same pitch, then silence. The stabs resumed and I shrieked, rolling once more—but this time, there were more, seven or eight at least. More were coming each time, and my evasive maneuvers were going to stop working pretty freaking soon. Think. *Think.*

Aldric hadn't known how to get away from the wolves. I hadn't either. A few more stabs plunged their way into my skin. I struggled to think of some part of the story I'd missed hearing from Old Man Granger, a useful tidbit about how to escape from a swarm of ravenous songbirds, but I had missed that legend, I'd missed that so—

Song. That song. Karla. There was a moment of silence and the pain began, too many different new wounds opened and oozing for me to count. I yelped and slapped a few more out of the way, kicking out blindly and throwing my body to one side. I landed on soft flowers and squirmed back onto the path. The birds were familiar. I didn't want to know what was off the path. The songbirds began to sing again and the stabs subsided, then all at once, they stopped.

Before a beat had passed, I shouted as loud as I could, trying desperately to make my sore, rasping voice sound pretty. "Past the branches gnarled and dark!" Silence, silence, *shit, shit, what were the other words, what was the rest?* "Where lie silent the singing lark!" I stumbled forward, pausing to spit out the blood from my lips.

There was a moment of nothingness. Two. I prepared for another round of agony, praying they wouldn't find their way to my throat or eyes. Up and down my arms and legs, all across my back, I was shredded with a hundred shallow cuts. Maybe they weren't deep, but they were enough. A dozen little rivulets of blood soaked through my clothes.

Then, a thousand different breeds of birds, all in sync, sang the melody back to me. A beat. Then another. Panicking, I continued with the next verse of the song, standing upright and daring to open my eyes. They all watched me from the branches of the trees, from in-between the slowly swaying flowers, from all around the dirt path before me.

They sang it back, children parroting back an elder's instructions. Not remembering the rest of the song, I began to walk forward, repeating the first few lines as I went, which were matched back in perfect harmony by all the birds around me. Even the butterflies seemed to be hovering to the beat, and the whole effect was…just horribly disturbing. Beautiful in such an awful way. They could've ripped my bones apart with those little beaks.

But instead they just felt like singing.

But then, that meant there *had* been some other way to bypass all the other trials. Summer and autumn and could I have outsmarted those wolves? Maybe…maybe then….

I whispered the next few lines, forcing my voice to stay steady. They followed, matching my warbled, choked tone. I continued as I walked along, repeating those same few lines over and over and over for the next few minutes, trying to forget about all the little wounds those damned things had opened on me. Trying to forget about a hell of a lot. *What… what would the other trials have even been? Maybe we were supposed to pick up that bear. Maybe….*

What if. What if. Wouldn't help me now. I had to keep going. I would have time to think all this through later.

That would be worse than anything the dragon could ever do.

After a few more moments of walking, the warm spring air began to swirl around me, stripping the endless field of flowers of their petals, which all came rushing inward, matched by a crescendo of birdsong. The sunlight was warm and seemed to thaw out the leftover winter frost in my blood. As the cloud of petals surged around me I took a few deep breaths, preparing for the worst.

The small vortex fell apart.

I was not prepared for the worst.

Layana's vision had been accurate, but at the same time, fallen entirely short of how awful this place was.

This will sound ridiculous coming from a guy who apparently talks with divine beings on a regular basis, but I don't buy into psychics. Just seems like a scam, whether it's crystal balls *or* knucklebones.

But I could feel something here, something my body was blind to, but my…oh, hell, my *soul* could feel. There was a weight to this place, and it was evil; it was wrong. Some kind of spiritual echo was at the edge of my awareness, the deaths of so many people, every ten years for millennia, begging to be released from this perdition.

I didn't want to haunt this place.

The rock beneath my feet was an unforgiving black. It wasn't shiny; it had no luster—just grimy, rough, all jagged edges and ugly curves. I was at the beginning of the path— if you could call it that—up the mountainside, and there was literally nothing behind me. I turned back and saw only a sheer cliff cutting off to a hopeless drop. I had no idea how far—there were thick storm clouds maybe a hundred feet down, and I had to fight down a wave of nausea and dizziness as I thought about just how high up in the air I had to be for that to be possible. A huge flash of light ripped through the cloud and the roar of thunder, not dampened by distance, blasted me against the mountain, leaving me cling-ing to the cliff for dear life as everything around me rumbled. Everything here dwarfed me. Every cloud and rock wanted me gone, wanted my feet to slip, wanted the blood they'd been waiting a decade for. .

Forward. Forward. Like the heart of a tornado, the red skies around me churned furiously, lightning tearing open the world every few seconds, instantly followed by deafening (and I mean that literally) peals of thunder.

As godsawful as the nightmare skies were, the ledge I was standing on was almost worse. The space that protruded from the rock was maybe a foot wide, uneven and rugged. I pressed myself flat against the cliff, turning my head to the side and trying to ignore the miles of open air that were wait-ing for me a few inches away. *No pressure. None. N-None at all.* There would be a wrinkle in the air, a cold rush down my skin, and I'd brace for the next blast of lightning, dig my fingers into the rock and pray the thunder wouldn't tear me off the mountainside.

The path curved horribly tight around the mountain, making it impossible to see where I was going more than a few feet in advance. There could've been a rock at the same level as my head, jutting out from behind a blind corner, or maybe even the dragon itself waiting for me. No warning. A dozen sharp edges clawed into my wounds from spring, and my windburns from winter kept my back raw and bloody.

I didn't want any of this. *This is not supposed to be happening.*

I kept quiet, because at least maybe if I could sneak up on the dragon, I could put out one of its eyes or...or something. I didn't know, but that wouldn't happen if it could hear me whimpering from half a mile away.

The incline grew sharper, and suddenly I was fighting not only to keep my weight against the cliff beside me, but on the path below me. My foot gave way at one point and I was crushed against the hard rock, my bruises from the temple steps turning a shade darker. I desperately clutched for a handhold, slipping down maybe a foot or so before I stopped myself. That hill outside of Hammerk had been nothing. *If I fall here, I won't ever stop.*

My fingers—blistered, burst open, and blistered over again—pressed against the rock and began to push me back up. I took maybe three whole minutes to stand upright, not trusting my balance to move any faster than that. Another deep breath. Then another. Oh gods. I reached a fumbling hand down for my waterskin and found nothing. Must've lost that in the avalanche too. My throat felt about as dry as the rock beside me, but I didn't have many options. *Heh. He died of thirst surrounded by rainclouds.* The irony. Irony. Dead ends. Aldric. I stopped, closing my eyes and shaking. *Gods, I'm...I'm so sorry...it....*

I rounded the corner and abruptly stopped, laughing hysterically at the fact the path had widened to a whopping two and a half feet. That was good news to me now. Dear gods, it meant I could walk to my death even faster. What a wonderful blessing. Before me was a rock face, mercifully only four or so feet tall. I shifted my position (carefully) to get in front of it, squatting down and jumping up, grabbing on to the ledge and pulling myself on up. I swung my legs clumsily and awkwardly, too tired and beaten up to move smoothly.

I…I knew there was no way in hell I could beat this thing. I didn't love Marisa. I didn't even love myself at this point. Had there been a blade powered by guilt, I might've been okay. There'd been one good chance given to me, and I'd ruined it, dragging my only friends down with me. They…they'd….

At least buying a few more seconds of life for Marisa and…damn. I didn't even know that guy's name. I chuckled again. I mean, c'mon? Dying for some asshole and you don't even know his name? Mom and Dad would be proud.

Oh Gods. Mom. She'd…she was already so worried and….

The smile was gone again. There weren't meant to be smiles here.

I came to another ledge, repeating the process. I realized vaguely that moving up higher like this meant I would be getting to the summit faster, which…which was not…which was not good.

Another corner. I had to gather my nerve with a few deep gulps of air before peeking around them. This one came to a ledge, but it was much larger than four or five feet. I'd guess and say it was at least twenty or twenty-five. I forced myself to keep my eyes on the wall in front of me and not on the very narrow ledge I was on, not at my battered hands, sliced to hell, and in no condition to be climbing mountains without any ropes.

Deep, deep breaths. Then before I could lose what little willpower had stayed with me this far, I grabbed onto the first handhold I saw and heaved myself up, clinging fast to that rock wall while my foot desperately kicked around for a ledge to rest on. After a heart-stopping moment, I found one. A few inches off the ledge. Deep breaths. Deep breaths.

Just a few hundred more to go.

Had I been able to scale that thing with my eyes closed, I would've done it. I craned my neck up, trying to find the next little pocket in the stone as fast as I could. I didn't trust my fatiguing arms to last long. Grunting, I pulled my weight up to the next ledge, then the next, finding it easier as I went along. I could rest my feet on most of the handholds, but each world-shattering thunderclap threatened to knock me off. With every foot higher I managed to climb, the wind grew more vicious, ripping me to one side or the other as I reached for another grip.

My right hand closed on the top ledge, and with all the strength I had left, I heaved, throwing my other arm onto the ledge and using the momentum to bring my legs up and over. I curled up, too exhausted to even move away from the edge. *Gods. Please gods, I can get eaten alive by the dragon just not another cliff.*

After a minute, I was able to shakily rise up, and I wished I'd stayed lying down. I was at the base of the summit, now, and the hurricane skies were somehow fouler than they were before. Closer, hungrier. The path, the more-or-less steps in the mountain were the only traversable part—everything else was razor pointed, obsidian spears angled to make climbing up any other way impossible.

The cliff jutted down sharply, carved out of the mountain by some unnatural force that wanted to see broken bodies go tumbling down. The clouds above whipped around faster than anything in Plagiar (had those spring birds been here, they would've been literally torn apart). Bolts of lightning flared constantly, curving down into the clouds hundreds of yards below and then off into nowhere. They came from above the peak, where the awful red light emanated like the devil's halo lording over the entire mountain. There was nothing living on this mountain. Nothing living that came here stayed that way for very long.

The incline was too steep to see what was waiting on the summit, but there was no doubt it was the end of the road. The path had finally finished. Had…had the priests in Drowduss, the portal in the open air—had that really only been an hour or two ago?

I waited for a moment, perhaps hoping the gods would let me off easy, send a gust of wind to throw me off the mountain, maybe vaporize me with lightning, but it didn't come.

My feet moved slowly and grudgingly ahead.

I wondered how many other people had walked up this path.

I knew how many had walked back down.

The steps were uneven, rough and crudely hewn into the rock.

The lightning and thunder, not a hundred feet above my head, was too loud to think, but not quite loud enough to keep me from being afraid.

This is where they were. Marisa and the other one taken in the Reckoning.

I stopped, my head almost level with the summit. I still couldn't see. I could still turn around and…and…I don't know. I don't think leaving this place alive was an option, but there was a choice. A horrible, morbid choice, but there was one nonetheless. I stared at the cliff behind me and the abyss on the other side for a full minute, thinking it through. No. No, I…I'd see this through.

I turned and stepped up onto the summit.

The mountaintop was flat, with only occasional ripples in the volcanic rock. But otherwise? Eerily smooth. It was wide, fifty or so yards long, and at the far side, I saw a thin spire of rock, jagged and slender. Marisa and the other guy were there, apparently bound to the spike by some material I couldn't see. Even from this distance, they looked…broken. Horribly emaciated, curled up in fetal weakness, still as statues.

But there was no dragon.

There was no dragon.

Could…could this seriously be it?

Could I get them and get out, find some way to escape this mountain, before this thing returned? It must've gone… somewhere. Maybe the gods distracted it or…it didn't matter. I could grab them and get back down the mountain and go. Something warm made me forget the stab wounds, the frost-nip, the cuts and sores. I was going to live. I was going to live. I took a step forward, then another, giddiness pushing me into a half-sprint as I heard my footsteps echo before me—

No.

No.

I shouldn't have been able to hear my footsteps. The sound of the wind should've drowned them.

I saw the two prisoners turn and lift their heads with the look and speed of dead men, hearing a human running, then suddenly stop. They could probably hear my own heart, thrashing hard enough to break through my aching ribcage. The skies above had gone silent like an attack hound waiting to be let off its leash.

Oh.

I turned around very slowly and saw the dragon.

The beast was massive beyond words. If I was lying on my side, maybe—*maybe* five of me would've stretched to the width of its face. Its eyes were the size of…gods, where its eyes should've been white there was only black, its pupils horrible yellow slits. Wide, thick scales, separated by the faintest of red lines, identical in shade to the hurricane above us. I couldn't get a glimpse of the rest of its body, but half its neck and head was at least fifty feet off the ground, and as it bared its teeth—all longer and thicker than my arm, whiter than the marble of Remos' temple—it spread its ungodly wings and blocked out the entire sky on either side.

The…whole sky.

The dragon opened its mouth and let out a roar that almost wrenched my bones from their sockets, crushed all other sound into nothingness. Just as I could feel, in my soul, that this place was some kind of sin, I could feel the power in this thing. It was like standing next to one of the goddesses, but…but this was harsher. They had radiated control and restraint, but this was all primal hunger, fury, like being sucked into an open oven. For the first time since humans had walked across the surface of Plagiar, I knew what it meant to be absolute prey, of looking at this beast and knowing there was nothing I could do but die. If the gods ever gave it leave, it would end every life in Plagiar without any challenge whatsoever. Its roar filled the sky, shaking the roof of the world and making lightning rip through the air. The noise was too loud for sound alone to convey; you could see the air twisting and rippling as the raw power of its scream poured through everything, shifting from sound into light and heat and force.

"Little mortal," it spoke—no, speak isn't right, it…its voice…it…. I got slapped down to the ground, thrown back ten or fifteen feet across the rock. I scrambled backwards, refusing to meet its horrible eyes, trying to fight down the splitting pain in my skull, the blood trickling out of my ears and eyes and nose. Some sharp pain burst deep inside both my ears. My bones ached and shook. My ribs, *dear gods my ribs*, they shook and pulsed with each syllable, trying to slow down the force before it got to my heart. "You have come to die."

"F-f-fuck you."

I wanted to die myself. Damnit I was a coward and a shitty friend and a hundred other worthless things but I wanted to go down showing that bastard some spite.

There was a moment where all nature was perplexed, and I could faintly hear Marisa say "Harkness?" either unbelieving that I was here or unbelieving that I was foolish enough to talk back to this thing.

It began to laugh, an earthquake of sound that was just as painful as its voice. "Your insolence is childish. Futile… as was your coming here. I will break you as I broke your forefathers."

Nothing witty came to me, no snarky reply. I struggled to get to my feet, but I couldn't. It was like standing up with some tremendous weight pressed against me. I realized vaguely that Marisa and the other guy probably weren't even tied down, just held against the rock by the psychic pressure the dragon gave off.

The dragon rose, higher and higher, revealing its full self. The…the size of this thing. It took up all the sky before me, muscles thick as trees under its scales. It shouldn't have been able to *be*. It should've been too heavy or too big but no one had bothered to tell it so, and as it drew up its whole form it just grew bigger and stronger. A tail, some thirty feet long, slithered back and forth in the open air, and with one massive flap of its wings (which sent me flying backward, crashing and rolling to a stop near the edge of the summit) the world-breaking storm above us began to rage again. The dragon opened its maw and let out a geyser of fire, the heat of which—from all the way across the mountaintop—flash-burned every exposed inch of my skin, blisters tearing open all down my arms and legs, my hair singed and scorched. The light was brighter than the sun, a white-hot that spewed out and snarled into the ferocious red as it poured into the storm clouds above.

"Mortal. I am the end."

I was curled up, trying to resist the sledgehammers of sound and pain that broke against me when this thing spoke. The dragon landed, the whole mountain tilting under its weight, setting its hind claws somewhere below the edge of the summit and pressing its face not fifteen feet from mine. The heat from behind its jaws began to roast me slowly.

"I shall grant you this. Decide. Who shall have the mercy of dying first?" the dragon roared, and being so close to its voice, to *it*—my body couldn't handle it. There was a twitching in my heart as it struggled to keep its rhythm. My vision blurred and flashed with spots. My skull throbbed, joints alight with the same pain old men feel when hurricanes are coming.

A voice sounded across the mountaintop, over the storms and the fire and the dragon itself. It carried clear and strong and pure. It was worn and hollow and weary but there was absolutely no fear.

"You will."

There was absolute silence on that mountaintop. Maybe the whole world.

I…I recognized that voice.

The dragon turned away from me, staring at the newcomer.

Hell had eaten her raw and spat her back out half-dead. Something cold and fierce shone in her green eyes, even sunken behind the deep purple bags from days without sleep. Her red hair was broken and messy in a thousand different ways, an unkempt mane blown back by the winds. Her lips were chapped, burst open as mine were, but they were pulled tight, stoic before the dragon. Deep bruises covered her arms and legs, and a hundred cuts and scrapes were etched into her face, her exposed arms, and I knew her entire body bore them from Remos' tests. No, from before. The journey.

She'd made it through the tests fine, hadn't she?

She didn't look like hell 'cause of wolves and birds and bears.

She had those cuts from stumbling through the woods.

From taking on bandits with a stolen sword—and *winning*.

Her skin was burnt as red as her hair from lying on that beach and talking a goddess into letting her go.

The tears on her clothes were courtesy of the Drowduss watch—guards who tried and failed to catch a temple thief.

The only thing that looked taken care of hung around her neck, rippling in the wind. A pink scarf resting around her neck. A…a small, cheap thing.

A small cheap thing that her fiancé had to work months to get.

It made my entire body break even more, but I started to laugh, coughing up blood from my burning stomach. The pressure of the dragon's gaze bore into the side of my skull as it turned back to look at me.

I couldn't choke out the words. I just shook, dying one wheezing bout of laughter at a time.

"Insolence." The dragon reared back, taking a whole second to open its jaws all the way, and I scrambled to get clear. I would've been boiled in my own blood if I stayed put.

The dragon's mouth exploded with flame, a river of hell pouring out toward Elaine, who simply reached up and tore off her cloak, undeterred by the thunder that had begun to shake the world once more, the furious lightning strikes that hammered the mountain below. The heat scorched my back as I crawled, burning my tunic to ash and scalding me beyond pain.

It did not faze her. She merely let the cape fall to the breeze as she reached over her back, grasping for something.

The dragon's fire parted clear around her as she pulled out Layana's Blade. The entire world shook, and I honest to the gods mean that *the whole world* rumbled at the force of the impact. The dragon's flames passed around the blinding pink aura that cloaked Elaine—*the exact same shade as her scarf.*

The dragon stopped, and I saw in its eyes—for what had to be the first time in its entire existence—fear. Confusion. Somewhere in its features, totally inhuman and monstrous, I saw it.

Doubt.

"You think that blade will save you? I will scatter your bones to the corners of Plagiar. And I will keep you alive as a—"

"Lizard," Elaine said, and the dragon stopped. Its voice just broke against hers. "I don't think you understand. You hurt Fenwick. I'm going to kill you."

The dragon roared as Elaine charged ahead, the fire once again splashing away. I howled (screams matched by Marisa and Fenwick on the other side of the mountaintop) as another scorching wave of heat roasted my skin, but Elaine didn't flinch. She dug her feet in, brandishing the Blade before her. She refused to retreat, forcing herself steadily forward. All her features were strained with exertion, her thin arms pushing for all they were worth. The dragon continued, breathing steady and hard, its flaming mouth opened as far as it could manage. She kept going, the Blade parting its flames like water on rock.

Then the dragon took a step back.

The flames sputtered out as the dragon pressed down into the mountain, pushing off into the air (once again, the mountain trembled, and even though Marisa and Fenwick and I were thrown to the side, Elaine kept her balance, the pink glow bracing her against the impact) and letting out a war cry that tore fissures into the rock beneath us. Elaine moved closer still, green eyes darting around the summit for a way to get up to its level.

The dragon looked down for a moment, snarling, thinking.

It couldn't kill Elaine.

But it could still kill her reason for coming all this way.

Swinging its tail—some gargantuan mace you could crush whole armies with—down at her, Elaine jumped to the side and rolled, dodging the blow. She popped back up, gripping the Blade in one hand, her whole form beginning to glow and flicker with pink light. The dragon turned its head toward its prisoners, drawing in breath. The furious clouds twisted and squirmed as it inhaled, the winds and breeze sucked in to fuel its next gout of flame. Elaine screamed in protest, her own voice somehow terrible and loud enough to match the dragon's, and she brought the Blade down on the dragon's tail.

The dragon wailed, this time in pure agony. Not once in its life had anyone ever caused it this much pain—*any* pain—and it had no idea how to react, how to cope. Stunned, it was clumsy turning back around, losing altitude fast and staring at Elaine, amazement and terror visible even on its alien features. Elaine got a running start and jumped, slashing through part of its back as she fell forward. The dragon, crying to the heavens, rolled over in some vain attempt to crush her, but Elaine let herself fall to the other side, landing with that same impossible grace. The Blade's light began to envelope her fully, a rose-colored star going supernova, and her feet righted themselves as her body touched the ground.

The dragon kicked out at her, striking with deceptive speed, but she casually sidestepped the blow, twisting her Blade up and splitting the beast's foot in two. Elaine followed with another strike, stepping in and plunging the Blade through to the hilt in the dragon's gut and twisting with all her body, ripping it out in one master stroke. The entire bottom half of the dragon's body seemed torn open now, screaming as it thrashed, legs kicking as it tried to get away from Elaine. Where her steel had touched it, pink fire licked the edges of its wounds, widening them further even as she drew away.

She kept going.

The dragon let out another useless burst of flame, but Elaine walked straight through, a look of cold fury about her. It pressed down against the mountain to flee but Elaine slashed at its wing, almost idly, tearing through the membrane and crippling it for good. The beast writhed, perhaps hoping to fall off the mountain and scamper off, to lick it wounds. Or, maybe, it just wanted to die on its own terms, rather than face death at Elaine's hands. I couldn't blame it either way.

Unfortunately for the dragon, Elaine had absolutely no intention of letting it live.

She ran forward, moving in for the killing blow, and I saw that bastard's reptilian eyes widen in fear, a feeble word of protest forming in its throat as she drove the Blade down into its chest, right where its heart should've been.

Layana's Blade shook and the dragon began to convulse, crippled leg and stumpy tail flopping aimlessly, jaw unhinged from shrieking and eyes rolling back into its head. There was a moment of stillness. Then two.

Then the dragon burst open with light, something that blinded me for a full minute. I screamed, a noise lost amidst the dying throes of the dragon, the earthquake beneath us, dozens of thunderblasts a second above, and total cacophony across Plagiar as every living thing felt the end of the Reckonings come at last. I felt the air change, the pressure in my head and bones tapering off, and I knew the storm was gone. The dark red skies had calmed.

When my eyes finally cleared, I saw Elaine standing over the dead beast with the Blade in her hand, breathing hard. Utter calm covered her features, only a hint of righteous anger in her eyes. Slowly, the pink flames began to cremate the great beast, blossoming out from the chest and devouring it inch by inch.

"'Laney?" Fenwick whispered, and for the first time I got a good look at the guy. Gods, they must not have had food or water in…in…days. It was a miracle they were still alive.

But miracles didn't seem very hard to come by lately.

Slowly, my muscles began to find themselves again. I rose up, trying to regain my balance. My whole body felt…brittle, wracked with bone-deep soreness.

Fenwick was trying to crawl to Elaine, his legs too weak to hold him. The Blade slipped from her fingers, falling and rattling against the stone as she hurried over, grabbing him, burying her face in his shoulder. "Fen. Oh gods. Fen I thought—"

"Elaine, you…."

They sat there, weeping and holding onto each other like there was nothing else in the entire world. They both shook, bodies racked with sobs and exhaustion and relief. Elaine broke away, fumbling for her wineskin. She held the tongue to Fenwick's mouth and oozed water into his bloodied lips, gently wiping up any that sputtered out when he wheezed and choked. She murmured something to him and drew out a summer wildflower from her pocket, tucking it into what was left of his tunic. Not three feet behind her was the most powerful weapon in all existence—entirely forgotten. The beautiful pink light had begun to die down, leaving just an average sword behind.

As I staggered over, soaking in the quiet (save for Fen and Elaine's barely comprehensible sobs), I watched the Blade for a moment. It slowly began to fade, breaking off into little bitty pieces and rising up into the air, nothing more than silvery dust. The last of the gods' great weapons had been taken away.

I looked down at my arms, charred and raw and oozing blood in a few spots. I couldn't help but laugh, sounding like a skeleton trying to hiccup. "Heh. I smell like…oh, the irony." I coughed, splattering a bit of blood and ash on the ground. My leg shook and I knelt for a second, taking deep breaths into my aching lungs.

I felt a bloody hand close around mine and I looked at Marisa. For the first time, I think, I really looked at her.

About half her dark brown hair was gone from fire and flame, the remainder singed and split and frazzled. Her eyes, her beautiful blue eyes, were haggard, sunken back in her skull. Marisa was never thick, but she'd lost so much weight— even the rags that remained of her clothes were too big for her, swallowing up the skeleton she'd become. Her face, cut up and bloody, ash pounded down into the skin, was close to mine. Somehow, she…she was prettier than I'd ever seen her, but at the same time, she also wasn't, and I didn't understand how. The paradox started rattling against my tired heart, and I didn't try to ignore the empty feeling that replaced it.

"I knew you'd come," she said. "You were so brave."

I looked down at her, at the…at the girl trembling in my arms. It would've been really easy to tell her what she wanted to hear. To invent some story that explained away my not having the Blade, my not saving the day.

To take her back home and marry her.

I doubted Elaine would care about how things were remembered, she was happy just to have Fenwick. I could take responsibility. Take credit. Take glory.

The legends would go down that Harkness had slain the worst monster ever to rear its terrible head in Plagiar, and in time, even Marisa would believe it, thinking her true recollection of what happened nothing more than a fever-pitch dream, some hazy result of being half-starved and half-dead.

It would've been really easy.

Everything in life I've ever wanted.

A pretty girl, if I let it happen. Lots of pretty girls. All the money and fame I could want. I'd never have to work again. I could go wherever I wanted. Be anything. Do anything.

She looked up at me, a watery smile on her face, and I brushed what was left of her hair back into place.

"Marisa," I said as gently as I possibly could, "I think we need to talk."

EPILOGUE

I'd been looking at my arms every day for more years than you could count, and I was still a little bewildered to see them all scarred to hell. Sometimes the old burns still felt hot, and I'd gotten real fond of sitting in rivers whenever I stumbled upon one.

The shallow parts, mind you. With some time, I got back on speaking terms with rivers.

Clump step. *Clump* step. *Clump* step. I lifted my head, continuing to rock back and forth in the wooden chair. Saw that wrinkled hand wrapped tight around a wooden cane that was almost as old and ancient as we were. Her silver hair tucked back into a little bun. Karla nodded at me, then turned to the codependent—*oh, who am I kidding, it was damned adorable*—lovers sitting next to me. Fenwick's face was as torn up and maimed as my arm where it wasn't covered with his scruffy grey beard. Elaine was on his lap, gently sleeping. The quiet roar of the crowd around us had been enough white noise to let the old girl drift off.

"Nerves?" I asked. Karla nodded, leaning on her good leg as she came to a stop.

"Yeah," she murmured. "Every time. Want to do right by him, you know?"

I shook my head. "You tell it better than I do, and I was there. You get all the little details right and everything. Granger'd be proud, wouldn't he?" Fenwick stayed quiet beside me, one trembling hand running through Elaine's hair.

Karla gave me a small smile, and I hoped I'd assuaged her, if only a bit. She stared at Elaine and Fenwick with a little jealousy, the sort of jealousy she really only got this time of year.

The crowd was starting to get restless. I beckoned to them and resumed my rocking. Karla took a few deep breaths and began making her way to the little stage, taking her sweet time. When she got up, she only had to smack the butt of her cane against the platform once to make everyone quiet down. There was silence, aside from a few torches being lit—Karla's story would run long after the sun had set, and nobody wanted to get up and move after she began. People sat and got comfortable, all their eyes focused on the same place. Karla took a few deep breaths, her cataract-ridden eyes looking out as far as they could over the crowd. I always got the feeling she was hoping she'd see him, see a face that matched his. Somewhere between the throng of eager listeners and the sun inching toward the horizon, she found her breath.

"Back," Karla began, "when I was still young and full of life like all of you, the world was a different place. Full of darkness, and pain…and love."

I saw Fenwick shift a little, getting comfortable. Elaine opened one eye and looked over at Karla for a moment. Fenwick squeezed her hand and whispered something to her that made her smile. She nodded her head against his thin chest and drifted back to sleep.

I saw a lizard scramble past my feet, dodging the legs of the rocking chair. I went to step on it but had a better idea.

"Hey Elaine," I muttered, not wanting to distract the kids nearby from Karla's story.

She glanced a sleepy eye up at me.

"Think you could take care of this for me?"

She snorted and rolled her eyes, leaning back against Fenwick. He, uh, didn't seem to find it as amusing.

Karla told her story, just as Elaine and Fenwick and Marisa and I had told it to her. She got all the little details right. The terror in that chase through Drowduss, the way the Old Gate burned with color against the temple wall.

The way Aldric had slain the dragon, dying in the process. The way they'd felt the ground rumble a thousand miles away, at the very edges of Plagiar itself.

And the way they'd lifted glasses to Aldric the Dragonslayer, every year since.

I leaned back in the rocking chair, watching the shadows behind Old Lady Karla grow longer and longer until night had well and truly fallen. They almost didn't need the torches: the stars were brighter than normal, as if the constellations were listening in too, and the occasional firefly danced along, perhaps by way of apology.

I crushed every single one I saw. *Fuck you, fireflies.*

Beside me, Fenwick and Elaine had both drifted off to sleep. We knew a different version of the story. One that was…a bit more accurate.

But nobody in the village slept as peacefully as those two did at night. And even though Karla teared up telling the ending, even after all these years, nothing made her happier than hearing another newborn son being named Aldric, another travelling minstrel coming through and singing his praises, a traveler coming to see the legend's hometown. Everywhere I'd been, they knew him.

I watched the two next to me, snoring lightly, an old wrinkled hand interlaced with an old scarred one. Their rings glowed in the firelight, and even I felt comfortable enough to drift off to sleep too.

ABOUT THE AUTHOR

Born and raised near Charleston, South Carolina, Benjamin Gamble always had a passion for writing. He has previously worked as a camp counselor and as a waiter, where he encountered monsters far more terrifying than the ones in this novel. He currently attends Furman University and tells his relatives he's considering graduate studies afterwards.

PERMUTED PRESS
needs **you** to help

SPREAD (THE) INFECTION

FOLLOW US!

f | Facebook.com/PermutedPress
🐦 | Twitter.com/PermutedPress

REVIEW US!

Wherever you buy our book, they can be reviewed! We want to know what you like!

GET INFECTED!

Sign up for our mailing list at
PermutedPress.com

PERMUTED
PRESS

KING ARTHUR AND THE KNIGHTS OF THE ROUND TABLE HAVE BEEN REBORN TO SAVE THE WORLD FROM THE CLUTCHES OF MORGANA WHILE SHE PROPELS OUR MODERN WORLD INTO THE MIDDLE AGES.

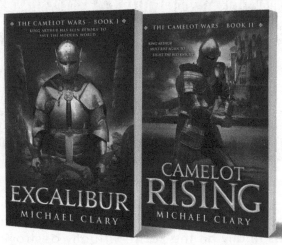

EAN 9781618685018 $15.99   EAN 9781682611562 $15.99

Morgana's first attack came in a red fog that wiped out all modern technology. The entire planet was pushed back into the middle ages. The world descended into chaos.

But hope is not yet lost— King Arthur, Merlin, and the Knights of the Round Table have been reborn.

THE ULTIMATE PREPPER'S ADVENTURE.
THE JOURNEY BEGINS HERE!

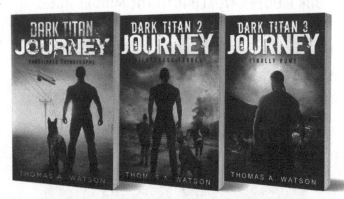

EAN 9781682611654 $9.99   EAN 9781618687371 $9.99   EAN 9781618687395 $9.99

The long-predicted Coronal Mass Ejection has finally hit the Earth, virtually destroying civilization. Nathan Owens has been prepping for a disaster like this for years, but now he's a thousand miles away from his family and his refuge. He'll have to employ all his hard-won survivalist skills to save his current community, before he begins his long journey through doomsday to get back home.

PERMUTED
PRESS

THE MORNINGSTAR STRAIN HAS BEEN LET LOOSE—IS THERE ANY WAY TO STOP IT?

An industrial accident unleashes some of the Morningstar Strain. The

EAN 9781618686497 $16.00

doctor who discovered the strain and her assistant will have to fight their way through Sprinters and Shamblers to save themselves, the vaccine, and the base. Then they discover that it wasn't an accident at all—somebody inside the facility did it on purpose. The war with the RSA and the infected is far from over.

This is the fourth book in Z.A. Recht's The Morningstar Strain series, written by Brad Munson.

PERMUTED
PRESS

GATHERED TOGETHER AT LAST, THREE TALES OF FANTASY CENTERING AROUND THE MYSTERIOUS CITY OF SHADOWS...ALSO KNOWN AS CHICAGO.

EAN 9781682612286 $9.99   **EAN** 9781618684639 $5.99   **EAN** 9781618684899 $5.99

From *The New York Times* and *USA Today* bestselling author Richard A. Knaak comes three tales from Chicago, the City of Shadows. Enter the world of the Grey–the creatures that live at the edge of our imagination and seek to be real. Follow the quest of a wizard seeking escape from the centuries-long haunting of a gargoyle. Behold the coming of the end of the world as the Dutchman arrives.

Enter the City of Shadows.

**PERMUTED
PRESS**

WE CAN'T GUARANTEE
THIS GUIDE WILL SAVE
YOUR LIFE. BUT WE CAN
GUARANTEE IT WILL
KEEP YOU SMILING
WHILE THE LIVING
DEAD ARE CHOWING
DOWN ON YOU.

EAN 9781618686695 $9.99

This is the only tool you
need to survive the zombie apocalypse.

OK, that's not really true. But when the SHTF, you're
going to want a survival guide that's not just geared
toward day-to-day survival. You'll need one that
addresses the essential skills for true nourishment of
the human spirit. Living through the end of the
world isn't worth a damn unless you can enjoy
yourself in any way you want. (Except, of course, for
anything having to do with abuse. We could never
condone such things. At least the publisher's
lawyers say we can't.)

PERMUTED
PRESS